JAMES R. TRAMONTANA

# Ace Tucker Space Trucker

*A Novel*

# Contents

# Dedication

For Diane, the love of my life and the only one brave enough to put up with my craziness.

# Free "Music of Ace Tucker Space Trucker" Album

1. Visit http://musicof.acetuckerspacetrucker.com
2. Add the album to the shopping cart
3. At checkout, use THE FIRST WORD OF **CHAPTER FOUR** as the coupon code
4. Bam! Get a FREE album
5. Rock out

# 1

# Ace Tucker Space Trucker

A ce Tucker wasn't surprised when Elvis Presley asked him for a beer. The surprising and the unexpected had always been a part of his life. As a baby, an unknown alien took Ace from Earth and left him on the doorstep of an outer space orphanage. There was no explanation and as far as origin stories go, well, that's all you're going to get.

The overtaxed nuns of the Galactic Church did their best to raise him, but Ace was a strange and difficult child. After eighteen years of frustration, they had finally had enough. The nuns sent Ace out into the galaxy with a half-assed blessing for his soul and the state-mandated fifty credits for bus fare, lunch, and tolls.

Now, ole Ace Tucker was a man of action and a gambling man. So, he spent twenty-five credits on a ticket to the nearest casino planet and used the rest to enter a high-stakes nebulacard tournament.

Eight hours later, he was the proud and improbable winner of the grand prize: a one-of-a-kind prototype Valdovian Ultra Space Freight Hauler smartship.

Ace spent the next ten years scratching out a meager living as a galactic cargo trucker. These days he worked the rock 'n' roll circuit as a roadie for Mustache Supernova, the greatest band in the known galaxy.

Yes, sir. In all his days, Ace thought he had pretty much seen it all.

But he hadn't seen anything yet.

Our story begins the night Ace Tucker and his best friend/business partner, Ivan Chimpanov, attended a swinging party at the palatial estate of famed galactic rock 'n' roll promoter, Sleazon Nebula.

Vibrant and raucous alien partygoers of all shapes and sizes milled about as Ace and Ivan sized up a man who was the spitting image of the one and only Elvis Presley.

"I dunno, Ivan," Ace said. "He sure looks like Elvis but what the hell would he be doing out here? Isn't he supposed to be dead?"

"Yeah!" Ivan said, drawing out the word to three syllables. "But there have always been rumors that he faked his death. It's possible that is him."

Ace narrowed his eyes and tilted his head as he tried to get a bead on the man. "Right, but... He could be a shapeshifter. You know as well as I do that odd lifeforms are part of the job. Remember that guy from the Large Kingdom of the Shiver who had no *true* physical form? He had some kinda low-level telepathy and would just take any physical shape he could cherry pick out of your head."

"Riiiight," Ivan said. "That was the day you had just finished watching the first two seasons of *Charlie's Angels* for the umpteen millionth time!"

"Yup. That ole boy took the form of Farrah Fawcett. Man, that was one hell of a day!" Ace said and took a sip from his beer.

"All I'm saying is it *could* be Elvis, yeah?" Ivan said as he stared at the man, ignoring his own beer.

"I dunno, man," Ace said after he swallowed. "If it was Elvis why would he be poaching drinks all night? I've seen him steal, like, four glasses of bubbly from waiterbots when they weren't looking."

"Hang on, Ace!" Ivan said with a gasp. "He's coming over here!"

"Say there, mister," the man said. "Can I have one of them beers there? Thank you. Thank you very much."

"Excuse me?" Ace said as he tapped his index finger on his bottle of Dark Star beer. *Tap, tap, tap.* "What was that?"

Ace's physical appearance made him an easy mark, he guessed. He tended to stand out in a crowd. He wore simple denim jeans, a black Mustache Supernova t-shirt, and biker boots. His shoulder-length wavy dark hair was kept in check by a black snapback hat featuring an embroidered patch with the word "Ace" written out in fancy white script front and center.

Sure, other lifeforms throughout the galaxy looked human, but most of them dressed like pansies.

"I said, can I have one of those beers, mister?" the man said.

Ace let out a quick snort and glanced at the six-pack he held like a briefcase. Two full bottles and three dead soldiers.

Ace raised up his bottle-in-progress and checked how much liquid joy remained. About four fingers worth. He brought the bottle up to his lips and took a long pull, draining the bottle in one gulp then shoved the bottle upside down in the empty slot of the six-pack like a gunslinger holstering his weapon. A few drops of beer ran along the length of the container and dripped onto the floor.

"Nope," Ace said with a slight burp. "Fresh out, buddy. Sorry."

"Aw come on, man. I can see right there you got two more full ones." The man pointed at the six-pack and gave Ace a friendly smile.

Ace furrowed his brow. "Tell you what. Me and my pal here have a little bet. You settle it for us, and I'll give you one of these. OK?"

"Sure, man! What's the bet?"

Before Ace could speak Ivan blurted out, "You're Elvis Presley, right?"

The man threw his head back and roared with a laugh that carried all the way across the room. A few party guests looked over. When they saw who was laughing, they looked away, annoyed. After what seemed like an eternity, the man stopped laughing and wiped away a few tears.

"Yeah, man. That's me. But jeez, man. I never thought anyone would ever ask me that again," Elvis said.

"See, Ace! What'd I tell you?" Ivan said, elbowing Ace.

"Watch where you elbow me, Ivan!" Ace said. "You hit me right in the sixer!"

"Great. You got beer all over my jacket!" Ivan said as he slapped at the beer drops in an attempt to keep the jacket pristine.

Right now would be a good time to explain that Ace's pal, Ivan Chimpanov, loved his leather jacket. It might also be a good time to point out that Ivan was, in fact, a Russian cyborg chimpanzee.

When they first met, the jacket first caught Ace's eye. It was not every day you see a leather jacket covered in punk rock band patches two hundred light years from the Solar System.

Ivan wore his affection literally on his sleeve. Sex Pistols, The Clash, Misfits, The Damned, Buzzcocks, and countless others running the gamut of classic punk littered every inch of the jacket. The area on the right shoulder, however, displayed Ivan's favorite: the Ramones. He had several patches commemorating the rebellious progenitors of punk. Ace always wondered if it was

4

the music or the title of the Ramones' third studio album, *Rocket to Russia*, that first grabbed Ivan's attention.

Ivan started as a normal Earth-bound chimpanzee until the Soviet Union shot him into space in 1985. Some sort of new propulsion system experiment. Mother Russia didn't care if Ivan lived or died. If it weren't for a group of bored Ruffinili college kids out for a joy ride, he would still be adrift somewhere in the depths of space.

Lucky for Ivan those dorks were engineering students and thought it'd be cute to have a super-intelligent chimp for a butler. The Ruffinili didn't account for Ivan's vicious temper, though. Once his new cybernetic systems came online, Ivan kicked those jerks' asses and stole their ship. Ivan never told Ace exactly what he did with them, though. Just that they "got what they deserved." Ace learned not to pry too much with Ivan. He'd tell you what he wanted when he wanted.

"There. That's better," Ivan said, satisfied his jacket was clean. "That beer could've stained my Ramones patches, Ace!"

Ace bit his lip to hide his smile, "Hey, man. You're the one that elbowed me. But, we're rude to our friend here, Ivan. Here you go, Mr. Presley. Have a bottle of Dark Star beer."

Ace pulled a beer from the six-pack, opened it with a church-key attached to his belt via a retractable chain, and handed it to Elvis.

Elvis took a long drink and said, "Ah! Thank you. Thank you very much."

"But answer me this," Ace said. "How did a supposed dead guy from Earth get into this exclusive after party? I mean, it's not every day that Mustache Supernova has a show in this sector of space. Me and Ivan here are on the road crew, and that's the only way we got into this party. How about you?"

"Aw, hell, man," Elvis said. "I wrote most of Nova's hits!"

Elvis showed a heightened level of cool by referring to Mustache Supernova simply as Nova, both as a form of lazy slang and as a nod to the band's frontman, Nova Johnson.

"No way!" Ivan said. "You're telling me you wrote *Blow That Neutron Out Your Starfish?*"

"Yup," Elvis said.

"How about *Psionic Isohammer Boogie?*"

"Yeah. I wrote that one, too," Elvis nodded.

"*The Thieves of Plasmatron?*"

"Oh yeah!" Elvis said.

"What about that one album where it was just four hours of orgasms and crying?" Ivan asked with a cringe.

"Nah, man," Elvis winced. "That's Nova Johnson's solo stuff. I didn't have anything to do with that crap."

"So what then?" Ace said. "You've just been a ghostwriter in outer space this whole time? Aren't you supposed to be dead?"

"And you don't look a day over forty!" Ivan added. "Shouldn't you be, like, seventy-something years old now?"

"Yeah. Funny story, actually," Elvis said after draining his bottle of beer. "Ahh...So there I was, on Earth. At my home, Graceland. I had just finished playing racquetball and was on my way to the john when these two guys just appear out of nowhere and...Oh, damn. Wait a minute—"

Elvis stopped. His face turned ashen, white and pallid. His lips trembled a few times like he was trying to speak, but all that came out was a low inaudible whisper. He looked past Ace and Ivan with wide eyes. Ace turned, following Elvis's gaze to the far side of the room. A man dressed from head to toe in an impossibly shiny metallic suit stood near the entrance waving off a waiterbot trying to get his drink order.

Ace had to squint to get a better look. "Whoa. That's the shiniest suit I've ever seen. It's...impossibly shiny."

It wasn't just the tailored three-piece suit complete with a shiny tie that was made of metal. The man's skin seemed to be made of the same impossibly shiny ultra-reflective chrome. He reflected and bent so much of the dim ambient mood lighting he appeared almost invisible. Yet, the man shined with brilliant iridescence at the same time. It made Ace's eyes water and his brain itch. When his eyes finally focused Ace saw the man held a laser revolver in his impossibly shiny hand. A split second later, the room erupted in laser fire and screams.

* * *

Five terrifying minutes later Ace dragged a limp and bloody Elvis Presley across the lawn of Sleazon Nebula's palatial estate. Laser blasts echoed from behind the mansion as Sleazon's security Killbots fought the impossibly shiny gunman.

Sleazon was the biggest concert promoter in Doucheon System and rumored to be an arms dealer on the side. His home protection measures were top notch, but the repeated explosions and robot screams didn't convince Ace it was enough.

When the gunman first opened fire on the party, he started by targeting Elvis Presley. Yet, Elvis evaded the first dozen or so shots without a scratch. He leaped. He crouched. He juked around furniture, party guests, and waiterbots all while laser bolts tore through the well-appointed great room of Sleazon's mansion.

Elvis almost made it outside when he slipped on a cocktail napkin. A laser bolt ripped through his midsection, and he dropped like a sack.

Ace and Ivan stayed low and moved slowly as the lasers flew

overhead. Ace knew keeping your head down was the best way to stay alive. No one liked a hero. It wasn't that Ace was a coward. He just liked being alive too much to do anything stupid like getting involved.

Moreover, he was unarmed. His sidearm sat idle in a gun locker on *Betty*, his spacefaring smartship parked out front.

When the shooting paused, Ace peaked up from behind a smoldering Jarkolounger. The headrest and most of the back were melted making the expensive lounge chair look like some sort of surreal modern art project. The stench of burning jarko fur hung heavy in the air, stinging Ace's nostrils.

Across the room, the shiny gunman loomed over Elvis with his laser revolver poised and ready to fire.

Elvis squirmed. He held one hand against the wound on his gut and the other up as a plea for an armistice.

"It's nice to see you, Mr. Presley," the gunman said. His voice was jarring and synthetic like his larynx was an ancient computer speech synthesizer trapped in a blender. "Andromeda sends her regards."

"Aww! Come on, man! Not now!" Elvis's voice quivered, and his hand shook.

"I'm afraid your time is up." The gunman cocked the hammer back on the laser revolver. Ace guessed this was mostly for dramatic effect. The hammers on laser revolvers did absolutely nothing, but tough guys loved to do crap like that to make a point.

"You know what I want," the shiny gunman said. "Give it to me, or you die. Here. Now."

Out of nowhere, an orange plasma bolt hit the gunman square in the back sending him flying out the sliding glass door and into a heavy-water swimming pool thirty feet beyond it.

Four armored Killbots carrying twin plasma throwers and bad

attitudes stalked into the room.

"Attention partygoers," the Killbots said in robotic and deafening unison. "Mr. Nebula regrets to inform you, due to unfortunate circumstances beyond his control, the party is canceled. Please gather your belongings and vacate the premises. Failure to do so may result in personal injury. Have a nice night."

The Killbots opened fire on the swimming pool all at once.

The gunman avoided the superheated plasma vaporizing the water around him by swimming like an eel and snaking in every possible direction.

The Killbots stomped past Ace and Ivan firing the entire time and hurling nasty insults in Robotese.

"We gotta save him!" Ivan said.

"What?" Ace shouted over the stomping, blasting, and swearing.

"Elvis! We gotta save him. He's hurt super bad!"

Ivan always had a soft spot for injured critters. One time, while on a run hauling Lemmium, Ivan found a tiny ralladog with a broken tail. Ace didn't see what all the fuss was about as the thing clearly had a second working tail. But Ivan insisted on nursing it back to health. It turned out to be a smart move because that ralladog happened to be Big Johnny's favorite pet, Feefi.

Big Johnny was the rotund and cash-flush proprietor of Big Johnny's Lemmium Emporium and a solid customer. Hauling Lemmium was notoriously volatile, and Ace was one of the only truckers crazy enough to do it on a regular basis.

After Ivan patched Feefi up using the advanced medical systems onboard *Betty* he posted a lost dog notice on Krang's List. Within two hours Ivan got a reply from Big Johnny himself, overjoyed that they found his beloved pet.

Big Johnny insisted they take two hundred credits as a reward.

Ivan split half the money with Ace as per their agreement to share all monies earned on the job, including tips and rewards.

Ivan bought a few credits worth of black market Earth media including some choice television shows and music albums from the mid to late 1970s—Ivan's favorite era.

Ace lost his share on a bad bet.

It was twenty to one odds, and Ace's bookie swore that Mugs Turntoil would take a dive in the tenth round of the fight. The winnings would've been easy money and help to clear part of Ace's sizable gambling debt. His lucky streak seemed to start and end with the nebulacard tournament he won in his youth. Since then it had been a series of small wins and big losses.

As fate would have it, Mugs did not take a dive in the tenth round as promised. Instead, he knocked the head off his opponent in the sixth round and won the fight. Ace was out a hundred credits.

Ace's tab on borrowed money had serious interest stacking up. The little shindig at Sleazon's was supposed to be a short respite between jobs. They were due to blast off within the hour and deliver several thousand metric tons of Mustache Supernova's sound equipment to the next tour stop.

"You're out of your damn mind, Ivan!" Ace said, amazed that Ivan would suggest helping a doomed stranger in the middle of an active shoot-out. "Leave him. The paramedics will be here any minute. Let's get the hell out of here! We're late already!"

Ace pointed at the front door, away from all the stomping and blasting, where the few remaining party guests scrambled for safety. In the distance, he could hear rescue and police vehicles approaching. Yet another reason to get out quick. Ace was not a fan of cops. They asked too many questions.

The initial onslaught of laser fire took out a dozen or so people.

Blood, spilled drinks, and snack chips covered everything. Small fires burned on mangled pieces of classy furniture. In the corner, a groupie puked and fished around for her phone, so she could post images of the horror on galactic social media. SpaceFace was going to have a field day with this, and she wanted to be the first to break the story.

"Come on, Ace," Ivan said. "We can get him to the ship. Plus! He's from Earth! Don't you always say we gotta stick together 'cause no one else gives a damn about us?"

Ivan was right. Ace did always say that. Living as a lone human in a galaxy full of trillions of alien lifeforms had its upsides. It was hardly a boring place to call home. But even with all the crazy numbers of people out there, it could get lonely.

Ace spent years on his own before he met Ivan, and species differences aside, they became fast friends. They were both from Earth and had a DNA-level bond stronger than any of their previous friendships. A shared genetic history that spanned their evolutionary differences and kept them thick as thieves.

Also, it didn't hurt that Ivan's cybernetic implants made him a super-genius and could riddle things out better than Ace could. If Ivan believed that they could make it out of there with Elvis in tow, then Ace was inclined to believe him.

"Alright, goddammit!" Ace shouted.

Ivan nodded in agreement and scurried over on all fours to where Elvis lay, passed out, in a pool of his own blood. Ace followed, cursing under his breath.

Elvis awoke and coughed up more blood. He clutched his abdomen, but the bleeding didn't look all that bad to Ace. Based on the caliber of the laser revolver he expected to see clear through the man to the floor.

"Jeez!" Ace said. "You'd think a guy who took a laser blast to the gut would've bled out by now. Look, Ivan! Where the laser blast hit. It's all covered with black plastic or something. What the shit?"

"Just relax," Ivan said to Elvis. "We're going to get you out of here."

"Thank you. Thank you very much," Elvis said, grabbing Ace by the arm. Elvis squeezed harder than Ace guessed a seventy-something-year-old with a laser wound possibly could.

"Please, m-man," Elvis sputtered. "Help me...Gotta get me to Graceland. Get...El...Dorado."

Elvis's eyes lost focus, and he passed out.

* * *

As the fierce battle raged below, Ace had a white-knuckle grip on *Betty*'s steering wheel and rocketed through the atmosphere at fourteen times the speed of sound. Everything shook like a paint mixer as the ship breached the atmosphere and blasted into outer space.

A few empty fast food containers rattled off the dashboard and floated up for a second before the artificial gravity kicked in. When the containers hit the floor, Ace kicked them over into the pile on Ivan's side of the cabin.

Ace engaged the dark matter hyperdrives and pushed *Betty* through a curtain of multidimensional light, slipping out of normal space and into hyperspace.

When Ace was satisfied they were safe he flipped an analog switch labeled "autopilot."

"All yours, Betty," he said.

"Confirmed, Ace. Autopilot engaged. We are trucking at eight million times the speed of light," *Betty* said in her somewhat robotic, yet soothing, female voice.

Years ago, when Ace first took ownership of *Betty*, she had a nerve-grating, sterile audio interface. "Welcome, new owner. This interface will guide you through customizing your new Valdovian Ultra Space Freight Hauler smartship." It sounded like nails on a chalkboard.

The voice was the first thing Ace changed. It took him almost an hour to get the cadence and timber of it right. When he was done, *Betty* sounded breathy and intimate yet firm and stern. Just the way Ace liked his women.

By the time Ace was ready to customize the exterior, his sobriety had long since been kicked to the curb. He had been celebrating his nebulacard tournament victory and sampling the fully stocked bar aboard his newly acquired smartship. The mix of booze and the bizarre set of circumstances that resulted in his triumph had left his head fuzzy and filled with strange thoughts.

Ace initially lost his money in the first round of the tournament and had to scheme a way to earn some quick cash to get back in the game. He figured if he could earn one hundred credits fast, he could re-enter under a hard-luck ruling and have a chance at the big win. In a twist of fate, he met a slagrunner at a bar who specialized in black market media from underworlds, the technologically backward planets not affiliated with the Galactic Union. Fetish collectors loved to get their hands on the media because it was forbidden to actually visit those planets.

The man never gave Ace his name, but prepaid two hundred credits and said the best way to transport the goods was by uploading the content in a living brain.

"A small device will be strapped to your skull," the slagrunner said. "It will store the underworld media in your prefrontal cortex temporarily. It is quite painless. You won't even notice it."

The process only caused slight brain damage (no more than the swill Ace was drinking) and it paid well so Ace figured why not.

Ace had no idea that his brain would be exposed to cultural artifacts from Earth. But there they were among Zentali opera, Mundial folk music, and Hodarki poetry slams. His first conscious encounter with Earth.

In a perfect scenario, Ace would have retained no memory of the media pumped into his brain, but a lightning storm raged that night on MegaReno. When the buyer strapped Ace into the retrieval unit, a power surge botched the process leaving bits and pieces behind.

Most of the stuff left behind were just impressions. Ghost images. A man hitting a ball with a stick and the roar of a crowd. Loud guns firing tiny solid projectiles. A bar full of men punching each other and throwing chairs. A mustachioed outlaw with an infectious laugh driving a black vehicle with a golden bird painted on the hood. Weapons of war raining hellfire down on sleepy towns. A child eating small grain circles covered in white liquid.

Whereas most of the visions were hazy, a few were more concrete. The clearest bit was a cinematic sequence of an eighteen wheeler rolling down a highway being chased by what Ace later learned were police cars.

The sequence always played the same in his mind's eye. The truck smashing through a barricade. Wood and metal splinters flying everywhere. Scores of black and white police cruisers in pursuit with sirens wailing and lights flashing. The driver yelling something unintelligible but clearly having the time of his life.

Another especially vivid bit was an animated rollerskating coyote with an exploding rocket strapped to its back trying to capture a speeding roadrunner.

His inebriated subconscious mashed it all together spitting out what the startup program used to build the exterior design of *Betty*. A perfect recreation of a 1974 Kenworth W900 truck with one cartoon rocket strapped to nacelles on each side of the semi-trailer.

Ace knew *Betty* wasn't exactly pleased with his design choice for the exterior. She asked him to confirm the design fifteen times. She eventually gave in and begrudgingly moved on to the next phase of the startup program.

*Betty* had top-of-the-line artificial intelligence with complete empathic and emotion circuit upgrades. She was as alive as any physical being and as such had her own little personality quirks. One of them being a short temper when Ace was slow to pick up on advanced concepts.

When it came time for the interior design phase, *Betty* informed him that the hyperdimensional nature of the interior space allowed for as much actual physical space as he desired. She had to rephrase this several times before she settled on, "The innards are way bigger than the ship looks from the outside. Put whatever you want in there."

Something in *Betty*'s tone hinted to Ace she was, in fact, a *spaceship* and should probably look like one in certain parts. He decided to go with the interior layout template for a Valdovian Galacto-Freight space cargo hauler.

It made Ace's head hurt when he thought about the dimensionally transcendental nature of *Betty*'s interior. He didn't even try to understand how the interior exists in a different relative dimension to the exterior. It was easier to just think of the ship as four decks and a large cargo bay that never got completely full.

The cockpit was at the head of the ship on the upper deck. Ace forced the issue and compromised with *Betty* on its design.

The cockpit looked like the cab of a standard eighteen-wheeler but with super advanced alien tech blended in. Cutting-edge Valdovian navigation and operational systems like 4D haptic touch computer holoscreens were inlaid upon the faux wood and vinyl dashboard right next to analog dials, switches, and pulls.

A single CB radio push-to-talk microphone hung from the ceiling and served as Ace's main communications interface. Below it was a large leather captain's chair behind a polished wood and chrome steering wheel. Accelerator and brake pedals were beneath the dash for use when *Betty* was in ground transport mode.

A second identical leather chair sat abreast to Ace's. This was Ivan's seat and where most of the fancy alien technology resided along with more round analog gauges and black flip switches.

Everything else throughout the ship was pure Valdovian Galacto-Freight design. Brushed ultra-titanium blended with subdued matte paint colors on the walls, floors, and ceilings.

Beyond the cockpit was a long corridor with ladders leading down to the crew quarters and a small airlock to *Betty*'s exterior via a side hatch. At the end of the main corridor was an elevator that connected the upper deck to the rest of the ship.

Deck two held the dining area, kitchenette, and recreation room. Below that was the engine room, a place Ace never went because every time he entered his brain wanted to scream. It was pure alien technology, and although Ace was handy with tools, he left the repairs and upkeep for the propulsion systems to Ivan.

Deck four was the cargo bay, main airlock, and the sickbay. Ace's next stop.

When Ace walked in, he saw Ivan attempting to stabilize Elvis Presley's condition with the super advanced medical support systems.

"How's he doing?" Ace asked.

Ivan shook his head as he looked up from a complicated med computer screen that Ace never could figure out.

"He's in pretty rough shape, Ace. I'm not sure he's going to make it," Ivan said.

A silver spike protruded from the top of Ivan's wrist and was jammed into a data port on the wall next to Elvis's bed. Ivan's cybernetic implants made it possible for him to interface with any computer. This made him the perfect co-pilot and business partner. There wasn't a computer system he couldn't crack or a ship he couldn't fly.

Ivan was also a whiz with languages. Ace had to rely on a second-hand translator implant to understand and communicate with the over seventy billion languages spoken throughout the galaxy. Ivan, on the other hand, didn't require one. The cyber tech writhing through his body had souped up his brain to an off-the-charts IQ. The languages he didn't already know, he could pick up in the course of an average conversation. Unless it was with one of the few species in the Outer Belt that communicates solely by touch. You have to hire a translator or risk being bludgeoned to death by a flurry of tentacles swatting at you like a drunk trying to put out a fire with their bare hands.

"Hang on," Ivan said as the screen started displaying a series of complicated computer code. Ivan's eyes rolled into the back of his head and started to flutter like a person deep in REM sleep, a physical manifestation of him hitting the computer systems hard, processing an onslaught of new information.

The screen stopped spewing code, and Ivan snapped out of his trance.

"Wow. Elvis has nanotech installed in his central nervous system," Ivan said.

"What? He's a cyborg like you?" Ace asked.

"Not really. It's different. Like nothing I've seen before. But it's definitely alien and super advanced. That would explain why the guy hasn't aged in the last few decades. The nanobots are constantly repairing his cells and enhancing his physiology."

"Well, shit. If he has onboard medical, why aren't the nanobots fixing him up?" Ace asked.

Ivan pointed at the wound covered in burnt plastic on Elvis's gut. "That spot there. It has a massive concentration of offline nanobots. It's like they all rushed in to take care of the wound and then were immediately shut down. I'm not sure why. It might have something to do with the gun that shiny guy had. I'm picking up all kinds of weird energy signatures, and they're strongest around the wound. So, I guess the blast had some type of effect on his tech. They were able to stop the bleeding before they conked out, but without something to kick the healing into gear, I'm not sure he's gonna make it."

"El...Dorado..." Elvis murmured. He reached out and squeezed Ace's hand. "Graceland...El...Dorado."

Elvis fought to open his eyes, and when he did, they lacked focus.

"Try and take it easy," Ace said trying to sound reassuring. "We'll get you to a hospital as soon as we can."

"No! No hospitals." Elvis's speech was shallow and haggard. "He'll get me if you drop me at a hospital. He'll be there. He'll get me."

"Who? Who's after you, Elvis?" Ivan asked as he tapped a few buttons on the medical computer.

"The Shiny Man..." Elvis whispered before passing out.

18

# 2

# Earth Can Eat a Turd Sandwich

After putting Elvis in a medically induced coma, Ivan sat in the co-pilot seat, jacked into a data port in the dashboard of *Betty*'s cockpit via his cyber implant.

Ace sat in the pilot's seat, drinking a beer and glaring out the windshield.

Ace thought hyperspace was pretty dull. Just a gray field in every direction and a dull ball of white light directly in front. Nothing like it was depicted on the science fiction shows in Ivan's media stash.

Ivan was a collector of Earth media but, unlike the slagrunner Ace muled for ten years ago, Ivan got his ephemera the old-fashioned way. He was part of a club that exchanged media at monthly underground swap meets. No live brains were employed. Just good old-fashioned zettabyte hard drives full of entertainment and information for Underworld civilizations.

In the years Ace had known Ivan his stash had grown to boast an impressive collection of music, movies, and television shows from Earth ranging from the 1920s through the early 1980s. Most of the time Ace would pull up something to watch on the heads-up display when they were in hyperspace. Today he merely glowered and sipped his beer.

The blockade around Earth made it impossible for Ace and Ivan to do any meaningful research on the GalactoNet. They had to rely on Ivan's stash to find information on Graceland and El Dorado. Ace was already familiar with the mansion Elvis called home but had never heard of El Dorado. Although it sounded familiar to him. Maybe he had seen a western with that title. He wasn't sure.

But that wasn't really what was bothering him.

Ace turned to Ivan and said, "I'm not going to Earth, Ivan. That place can eat a turd sandwich. Being a fan of Earth stuff is one thing. They make great shows and music. OK. Fine. I like them. You like them. Great. But screw going there. I ain't doing it."

"Listen, Ace," Ivan said, "I swore I'd never go back there either. Remember they gave me a one-way ticket to freeze to death in space. I was just a science experiment to them, and they threw me away."

"At least they sent you up with six bottles of Stoli! More than I got," Ace said.

"If you're referring to the bottles of vodka the Soviet scientists put in the capsule with me when they literally blasted me out into Hell...Let me tell you that was not enough to make up for..." Ivan sighed and regrouped himself. "Listen, I know how you feel. Really, I do. But think about it this way. Maybe we'll find a clue as to who you really are."

"I know who I am, goddammit. I don't need to find anything out." Ace tilted the beer back and shook the last few drops into his mouth before tossing the bottle at a garbage chute behind his chair. It missed and hit the ground, rolling into a corner.

"Ok. Safe to say we both have abandonment issues. OK?" Ivan said. "But hasn't it ever bothered you? I mean, it's not every day that a human baby is plucked off Earth and deposited at a prestigious orphanage in the Gloweron Sector."

"That place was a dump, Ivan. Don't believe what they say on the brochures. There's nothing glamorous about being an orphan," Ace said. "And they told me plenty. They said I was left for dead in a parking lot. Then a kind alien took pity on me and thought I could lead a better life off-world. Big deal. Shit like that happens all the time."

"No it doesn't," Ivan said. "Stuff like that does not happen all the time. I've never heard of that ever happening. Ever. And I've been places, Ace. Remember I was out there on my own, mixing it up for years before we met. Almost no one had ever heard of Earth."

"Whatever. Don't meet your heroes is all I'm saying." Ace reached into the cooler on his side of the cab and pulled out a fresh bottle of Dark Star. He popped the cap off using the dashboard-mounted bottle opener then resumed glowering out the window.

"Don't 'whatever' me." Ivan retracted the spike from the data port, and it receded into his arm like a saucy noodle being slurped up. "OK. Forget about personal discovery then. How's gold strike you?"

Ace perked his head up. "What do you mean?"

"Well, I just got done reviewing my stash for any mention of El Dorado and as far as I can tell it's a legendary city of gold. There was a public access program called *Mysterious Mysteries* that did an entire show on it."

"So, you're saying that the guy we have on board, on top of being the not-dead King of Rock 'n' Roll and a cyborg, also owns an entire city made of gold?"

"No, not exactly," Ivan said. "What I'm saying is that this guy is super rich and he's hurt. And he wants us to take him back home for help. He's probably got a huge cache of gold and is offering to pay us off for helping him."

Ace tapped his index finger on the beer bottle with one hand and beat the steering wheel with the index finger on the other. He tended to drum on things when he was lost in thought, and right now he was tapping the drum solo from the surf rock anthem *Wipe Out.*

"I dunno, man. Betty, what do you think?" Ace asked.

"I don't have any further information on Earth other than what's in Ivan's media archive, Ace." *Betty*'s soothing voice filled the cabin. "The Galactic Union blockade has made any information scarce at best. I agree with Ivan's supposition, however. Elvis is asking you to take him to Earth, to his home at Graceland."

"Hang on, Betty. You breezed by the best part," Ace shouted. "The blockade. Doesn't that prevent spacecraft from landing on Earth?"

"That is correct, Ace," *Betty* said.

"Well, that settles it then. We can't go. Betty says it's impossible to get in. Too bad, so sad. We take that nice fella bleeding all over my sickbay to the nearest hospital and call it a day," Ace said. He took a long pull from his beer.

"Betty?" Ivan said with a proud smile. "Doesn't the blockade matrix specify that nothing *non-native* can enter the system?"

"That's correct, Ivan," *Betty* said.

"And this was put in place after the Hasselhoff Incident in 1988 to prevent further cultural incursion from the rest of the galaxy, right?"

"That is what the Galactic Union mandate specifies, yes," *Betty* said.

"But it was designed so that once Earth develops hyperdrives, humans will be able to leave and make contact with the rest of the galaxy. Isn't that right?" Ivan asked.

"Correct," *Betty* said. "The positron field surrounding Earth is tuned so that Earth beings can pass freely through it. Only beings with terrestrial DNA may traverse it."

"See, Ace?" Ivan said. "We are literally the only people in the galaxy who can get in."

"Well, isn't that just frickin' convenient. I still ain't going," Ace said.

Ace was just about to take another tug from his beer when something exploded directly in front of *Betty*. Ace dropped his beer, and the ship fell out of hyperspace.

"Son of a —!" Ace scrambled to pick up the bottle of Dark Star as it sloughed beer out onto the floor.

Alarm klaxons blared, and warning lights flashed everywhere. Ace stood the beer bottle upright then started flipping analog switches and tapping on the holoscreens closest to him.

One screen to his left showed a blue dashed line surrounding a vector graphic of *Betty*'s hull. Her shields just went up. Typically while in hyperspace there was no need for them. Ace looked over at Ivan jacked into the data port via his cyber-implant spike.

"What the hell was that?" Ace asked. He punched up a visual display of *Betty*'s exterior. The screens were static.

"Something exploded in front of us and knocked us out of hyperspace!" Ivan shouted.

"I can see that. What the hell could've done that? That's impossible. Betty! Status report."

No reply.

Only static and alarms.

"Betty!" Ace shouted again. "Goddammit. Ivan, turn off those friggin' alarms!"

Ivan's eyelids fluttered as he sent the command to silence the klaxons. He shifted in his seat and straightened up like a kid paying attention to his favorite cartoon.

"What the hell is going on?" Ace asked as he watched Ivan squirm.

"Betty's higher logic functions are down, Ace," Ivan said. "Life support and basic systems are running, but everything else is in the process of rebooting. I've taken over and raised our defense shields. Scanners are reading a ship approaching from the rear at an insane speed. I've never seen anything move like that before. It'll be here in ten seconds."

"Well, thank space Jesus for your cyborg innards!" Ace said. "Do we have weapons?"

"Yeah! Bringing them online now," Ivan said.

"Good, spin us around and let's say howdy to this asshole," Ace said.

Exactly ten seconds later a ship appeared in front of them. It was unlike anything either of them had seen before. It was smooth and covered in a silvery metal so shiny that it reflected starlight from hundreds of light-years away in a dancing iridescent cloud. There were no running lights, no hatches, no ports, no obvious seams or markings of any kind. It was a like a shiny silver egg crapped out of a giant metal space bird.

"What the shiny shit is that?" Ace asked.

"I have no idea," Ivan said. "I am hitting it as hard as I can with the scanners, but I'm barely getting a reading. I mean, the systems see that it's there, but it can't make out exactly what *it* is."

"Do we have comms?" Ace asked.

"Yes. What do you want to say?" Ivan replied.

"Don't worry about it. I got it." Ace grabbed the push-to-talk CB-style radio handset that hung from the ceiling of the cab as

Ivan initiated the ship-to-ship communication link.

"Alien vessel. This is Ace Tucker, independent long-haul space trucker. I don't know if you realize this, but I'm sitting in a Valdovian Ultra Space Freight Hauler. The Valdovians are known for their fine craftsmanship as well as their affinity for high-powered energy weapons. This ship might not look like it, but we're packing one hell of an arsenal. I suggest you back away slowly and get the hell out of this sector of space before I blow your shiny ass to Kingdom Come."

After a long pause, Ace shifted in his seat and pressed the push-to-talk button again. Then immediately released it and said to Ivan, "You have us patched into them, don't you?"

"Yeah. We have a stable comm-link. I have confirmation that your message was received. They're just ignoring us."

"Sonsabitches," Ace said under his breath. He pressed the push-to-talk again and was about to speak.

A voice, louder than anything he'd ever heard before, blared out in every direction around Ace's head. It was like standing in a giant bucket with a thunderstorm of chainsaws. Ace dropped the CB handset and put his hands over his ears.

"Ace Tucker," the grating synthetic voice boomed. "Relinquish your passenger. The one who calls himself Elvis Presley. You have five minutes to comply. If you do not, I will reduce your ship to a cloud of burning vapor."

When the audio onslaught ended, Ace's ears rang so loudly it was physically agonizing. He grabbed his nose and blew air hard through it in an attempt to make his ears pop. It did not help. He worked his jaw several times and tried to yawn. This also did not help.

*Great. I'm freaking deaf now,* Ace thought.

Ace turned to Ivan and shouted, "Great! I'm freaking deaf

now!"

Ivan was in a trance, jacked into *Betty*'s computer system.

"Hey, Ivan!" Ace shouted again, louder. "I think I'm freaking deaf now!"

Ivan reached under his seat with his free hand and pulled out a small device. Without looking at him, Ivan pointed the device at Ace and projected a red beam that hit Ace in the side of the head.

Ace immediately heard drums beating on the back of his skull. After about forty or so beats, the drums and the ringing in his ears stopped.

"Yow!" Ace said. He rubbed his temple where the beam had hit him. "What the shit, man?"

Ace realized that his hearing had returned to normal. "Oh. Thanks, man."

"No problem," Ivan said without looking at Ace. "Your brain was reacting like you had tinnitus. Somehow the bad guy projected sound directly into our skulls, and it damaged some of the little hairs in your cochlea, which caused inflammation and stimulation of auditory nerves. Your brain interprets this inflammation as constant ringing or buzzing."

"Thanks for the medical lesson, doc," Ace said with a grin. Ivan always felt the need to be the smartest person in the room. He loved spouting knowledge and facts even in life-threatening situations.

"Don't mention it." Ivan's eyes opened, and he gave Ace a look that meant business. "I was trying to work out where the audio had come from, the alien ship's defensive capabilities, and the amount of time it would take to get the hyperdrives back online."

"Ok?" Ace said trying not to sound impressed with Ivan's multitasking.

"We have to get out of here, Ace. I'm not sure I understand

26

what the hell that ship is or where it came from, but I'm pretty sure the driver is the same guy that shot up Sleazon's party. The ship's construction is of the same metal as the shiny stuff he was wearing. I can't get a solid lock on the ship. It's like it's phasing in and out of existence. It's super weird. The only thing I am certain of is that it's powered up some kind of a weapon. The energy signature is..."

"Lemme guess. Super weird," Ace said.

"Yeah. It's going to take me some time to figure out what it is we're looking at here," Ivan said.

"It's Andromedan," Elvis Presley said from the back of the cockpit.

Ace ducked like Elvis had thrown a water balloon at his head. Ivan jumped up, spun around, and assumed a fighting crouch on his seat.

"Jesus on a cracker, son!" Ace said when he caught his breath. "You can't just sneak up on people like that, man!"

"Sorry, fella. I'm still a little woozy from the drugs, ya know?" Elvis said, swaying. He shook his head a few times like he was trying to clear water out from his ears.

"I'll say. I put you into a coma. You should be out!" Ivan said.

Elvis ignored him and said, "Listen. We got bigger fish to fry, man. That guy out there is gonna blow us to hell if we don't get out of here. Like, now, man."

"What do you suggest we do?" Ace settled back into his seat and pulled up a status report on *Betty*'s weapon systems.

"Well, not that. If you shoot at him, you'll just piss him off more," Elvis said to Ace. Then to Ivan, he said, "Are your hyperdrives online? He probably tried to disable them, huh?"

"Yeah!" Ivan said. "The initial blast knocked us out of hyperspace and would've shut them down completely, but I was able to maintain the dark matter reaction manually."

"Manually?" Elvis whooped. "Wow. He probably never saw that coming. Probably thinks we're sitting ducks right now. What are you some kind of robutt?"

"Well for the moment we *are* sitting ducks," Ivan said. "We'll have hyperdrives back online in a few seconds. And the term is ro-*bot*. And no, I'm not a robot. I am cybernetically enhanced. Like you."

"Shoot, man," Elvis said. "I can't talk to computers or hyper-drives or nothing. I just heal real fast."

"Hey!" Ace shouted. "Can we maybe have the gear queer chitty chat another time? We've got seconds until this guy starts shooting!"

"Alright. Lemme think for a minute," Elvis said. "Umm. This happened once before I think..."

"You think!?" Ace was beside himself. "What the shit does that mean?"

"Aw man. It's been a rough life out here. With the space booze and space pills. My mind ain't what it used to be," Elvis said with a smile.

"Listen! I don't care who the hell you are or how rough a life you've had," Ace said as he swung out of the driver's seat and lunged towards Elvis. "If you know how to beat this asshole, tell us...What the—"

Ace reached for Elvis's shoulder with the intention of shaking the ever-loving shit out of him. But that didn't happen. Instead, Ace's hand passed right through Elvis. This had the uncomfortable result of knocking Ace off balance.

Ace plowed forward straight through Elvis and landed hard on his knees with his arms flailing around for something to grab onto.

"He's a hologram!" Ivan said and jacked back into the data port on the dash. "Dude. Ace. He's still in the infirmary. Take a look."

Ace got to his feet and stared at a video feed from the infirmary projecting on the windshield's heads-up display. Sure as shit. There was Elvis, zonked out in a coma. Ivan patched in the audio from the infirmary, and they heard the tell-tale slow beeping of the heart monitor and evenly paced robotic breathing of the ventilator. A low whispering could be heard coming from Elvis on the hospital bed.

A moment later the hologram of Elvis spoke, "Oh. Sorry guys. Did I forget to mention that I was astral projecting? Sorry about that."

"What the shit?" Ace said and inched around the astral projection of Elvis with his back pressed firmly against the wall like Elvis was a pissed off snake.

"Yeah. I'm tore up pretty good," Elvis said. "Y'all got to get me out of here and back to Graceland. You gotta find...*bzzzzt*...El...*bzzzt*...Dorado...*bzzzzt*...aw, man...*bzzzzt*...not again."

They could see Elvis's mouth move, but no new sound was audible.

"Ace. Something's happening," Ivan said. "I'm getting a really weird energy signature off that ship!"

"Do we have hyperdrives?" Ace asked as he plopped down in the captain's chair.

"Ummm...Yes. Hyperdrives are fully restored," Ivan said.

"Then get us the frig out of here!" Ace barked.

"Where?" Ivan asked.

"Anywhere! Just pick a destination that's not inside of a star or asteroid field and punch it!"

"You got it." Ivan engaged the hyperdrives and *Betty* winked out of normal space just as an energy blast erupted from the shiny silver ship.

# 3

# We All Screw the Pooch Every Now and Then

"What do you mean we're locked out of the nav system?" Ace asked.

"Just that. We're locked out. I can't alter the course heading," Ivan replied. His eyelids stopped fluttering, and he glanced around as if the answers would jump out at him.

"Aren't you interfaced directly with Betty's computer?" Ace asked.

"Yes," Ivan said.

"Then, why can't you alter the course?" Ace asked.

"I. Don't. Know!" Ivan's eyes bugged, and for a moment he looked more like a normal, primal chimpanzee rather than a super intelligent cyborg.

Ace took the hint and backed off. Ivan was his best friend and apparently stressed out. It didn't do them any good to fight.

"Alright, alright!" Ace conceded. "It's just that...I've heard stories, ya know? About people trying to get through the blockade. Like, I've heard of Blagovian raiders who tried to sneak in and conquer Earth right after it went up."

Ace shuddered and continued, "The story goes that one of them infiltrated the Galactic Border Patrol and posed as an office clerk to get the codes to drop the positron field keeping everyone out. After months of work, he finally got access, and his crew was on their way to raid Earth. They got as far as the moon before something ripped their ship to shreds. One Blagovian escaped in a lifeboat and got picked up in the Delexian System. They got the story out of him, but he went nuts from the trauma. They had to lock him away in a looney bin. It's pretty clear The Powers That Be don't want anyone messing with Earth. And just 'cause we were born there doesn't mean we can just slide on through like nobody cares."

"We're gonna make it through, Ace," Ivan said. "Don't worry. And I'm certain that once the nav program runs its course, we'll have control again."

Ace shook his head and said, "Yeah, well. You know. It's just that it's illegal for anyone outside to go to Earth. And I'm just not real keen on breaking the law and—"

"Since when?" Ivan interrupted. "Ace, before we started touring with Mustache Supernova you were basically a smuggler! You break the law all the time. Why now, all of a sudden, are you worried about it? I'll tell you why. It's because you're afraid of going back to Earth."

"I ain't afraid of nothing, Ivan." Ace held a mug of cawfeen, a hot brewed stimulant beverage. It was going to be a long night, and Ace decided to switch from beer to a beautiful cup of steamy go-go juice for a recharge.

Annoyed by Ivan's comment, Ace accidentally took too large of swig and burned his top lip and tongue.

"Dammit," Ace said under his breath as he set the cawfeen in a cup holder that slid out from the dash. He tapped a button on the touchscreen nestled among vintage-looking big rig dials and switches. The heads-up display showed an image of the Solar System and a little blinking dot that represented them approaching it. The readout in the corner reported they had three hours until they reached the Oort Cloud, the shell of icy objects that defines the outermost border of the Solar System.

Ace let out a prolonged sigh and brought up the itinerary for the rest of the Mustache Supernova tour. The party at Sleazon's was intended to mark the halfway point of the tour. They still had sixteen weeks to go, and now they would be late rendezvousing with the rest of the massive caravan. If they didn't wrap up this little trek to Earth quickly, they'd be on the hook for the millions of credits worth of sound and light gear in *Betty*'s cargo bay.

"Call me crazy, but I'm not feeling particularly happy there is a homicidal maniac after us, and there's some kind of astral projecting dead-not-dead rock star asleep in our sick bay, Ivan. And we're hurtling through space towards Lemmy knows what. The one thing..." Ace paused for effect. "The one thing that is keeping me from completely freaking out is this El Dorado business. You really think Elvis has some sorta stash of gold?"

"I think it's a real possibility," Ivan said. "I can't imagine what else he means by El Dorado."

Gold was precious in every part of the galaxy and a standard form of currency that everyone coveted. None more than Drags Vlorgo, Ace's bookie and loan shark. Vlorgo was a particular kind of butthole who loved to deck every inch of his body in gluttonous displays of wealth. Even a little bit of gold would be enough to satiate Vlorgo for a while and buy Ace some more time to pay off his debts. It would also save him from a very uncomfortable leg breaking. Or worse.

"Plus, man," Ivan said. "He's the King of Rock 'n' Roll. We gotta help him, right?"

Ivan's media stash included several examples of Elvis's music and movies. Ace was familiar but more a fan of heavier stuff like Black Sabbath, Motorhead, AC/DC and Led Zeppelin. Ivan swore all that stuff owed its existence to Elvis. Even Ivan's beloved Ramones owed Presley a colossal debt. That was really saying something. Ivan believed wholeheartedly the Ramones were the pinnacle of musical perfection.

Ace yawned. The cawfeen was not doing the trick.

"Listen. I'm gonna go take a power nap. Wake me up when we hit the border," Ace said.

"You got it, Ace. Nighty-night," Ivan replied.

On the way to his cabin, Ace stopped at a computer panel on the wall and pulled up a video feed of the infirmary. Elvis was still out. There had been no new Elvis apparitions since they escaped the Shiny Man two hours ago. Whatever means Elvis had used to communicate with them were not available to him now.

Ace shook his head as he continued to his cabin. He'd seen some wild stuff in his day, so he wasn't particularly freaked out. What did unnerve him, however, was the thought of setting foot on Earth.

When Ace was a small child, he asked a nun at the orphanage about where he came from. He was beginning to suspect that he was different from the other children.

"A backwater planet called Earth," the nun said. "It is a dreadful and awful place. They threw you away. A sweet dear child like you. Threw you away like garbage. An awful and terrible place."

When Ace pressed the issue asking for more information about Earth the nun locked him in a closet for three days. The orphanage had a pretty liberal punishment policy. Ace had known some kids who lost fingers from particularly militant stick-wielding nuns.

Ace's time in solitary planted seeds of resentment that blossomed as he got older. Around that time the other orphans became cruel and began segregating themselves into cliques. Ace was always on the outside. Alone. The other kids mostly ignored him. Sometimes they would laugh at him or hurl confusing insults when he would try and fail to answer a supposedly easy question in Quantum Engineering or Fractal Geometry class.

Resentment continued into adulthood when Ace learned that the rest of the galaxy was much harsher than the orphanage.

He considered trying to go to Earth, but when he found out about the blockade, he figured that was that. Just another expanse he couldn't traverse. Another reminder that he was a man without a home.

The solitude hardened him, and he stopped telling people what planet he was from. It wasn't until he met Ivan that he started to feel a little more normal about the whole thing. If you can call having a Russian cyborg chimp as a friend "normal."

Ivan's knowledge of Earth and burgeoning media stash helped rekindle Ace's sense of wonder. It had already been piqued a bit from the botched media dump but actually seeing and hearing real humans behave on screen had a profound effect on Ace.

It was Ivan who got Ace into Earth music. Starting with the Ramones, of course. The energy and excitement in those songs stirred Ace's blood in ways he couldn't even describe. The danger of pounding rhythms and raging guitars spoke to him on a primal level.

Yet, the feeling of loss and resentment always remained beneath it all.

Ace called himself a casual consumer of Earth media very different from the fetish collectors and die-hards like Ivan. But deep down he loved it all every bit as much as Ivan did. It repulsed him while at the same time enriching him. Like a pacifist who loved watching graphic bloody horror shows.

In his cabin, Ace mumbled to himself as he climbed into bed. "As much as I resent Earth for abandoning me I gotta admit, I am a little excited to finally see it. It'll be cool to see all the car chases, the barroom brawls, big rigs, the music that is always in the background of every conversation..."

Ace drifted off into sleep and dreamed of being escorted by three beautiful lady private investigators. One redhead, one brunette, and one blonde with hair so feathered it looked like the down of a beautiful golden garble goose.

The three kept calling him Charlie and said they had a secret mission for him.

\* \* \*

Ace woke with a start. He could feel *Betty* shaking, which was weird because the inertial dampeners kept vibrations to a minimum while in outer space. The ship only felt like that when they were flying through a planet's atmosphere. Or driving on the ground.

"Sumbitch!" Ace jumped out of bed and tapped a few commands on the data screen next to his bed. He called up the vital stats on the ship and wiped the sleep out of his eyes. He blinked hard and rubbed his eyes again. The screen read:

*System calibrated and reading in local nomenclature*
*Elevation: 337 feet above sea level*
*Locale: 35.514377, -89.262863 - Interstate 40 - "Music*
*Highway," Hatchie National Wildlife Refuge, Brownsville,*

*Tennessee, United States of America, North American Continent, Northern Hemisphere, Earth, Off Limits Sector of Space, Solar System*
*Ground speed: 74 miles per hour*

"That crazy son of a bitch!" Ace tripped over his boots as he stormed out of his cabin. He continued cursing as he bounded down the corridor, in his socks and underwear, towards the cockpit.

Ace burst in and was shocked to see a strange man sitting in the driver's seat. The driver was an older human male with gray-blonde hair sticking out in tufts under a used-to-be-white mesh backed hat. Emblazoned on the hat was an anchor and the words, "Pussy Admiral" written in puffy letters. He had a pot belly covered by a wrinkled flannel shirt and jeans with engine grease stains on the thighs. The man didn't notice Ace had barged in because he was singing *Rockaway Beach* by the Ramones at the top of his lungs.

"What the shit is this?" Ace yelled.

The man glanced back at Ace and giggled when his eyes passed over Ace's underwear, then turned back to the road. He never stopped singing. When the final cymbal hit rang out the man finally spoke.

"Glad you're up! Have a seat, man!" It was Ivan's voice.

"Ivan?" Ace sat down in the co-pilot seat.

"Yup!" the old trucker—Ivan—turned and flashed a smile. A few teeth were missing, and he hadn't shaved in about a week.

"Yeah! I pulled out one of the dazzlers from the Mustache Supernova gear we're hauling," Ivan said. "I rigged it to make me look like a real Earth trucker!"

Mustache Supernova were known throughout the galaxy for their epic stage shows. Ace and Ivan's job was to haul most of the stage gear from one show to the next. This included the personal holographic projectors (or "dazzlers" as they were more commonly known) that each member wore on stage. Every few songs the band would morph into different mythical beasts, and now Ivan had used a dazzler to disguise himself as a human trucker.

It was a smart move. A talking chimpanzee would raise a lot of eyebrows, but it didn't change the fact that Ace felt betrayed.

Ace looked out the window next to him and saw a lush forest whisking by at seventy miles per hour. On the road ahead was the tail end of a semi-tractor trailer that had mudflaps depicting a little mustachioed cowboy holding pistols. The words "Back Off" were written in fat block letters above the image. The bumper sported a rectangular sticker that read, "How's My Driving? Call 1-800-EAT ME." The fact that Ace could read the words meant his translator implant was working. Although he didn't really understand what it actually implied.

"We gotta get some of those," Ivan said.

"What?" Ace asked.

"Some of those mudflaps. They're hilarious!" Ivan reached over and hit a switch. Windows on the driver's side of the cabin started to open, and fresh air whooshed in.

Ivan closed his eyes, breathing in. "Ah! Smell that? That's fresh Earth air! We're here! Oh wow, I love this song!"

Just then another Ramones song (*Beat on the Brat*) started playing on the sound system.

Ivan sang and tapped on the steering wheel.

"Ivan! What the shit, man?" Ace yelled.

"Oh! Yeah," Ivan turned the volume down, so he didn't have to shout. "They've got a worldwide data network up and running now! There's so much music on there." Ivan drew out the word "so" to be three syllables long. "Did you know the Ramones have *fourteen* studio albums!? Four-teen, man! All I have in the stash are the first three!"

"What?" Ace asked.

"Yeah, man. And there's more than just music. It's got a little of everything. TV and movies, too. And lemme tell you, there are some movies out there that are way racier than *Deep Throat*. I've got Betty plugged into it, and we can access everything and—"

"Pull over," Ace said.

"What?" Ivan asked.

"I said pull over, goddammit!"

Ivan pulled *Betty* into an open parking space of the next rest stop and put her into park.

Ace opened the passenger side door and hopped out. The gravity was lighter than he expected it would be. The fresh air felt good on his skin, but he didn't want to admit it. He was super pissed off.

A few yards away a family rushed and fussed outside of a van. The father tried to get his kids into the restroom before one of them puked. The little guy didn't make it and wound up hurling all over Dad's jeans.

"Sorry, Dad," the kid said and wiped off his mouth. "Whoa. Look at that." The kid pointed directly at *Betty*. Ace turned around to get a look at what the kid was aiming at.

The rockets that straddled either side of *Betty*'s semi-trailer were now tucked mostly into the hull. When *Betty* was set for ground transport, there was no need for the rocket nacelles to be extended. For the uninitiated, it could be an odd sight. The rockets came straight out of Ace's imagination and had a distinct unreal look to them. Even though they were solid and real, they looked just like animated cartoon rockets. Only about a quarter of the rockets stuck out beyond the perimeter of the trailer; the rest of their bulk was tucked within.

Ace smirked and looked back at the kid. Then he realized that the kid was not, in fact, pointing at *Betty*, but was pointing at Ace himself. He looked down at himself and understood what all the fuss was about. In his haste, Ace failed to remember that he was dressed in nothing but tube socks and underwear.

Now, if Ace were a boxer short kind of guy—or even a boxer-brief kind of guy— this wouldn't be so much of an issue. But, as it turned out, Ace was a bikini-brief kind of a guy. Again, not so entirely shocking. However, he was not used to the lighter gravity on Earth. Galactic Standard Gravitation was about one and a half times that of Earth. As a consequence, his body circulated blood more freely than it otherwise would. The result? A show that Ace was not entirely thrilled to be giving at the moment. Yet, to an innocent bystander, Ace looked exceptionally...*thrilled.*

"Honey!" the father called to his wife. "Get in the van! Now!"

"But Bella hasn't gone yet!" she called back, almost at the Ladies Room entrance.

"I don't care! We're going to the next rest stop down the road!" Dad said as he shooed his son back in the van and did his best to brush off the puke from his pants.

"Why do we have to—oh my God! Bella! Get in the van! Get in the van!" Mom put her hand over her daughter's eyes and quick-walked her to the van. They all piled in and peeled out like their lives depended on it.

Ace blushed, covered his crotch, and shuffled back to *Betty*'s cab. He hopped up into the passenger seat and crossed his legs, resting his hands on his lap.

"Yeah," Ivan said. "That happened to me when I started walking around, too. Lighter gravity, you know?" Ivan let out a semi-silent guffaw. "Hey, man. What's the problem?"

"What's the problem? Where do I begin?" Ace shouted and was about to lay into Ivan when five triple black sedans tore into the rest stop and surrounded *Betty*.

"What the—?" Ivan said.

A man in an expensive-looking suit stepped out of the lead car holding a bullhorn. He wore sunglasses and had a tightly cropped all-business haircut. He flicked a switch on the side of the bullhorn and brought it to his mouth.

"Vehicle occupants! This is Special Agent Randall Calhoun of the United States Federal Bureau of Investigation. Power your vehicle off and step out with your hands up. Do not attempt to flee or make any sudden moves or provocations. We have you surrounded!"

Men with shotguns and bulky vests popped out of the jet black sedans and trained their weapons on *Betty*'s cab. A black helicopter with twin machine guns mounted on the front swooped out of the sky and hovered above them. The pilot spun up the guns with menace.

Tight red beams of light danced across *Betty*'s windshield. Ace winced expecting a blast of laser fire. *Betty*'s autonomic systems engaged and a tint washed over the windshield as soon as the focused beams of light struck it. From the outside, the windshield would appear one hundred percent opaque, but Ace and Ivan could still see out from within.

Ivan reached out and tapped the glass where the laser reflected in a bright red blotch.

"Wimpy laser," Ivan said with a shrug. "Must be some sort of targeting system."

The man with the bullhorn continued, "F-22 Raptors have been scrambled from Langley Air Force Base and will be overhead in approximately fifteen seconds. Any more funny business and they will unleash the fury of God Almighty upon you. Exit the vehicle. Now."

Ace turned to Ivan and said, "Who's this asshole?"

"Beats me," Ivan said. "Some kind of cop or something?"

"Were you speeding?" Ace asked.

"No," Ivan said.

"Shit." Ace didn't like cops. In his experience, the galaxy was just variations on a single theme. Everywhere was pretty much like anywhere else. Each planet with a certain level of technical sophistication looked and behaved pretty much like every other one. Sure, physical appearances were different, and each had its own unique cultural quirks. Some planets had better food, cooler tech, faster music, et cetera.

Ace's line of work sometimes straddled the technicalities of the law and cops were always cops throughout the galaxy. And always a pain in the ass.

Since Earth was hundreds of years behind the most infantile members of the Galactic Union, this local yokel was sure to be a double pain in the ass.

Just as Ace was about to jump out of the cab and do something stupid, Ivan said, "Hang on. I have an idea."

Ivan reached over to a data port on the dash and jacked into it. The grizzled old trucker hologram shimmered a little around the metal spike as it tried and failed to disguise the cybernetic metal. Diggs Bellavort, the bass player for Mustache Supernova, always complained about the dazzler's inability to handle cyber-metallic objects. Diggs had a somewhat unusual implant, an "upgrade" he called it, in his nether region. He religiously complained his dazzler couldn't make it look even larger and more voluptuous when he morphed into a giant bass-playing fire-breathing dragon on stage.

"The ladies expect the goods! I want to show them the goods!" Diggs would say when the dazzler failed to project the adequately proportioned dangling monstrosity between his legs.

Ivan let out a few subtle laughs as his eyes fluttered. "I'm searching the Internet for that cop...He's part of something called the Federal Bureau of Investigation. Some sort of national police force. Stand by, I'm cracking their computer systems...Man. They've got terrible security...OK. I've pulled up a personnel report on Agent Randall Calhoun. Hmmm. Interesting."

Ivan unjacked from the data port and started tapping his fingers on his belt buckle—a silver and gold oval with a sizeable mouthed fish at the center. Ivan's holographic disguise stuttered, revealing Ivan's fingers tapping on the control pad of the dazzler itself.

Ivan pulled a cable out of his wrist and plugged it into the side of the belt buckle. The holographic projection exploded in a rain of multicolored lights. Ace had to shield his eyes from the brilliance.

When the light show subsided, the haggard trucker was gone. A new man in a dark navy suit and red tie appeared in the driver's seat. The man had a friendly uneven smile, graying hair, and looked to be in good physical shape for an older man. He unplugged the cable from the conventional looking prong-style belt buckle. The oversized oval buckle with the fish was replaced by a sensible traditional dress belt. He reached into a bag next to the driver's seat and pulled out a second dazzler and plugged the cable into the side of it.

"She sells seashells by the seashore..." Ivan spoke as he tapped on the control pad of the second dazzler. Each syllable began to modulate and distort as he spoke. He was changing his voice, a trick Ace had seen before but found particularly unsettling now because of the amount of spit Ivan produced on each *sh* sound.

"She sells seashells by the seashore...The lips, the teeth, the tip of the tongue, the tip of the tongue, the teeth, the lips." Ivan got closer to the sound he liked. "A box of biscuits, a box of mixed biscuits, and a biscuit mixer. Mission accomplished. Mish-shun ah-comm-plish-duh. Mission accomplished...There, that oughta do it. Whatdya think, Ace?"

"I think you sound and look ridiculous. Who the hell are you supposed to be? That guy's father or something?" Ace asked.

"Something like that. Here. Put this on." Ivan unplugged the cable and handed him the second dazzler. The cable retracted into Ivan's wrist.

The dazzler itself was an unassuming device about the size of a deck of cards and worked by projecting a three-dimensional image over whatever it touched. When Ace clipped it on the waistband of his bikini briefs, a sudden burst of light made him squint.

His vision cleared but everything looked a bit darker. He looked down and found himself dressed in a black business suit. He wore a black tie and saw in the ghost reflection of the window next to him he wore black sunglasses. A coiled wire ran up along the side of his neck from within his suit jacket and terminated in a small earpiece stuck in his left ear.

"What are we supposed to be? Businessmen?" Ace asked Ivan.

"Just follow my lead," Ivan said, opening the driver's side door. Before Ace could protest, Ivan had his feet on the ground and his hands up in the universal "don't shoot" gesture.

Ace let a flourish of obscenity fly then opened his own door and exited with his hands up.

When Agent Calhoun saw the two of them he held up his own hand, motioning to the others with the shotguns to hold their fire, Ace guessed. He hoped.

"Don't shoot there, kemosabi," Ivan said in his new spittle-filled voice. "We come in peace. Heh heh heh."

"Sir! What are you doing here?" Agent Calhoun called out. He dropped the hand holding the bullhorn to his side and stared slack-jawed.

"Ah. That's on a need-to-know right now, Randy," Ivan said. "Can I call you Randy? It's kinda my thing. Giving people nicknames. Ya know? How about this, Randy? You and your men back on outta here and let me and *my* team handle this." Ivan gestured to Ace who just nodded.

"Whatdya say?" Ivan said. "Maybe I can upgrade that nickname there. How's that sound? Howsabout Randle Bar? Or! Or, how about Rando Calrissian? Man! I love them Star Wars movies. What a hoot they are. I love them Jed-Eyes. And those lightsabers. Big ole laser swords. Why don't we have those yet, Rando?"

Agent Calhoun was stunned. "I—I don't know, sir."

"I'll tell you why," Ivan quipped. "It's 'cause we don't spend enough on dee-fense. That's why. Now, I know this is a bit unorthodox, and you probably didn't know that I work on some black book projects nowadays. Secret stuff, ya know? Haven't seen me in the media too much these past few years. Have ya? Well, it's all because I'm working on some top secret stuff, son."

Ivan pointed at himself and continued, "So, how about you trust ole George? Huh? I've got it under control, and you stand down these men and let us get to it. We've got the situation under control."

Agent Calhoun hesitated for a moment then yelled into his

bullhorn, "Blue Team, disperse and meet back at the field office!"

The shotgun-wielding cops climbed back into their vehicles and one by one pulled out of the rest area and sped down the interstate. The black helicopter took off into the sky and flew away.

When all but Agent Calhoun's sedan remained, he gave a little wave and said, "Sorry for the trouble, sir. I just didn't know you were here. When we got the call, I didn't know what to expect. Sorry, sir."

"Aw. Don't worry about it, Rando," Ivan said. "We all screw the pooch every now and again. Am I right? Heh heh heh. Go on now. Scoot. They'll be a debriefing document waiting for you when you get back to your office."

"Thank you, sir," Agent Calhoun said and climbed into his sedan. Then, before speeding away, he popped out and said, "It was an honor to meet you, President Bush."

# 4

# The Smell of Pure Happiness

T wo hours later they arrived in Memphis. Ace was driving and fully clothed in his signature Mustache Supernova t-shirt, jeans, and snapback embroidered hat. Ivan had resumed his gnarled old trucker disguise.

Once they were satisfied the cops were gone, Ivan took Ace's dazzler and affixed it to *Betty*'s front bumper. A few button taps later he had it programmed to disguise *Betty* to look like a recreational vehicle called a Winnebago. Ivan told Ace they passed a bunch of them on the road and figured it would be the most common vehicle they could use. If the cops were still looking for them, they wouldn't be able to identify them by sight.

Not that Ivan was entirely sure how they identified them in the first place.

Ace had a pretty good idea, though. Maybe someone spotted a semi-truck with cartoon rockets strapped to its sides descending from the sky. A flying truck was not something people were used to seeing every day. One of the many reasons Ivan was on Ace's bad side at that moment.

"I said I'm sorry," Ivan said.

"I know," Ace said through a clenched jaw. He was still pissed off that Ivan didn't wake him when they hit the border.

"It was really super simple. Nothing fancy," Ivan said.

"That's what you said." Ace took a deep breath and held it in.

"It was a just a probe sitting there. It hailed us and told me to turn around. I replied to its hail and said we were from Earth. It scanned us. Detected Earth DNA then let us through. No biggie."

"OK. I'm not mad." Ace was definitely mad. He wanted to see Earth with his own eyes from space. He wanted a chance to back out of this ridiculous mission, too. The prospect of a considerable payoff would probably have made him carry on anyway. But he wanted to be the one that made the call. He and Ivan were partners, and Ace didn't like significant decisions happening without him.

"Well! Would you look at that!" Elvis said from behind. Ace and Ivan both about jumped through the roof. Ace jerked the steering wheel, and *Betty* swerved a few feet outside the lane. A guy in a flatbed truck attempting to pass them laid on his horn and shot a middle finger out the driver side window.

"Jeez! C'mon! You can't do shit like that, man!" Ace shouted at Elvis when he regained control and the flatbed truck accelerated ahead of them.

"Sorry, man. I don't really have much control over this. It just kind of happens, you know?" Elvis said.

"No, I don't know!" Ace said. "What the hell *is* happening? You're still in sickbay, right? This is another, what'd you call it, astral projection?"

"Yeah. I'm in a coma, man," Elvis said. "It's kinda terrible. Look I don't know how this is happening. OK? But what I do know is I don't have much time to talk. Don't ask me how I know. I just do. I can't hold this projection for long. It's real hard. So listen. You guys gotta get me to Graceland. Or I'm done for, man."

"Well, that's the general idea. We're heading there now," Ace said to Elvis and then to Ivan, "How much farther do we have?"

"About five miles," Ivan reported.

"Man! Look at this place!" Elvis said as his apparition floated towards the windshield. He bent down so he could get a better look. "This place is all built up! Doesn't look a thing like it did in seventy-seven!"

Ace watched Elvis out of the corner of his eye, keeping his eyes on the road, but taking quick glances at the ghost man next to him. It was very unsettling.

"You wanna tell us what we're doing here?" Ace asked. "And what's this business with El Dorado? You have a huge gold stash or something? 'Cause let me tell you, pal, time is money and the longer we're here, the more money I'm losing."

Elvis shouted, "Oh man! We're close to Libertyland! Man, I love that Zippin' Pippin! You ever been on a rollercoaster? That's my favorite rollercoaster of all time, man. Maybe once you get me fixed up, we can ride the 'coaster a few times. There ain't nothing like an old wooden rollercoaster. You know, one time I rented out the whole park just so me and my buddies could ride the Zippin' Pippin all night long. What a hoot! Man, that was a fun day, I — "

And then he was gone. Elvis disappeared mid-sentence.

"Goddammit!" Ace shouted and hit the steering wheel. "What the shit is going on here? Do you have any idea?"

"Not really," Ivan said. "But I can tell you the projections happen at semi-regular intervals. While you were sleeping, he appeared a few times. About every two hours. After the first time, I set up the scanners to start recording everything they could. When he appears, there's a super weird energy signature. I can't identify what it is or where it comes from, but I've got Betty working on it. It seems like he can only hold the projection for a few minutes."

"Wait. Betty's up and running? Since she's been quiet this whole time, I assumed she was down, and you rigged something in her place," Ace said.

"Not completely," Ivan said. "Her logic functions are there, but the artificial intelligence personality matrix is still a little weird. We might need to take her to a service station when we leave Earth."

"Weird how?" Ace asked.

"Betty?" Ivan asked.

"I'm busy, asshole!" *Betty* sounded like a quark-dust junkie who just crawled out from beneath a cardboard box.

"See?" Ivan said. "Her computer systems are fully functional. It's just her artificial intelligence is a little messed up right now."

Ace had stiffness in his jaw, and he clenched his teeth. *Betty* was supposed to be the voice of reason when he and Ivan had disagreements. With her personality matrix scrambled he'd have no one on his side to back him up.

He decided to let it go and get back to the task at hand.

"Did Elvis make any sense the other times?" Ace asked. "Or was it more rambling about goddamn rollercoasters?" Ace asked.

"Sometimes," Ivan replied. "His thoughts are super disjointed. It's like he has a hard time focusing and concentrating on the real world. According to the med computer, though, his condition is deteriorating. He's dying. So, that might have something to do with it."

"Well," Ace said with a sigh. "It looks like we're almost there. So maybe we can start getting some goddamn answers."

Ivan began reading a report he gleaned from accessing the Earth-wide data network. "Alright. Here we go. According to something called Wikipedia, Graceland is a mansion on a thirteen point eight-acre estate in Memphis, Tennessee that was home to Elvis Presley. It is located at three seven six four Elvis Presley Boulevard in the vast Whitehaven community about nine miles from downtown Memphis and less than four miles north of the Mississippi border. It currently serves as a museum. It was opened to the public on June 7, 1982. The site was listed on the National Register of Historic Places on November 7, 1991 and declared a National Historic Landmark on March 27, 2006. Graceland has become one of the most visited private homes in America with over six hundred and fifty thousand visitors a year."

"Good to know," Ace said. "Looks like we're here."

Up ahead on the right a blue and white sign read, "Graceland. Home of Elvis A. Presley." Ace pulled *Betty* into the entrance and rolled up to a small white guard shack. A man stepped out and waved at Ace to slow down and roll down his windows.

"Hi there!" said the man. "Nice Winnie. Oversize vehicles are fifteen dollars."

"Excuse me?" Ace asked.

"Fifteen dollars. For parking."

"We just want to go inside Graceland," Ace said. "This is it, isn't it?"

"Well," the man said, "This is the visitor center and the parking lot. Graceland is across the street over there. You park here and get your tickets right over there, and then you can go in and tour the mansion."

"We don't have any money," Ace said.

"Well, now that's a problem," the man said. "If you want to park here, you have to pay. And if you want to tour the mansion, you have to pay. There's free walk-ups to the meditation garden from 7:30 to 8:30 every morning so if y'all want to come back

51

tomorrow that's a freebie."

Ace didn't like being told "no." He contemplated beating the man to a pulp or driving over him but thought that might attract too much attention. They already had one run-in with the law and didn't want another.

Ace couldn't shake the feeling that he would see Agent Calhoun of the Federal Bureau of Investigation again. Although he looked nothing like the sheriff from the movie *Smokey and the Bandit*, there was something in Agent Calhoun's eyes that lead Ace to believe he had the same blind conviction to duty.

Ace had run into lawmen throughout the galaxy, and although pains in the ass, most were pretty alright people when you got right down to it. Reasonable. Every now and then you had to grease a palm so they would look the other way. Rarely did he meet zealots with the conviction to pursue a wanted man to the ends of the galaxy. But that was the look he saw in Agent Calhoun eyes.

*What would Bandit do at a time like this?* Ace thought. *He'd turn on the charm!*

"So, what do you suggest we do, sir?" Ace flashed a friendly smile hoping to coax the man into letting them through.

"Well," the man said. "There's a KFC up the road. You probably passed it on the way here. I know they let buses park there sometimes."

"KFC?" Ace asked.

"Yeah. You know. Kentucky Fried Chicken. It's just a few blocks away."

Ace thanked the man for his time all the while wanting to smash his face in. He backed *Betty* out into the street and drove forward looking for a place to turn around. On the other side of Elvis Presley Boulevard sat Graceland, a picturesque colonial style mansion set back from the road surrounded by a six foot tall stone wall.

Shuttle buses ferried tourists from the welcome center and into the open gates of Graceland. Ace did a U-turn and eyeballed the sprawling grounds of Graceland through Ivan's passenger side window. The stone wall surrounding the property was covered with graffiti; thousands upon thousands of messages to the King from fans.

Ace slowed as they rolled past the open gates made of wrought-iron and shaped like a book of sheet music complete with green-colored musical notes next to a silhouette of Elvis himself.

The open gates welcomed shuttle buses, but a guard at a small shack turned away everyone else. Ace brought *Betty* to a slow stop, much to the chagrin of the honking cars behind him. At first, he thought it was because he was blocking traffic. Ivan's shouts told him otherwise.

"Whoa! Ace. The dazzler is failing." Ivan hung out the window looking down the side of *Betty*. Ace stuck his head out his own window and confirmed it. The holographic image projected by the dazzler flickered like a broken video billboard.

Ivan sat back into his seat. His own dazzler was malfunctioning as well. Every few microseconds a polygon of old man face would blink out of existence and show part of Ivan's chimpanzee face underneath.

"Betty!" Ivan said. "What's happening to the dazzler projections?"

"Don't. Know." *Betty*'s voice was disjointed and oddly robotic. "Error. Interference. Some kind—interference emanating from—mansion—left. —Unknown energy source. Something powerful. It's dis—rupting—all—systems *bzzzt*." Lights and computer displays flashed like all-night Manzallian discotheque.

"Sheeeit!" Ace stomped on the accelerator and *Betty* inched forward. Within a few seconds, they passed the entrance of Graceland and the end of the stone wall surrounding the property. As soon as *Betty* cleared the property line, all systems blinked back to normal. They sped past a souvenir shop almost ramming into the back of a pickup truck. Ace slammed on the brakes and brought *Betty* to a complete stop. Ivan flew out of his seat and smacked his head against the dashboard.

"Yo!" said Ivan. "I'm not buckled in!"

Ace winced. "Oh. Sorry, man."

Ivan rubbed his disguised forehead. "I'll live. But we need to run a system diags to see what's going on, Ace. There's the KFC the guard told us about. Pull in there."

As Ace pulled into the KFC, he looked up at the red and white sign depicting a smiling bearded man with glasses enticing people to enter the parking lot.

"This looks like a good parking spot," Ace said as he brought *Betty* to rest behind the restaurant and powered her off.

"Yeah!" Ivan said as he extended his cyber-implant and jacked into the data port in the dashboard. "I'm starting the diagnostics now."

"Cool," Ace said. "Well, I'm going to hop out and stretch my legs while you run those diags."

"Yeah," Ivan said as his eyes fluttered from the computer interface activity. "I'll be a few minutes here."

Ace hopped out of the cab and was immediately hit in the face with the smell of something mouthwatering and delicious. The scent was unlike anything he'd smelled before. It was earthy, sweet, and savory. He inhaled deeply and became overwhelmed with a warm and delightful sensation flooding his body.

"Mmmm," Ace sniffed and spoke to himself. "Man! What is

that smell? Oh. My. God. It...It...Smells...Delicious!"

A desire began to stir within him, a ravenous craving that went beyond standard hunger. Like the smell was somehow calling to his soul itself. It was a near-religious experience. Like being wrapped in the arms of the Creator himself and having His delicious perfume fill Ace's nostrils and very essence.

"Oh man!" Ace said. "I have got to see what's going on inside that KFC!"

Ace followed his nose and walked into the KFC salivating like a starving ralladog.

When Ace stepped into the KFC the scrumptious scented air flooded his senses. He was so moved emotionally he had to pause for a moment, close his eyes, and just stand there inhaling. His knees weakened for a moment.

*If pure happiness had a smell*, Ace mused. *This must be it.*

The restaurant had a few occupied tables where people sat and picked at their meals. It looked like the main attraction was a sort of meat with a golden crispy outer layer. Everyone had some of that. Most everyone had biscuits (easy for Ace to identify because every culture in the galaxy has biscuits) and white pasty mush covered in a brown sauce. Some people had what looked like little bent tubes covered in sticky orange goo. But the meat—that had to be the fried chicken. There were pictures of it everywhere. On the windows, on hanging signs, everywhere.

A counter sat prominently situated to Ace's right with a large menu on the awning above it. A customer was ordering, and Ace strained to hear.

Behind the counter stood a young woman with shoulder-length jet black hair and bangs that stuck out from under her KFC visor hat. She wore a red knit collared shirt with KFC embroidered on the chest. Ace was intrigued by the way she yelled at the customer.

"Jesus Christ! Not again!" she yelled. "You guys just hit us last week!"

"Shut up!" the customer barked back. "Put it all in the bag!"

Ace worried the customer was going to get all the chicken before he had a chance to get some. When Ace got closer, however, he noticed the woman pulling out paper money from the register and shoving it into a plastic KFC bag. He had seen money loads of times on various TV shows and movies but was still taken aback by how small the paper notes actually were.

"Hurry up!" the customer yelled, gesturing with something in his hand. Not any something. A gun.

*Is this guy robbing the place?* Ace thought.

Ace watched as the woman behind the counter shoved more cash in the bag. She had tears in her eyes, and her voice trembled as she said, "Goddammit," with every thrust of her hand. She had a strength in her voice, but it also dripped with fear and sadness.

"Shut up, bitch!" the gunman yelled as he reared back the gun about to pistol whip the woman. He threw his hand forward, and the woman reared back, anticipating the blow.

It never came.

Ace snatched the man's wrist just as the gun was about to hit the woman's face and he squeezed hard. The thief yelped. Ace heard bones crunching over the *thud* of the pistol dropping to the counter.

Ace grabbed the man's other arm and pinned it behind his back with enough force to snap it at the elbow. As the thief cried his knees gave out, and Ace held him up without strain.

Ace thought the man had some kind of bone disorder that made him so brittle, but he appeared to be of an average build. A little pudgy even.

*Maybe it's the lighter gravity?* Ace thought.

Ace had spent his whole life living under Galactic Standard Gravitation, about one and a half times that of Earth's. As a result, Ace's muscle density was much greater than typical humans. He wasn't Superman, but he was definitely stronger than the average Joe.

"Holy shit!" the woman said.

When she realized the robber was immobilized, she leaned forward over the counter. "Eat it, dickhead! That's what you get. I hope this guy breaks both your arms! Johnny! Call the goddamn cops!"

Her face lit up with a glow, and she stood in a wide stance, fists on her hips, elbows wide.

Then to Ace, she said, "This asshole has robbed us *four* different times! You got a good hold on him? I'll get some shit to tie him up."

"Yes, ma'am. He's not going anywhere," Ace said with a grin. Her excitement was infectious and overshadowed the concern Ace felt when she mentioned calling the cops.

"Psh! Ma'am? Who you calling ma'am?" the woman giggled then bolted out of sight. Ace sured up his grip, and the robber yelped out in pain.

From around the corner, the woman called out, "Yeah! Feel free to fuck him up a little until I get out there."

The woman reappeared with a long orange cord and walked from out behind the counter to tie up the whimpering would-be robber.

"My manager called the cops. They're on their way," she said to Ace. "Keep his hands behind his back."

Ace held fast as she tied the cord around the man's wrists. The work was all close quarters, so the woman had to bump up against Ace as she worked. Her hips touched his hips, and her hands brushed over his hands a few times. Ace felt slight tingles with each accidental touch.

After a few moments of work, she squatted and worked at the man's ankles. Ace felt nervous. He'd never been this close to a human woman before.

Sure, he'd known alien women throughout the galaxy and thanks to some fluke of nature most were surprisingly human-like. Nearly all the right parts in the right places with some variation, of course. But this was the first time he'd been touched by another human being.

And a human woman.

And an attractive human woman.

Ace's pulse quickened, and he found himself clearing his throat a few times uncontrollably.

The woman's brow furrowed as she worked. She jerked her hands with strong, deft precision.

"Grew up on a farm." She looked up as if to answer Ace's unspoken question. "'Been hogtying critters my whole life." Then she stood and jerked the man's hands up to check how secure they were and to punctuate the next point, "Never tied up a jackass this big before, though." When the man cried out in pain, she yelled, "Shut up! Ass bag."

Her face softened, and she relaxed her posture. "Don't creep out on me, man."

"What?" Ace said and looked away. He didn't realize he was staring.

"I'm just messing with you. You can let him go now. He ain't going nowhere."

Ace released the thief and stepped back to admire her handy

work. Both hands were secure in the middle of his back, and the rest of the cord ran down the length of his leg and circled both ankles in a tight knot.

The thief wobbled before falling over with a giant thud. As he lay there, moaning, the woman held out her hand for Ace to shake it.

"April," she said. Ace looked at her hand, and she wiggled her fingers.

"Oh! Umm, hi! My name is Ace." He reached out and shook her hand. It was soft and firm at the same time. Ace unconsciously held the shake a little too long. When he noticed he pulled his hand back and blushed.

"Ace, huh?" April said with a wink. "You in the business of heroics and thwarting robberies or something?"

"No," Ace said, "I'm a trucker. Just got into town. He looked like he was going to hurt you."

"Well, my hero!" she said with a melodramatic flourish.

A fat man in a red KFC shirt two sizes too small waddled out from the back of the restaurant.

"Jiminy Christmas!" the man squealed. Then to the customers who were gawking from the dining room, "It's OK everyone. Everything is under control. Please stay calm."

"Everyone *is* calm, Johnny," April said.

"You hush up April Massey! I called the police, and they're on their way." Johnny stressed the first syllable as "POH-lease."

"Good! This asshole needs to go away for a long time." April gave the robber a little tap with her foot.

"Language, April! For heaven's sake!" Johnny said and threw up his hands. When he composed himself, he turned to Ace and said, "I saw the whole thing from the back. You, sir, are a bonafide hero! Thank you for your help. This little miscreant has robbed us *four* times in the past few months."

Johnny stuck out his hand, and Ace shook it. Johnny's hands were clammy and a little too soft. Like he hadn't worked a hard day in his life. From the look of his bulbous belly Ace figured Johnny's job was to just eat all day.

"That your Minnie Winnie parked out back?" Johnny asked.

"Huh?" Ace replied.

"The Winnebago. A Minnie Twenty Four, right? Pretty sweet. Me and the missus rented one of them a few times. We like to RV it down to Florida every now and then."

"Yeah. That's ours alright." A voice called from behind them.

Ace turned and saw a man standing about five and a half feet tall with spikey brownish-red hair and a youthful five o'clock shadow's worth of facial hair. He had a friendly smile and mischievous blue eyes. He wore a black leather jacket covered in punk rock patches. Ivan. He'd changed his appearance with the dazzler again.

"Holy shit! You're Seth Green!" April shouted and pointed at Ivan.

"Jeez Louise, April!" Johnny said. "Language!"

"Nah. My name's Ivan. I'm Ace's friend," Ivan said and stepped up alongside Ace.

"Well, you look just like Seth Green, man. Like, exactly. Spitting image!" April said, looking him up and down. "You could be his twin!"

Ivan laughed off the comment and gave Ace a nervous glance. Ace had no idea who Seth Green was but guessed Ivan picked the disguise from a media database.

*This Seth Green guy is probably some sort of celebrity or something. Way to keep a low profile, Ivan,* Ace thought.

Ace later learned after they pulled into the KFC parking lot,

Ivan's dazzler refused to hold the image of the old trucker. Every time Ivan tried to engage the disguise, it would pixelate and malfunction. Same with the dazzler on *Betty*.

After some tinkering, Ivan stabilized *Betty*'s dazzler first by picking a different model Winnebago. He had to work fast. Luckily they passed a white Winnebago Minnie 24 on their way to the KFC. Ivan scanned it and overlaid its image as soon as they were parked.

Ace tried to change the subject. "Umm. So, how about some chicken?"

"Sure! Sure! Anything you want, Mr. Hero," Johnny said, stepping over the moaning thief as he went around the counter to take Ace's order. "What'll it be? On the house."

"Great. Because we don't have any money," Ace said.

"Well," Johnny said. "If you had any it'd be no good here, sir. You just saved my bacon. How about a bucket of Extra Crispy? Our cooks hand bread our freshly prepared chicken seven times, then seven more times to make sure every tender, juicy bite starts with a crispy, flaky crunch."

"Ok," Ace said. "Sounds good."

"Coming right up," Johnny said.

Johnny shouted some instructions to an employee in the back, and within a few moments, he presented a bucket of crispy chicken to Ace.

Ace's mouth watered as he inhaled the heavenly scent and didn't notice that Johnny was speaking to him.

"What?" Ace asked.

"I said, since you ain't got no money, how about a job? How long you in town for? I'd sure feel better if you stayed around for a while and kept an eye on the place. You could park the Winnie out back and be security guards. What'd you say?"

Before Ace could answer, Ivan jumped in and said, "Yeah! We'll do it!"

# 5

# Be a Ritz, Find the El Dorado

Now that Ace was a bonafide hero in the eyes of the employees and management of the KFC on Elvis Presley Boulevard, he was allowed to sample the entire menu at his leisure. He'd already had some Extra Crispy and began work on a bucket of Original Recipe. Both had an amazing flavor that was near orgasmic, but the Extra Crispy had the added fun of a crunchier mouthfeel.

Ace bit into the delectable pieces of crispy meat with ravenous envy. His eyes rolled back in his head as he chewed. The delicious juice exploding in his mouth was unlike anything he'd ever eaten. A tingle of electricity wiggled through his body as he swallowed and greedily took another bite. There was a feeling of completeness inside of him that he'd never felt before; a oneness with the universe on a near spiritual level.

"If pure love has a flavor," he said aloud to himself. "This has to be it."

It was damn good chicken.

Johnny boasted about the secret blend of eleven herbs and spices that seasoned the hand-breaded pieces of chicken. A blend so secret not even the people who make it know its composition. Ace figured he could have Ivan analyze a drumstick with *Betty*'s culinary computers if he needed to know. Right now he was just enjoying the succulent ride.

After polishing off his second bucket Ace decided he needed to stretch his legs and asked if he could take a peek behind the scenes.

"So, you really want to know how the sausage is made?" April asked as she led Ace into the kitchen.

"Sausage?" Ace said. "I thought it was chicken."

"It is, dude. It's just an expression," April said. "Honestly it's not all that exciting. It's pretty much how your momma makes it, just on a larger scale and with fancier equipment."

Ace considered telling April he was an orphan and this was the first time he'd ever eaten fried chicken but decided against it. He didn't want to bum her out, and he really wanted to know how the stuff was made.

"Ok. So there's Rico over there inspecting the chicken," April said. "It's real chicken. Don't believe what they say on the Internet."

"What do they say?" Ace asked.

"That KFC uses some kind of genetically modified mutant chicken monstrosity with fourteen legs and no beak or some shit."

Rico opened a plastic bag filled with chicken parts. They appeared cut and cleaned but looked like way more than one bird's worth of parts for sure.

"So," April continued. "After he checks them to make sure they look alright he puts them in a basket and dunks them in a brine. That's to get the breading to stick. Dunk that shit, Rico!"

Rico performed the motions as April narrated.

"Next, he dries off the chicken a little by tossing the chicken in the basket seven times. Not six times. Not eight times. Seven times. It's kind of a freaky, but KFC is obsessed with doing things seven times."

After Rico tossed the chicken exactly seven times, he spread out the pieces in a large tub filled with breading. He began covering the chicken with an exaggerated motion.

"Check it out," April said. "He does a swimming, swirling motion seven times in the breading. Count 'em. We make the dudes with OCD do this 'cause they seem to get off on the counting thing."

Rico stopped when he reached seven strokes then put the chicken in a rectangular basket. He rocked the basket back and forth in a seesaw motion.

"One, two, three, four, five, six, seven rocks back and forth," April said. "The excess breading falls off, and the perfect amount is left on the bird. Now, if this was Extra Crispy, he'd dunk it back in the brine and do the breading procedure a second time. And I know what you're gonna ask. No, you can't bread it a third time for super duper Extra Crispy. It just flecks off and it cooks weird and nasty. You don't want to eat it."

Rico started laying the breaded chicken out on a rack, arranging the pieces, so they all fit.

"Once the chicken is racked he shoves it in that scary-ass pressure fryer over there," April said, pointing. "Ya know, Colonel Sanders himself invented the pressure fryer. Before they used to do it the old fashion way with big ass skillets and oil on a stove top. This scary awesome pressure fryer is a modern version of Sanders' original model. It has a super heavy hydraulic lid and rack system that drops the chicken in three hundred and seventy-five degree scalding ass hot oil and locks in under pressure to cook faster. You gotta be careful over there, man. That oil is so hot it will melt the skin right off your face. Believe me. I've seen

ACE TUCKER SPACE TRUCKER

it happen. Don't fuck with the hot oil."

Ace nodded like a schoolboy as Rico slid the rack in the empty slot below three full racks in the pressure fryer.

Rico grunted and pushed down on a large handle. The whole apparatus collapsed and lowered into the oil. When the racks of chicken hit the oil a chorus of sizzles and pops rang out. At the end of his swift downward motion, Rico locked the pressure fryer lid into place, sealing it, and hit a timer button.

"Now we wait ten minutes until those suckers are golden brown. Just like the Colonel would've wanted." April put her hand over her heart and giggled.

Fifteen minutes later Ace was eating a piece of the freshly cooked chicken. April warned him that it still might be a little hot, but Ace dove in anyway.

He took a bite of the piping hot chicken. It was even better fresh but very hot. He made an O with his lips to blow air out to cool the hot, delicious meat burning the roof of his mouth. He didn't mind.

Ace thanked April and Rico for the lesson and took a fresh bucket out to his folding chair in the parking lot near *Betty*.

An hour later April exited the building with her KFC shirt untucked. She had a purse with her, and she paused to root around in it until she found a ring with little metal keys on it.

"Hey, Ace!" April called out as she walked toward him. "Man! You sure can put it away. What? You got a hollow leg or something?"

Ace gnawed on a thigh bone, trying to pick every last delectable bit from it. Then said, "Huh?"

"You're still at it with the chicken," April said. "I've never seen someone eat so much chicken in one day. It's like you're not human."

"What do you mean by that? Of course, I'm human."

"Well, duh. Obviously," April said with a wink. "So. I saw your pal, Seth —"

"Ivan."

"Yeah. Ivan. Seth Green's clone. Whatevs. So, I saw he had a pretty sweet jacket on. He's way into punk, huh?"

"Yeah," Ace said. "We're both pretty big fans of the rock and the roll."

"The rock and the roll, huh?" She let out a little giggle. "Well, anyway. If you guys want, you should come out to Murphy's tonight. My friend's band is playing. Based on your pal's patches, I think you'll dig his band. They're called Joey and the Lawrences. They're punk as balls."

Ace tried to riddle out what about balls were so punk. That didn't make any sense. He tapped a finger behind his right ear, the place where his translator was implanted. Maybe it was having trouble with her dialect or something.

The translator replied to his tapping with a tri-tone chime only he could hear. The chime meant it had run a full diagnostic and was functioning at one hundred percent accuracy.

Ace shrugged and decided to change the subject.

"What about watching the KFC?" Ace gestured with the thigh bone.

"Shit, man," April said. "I think it'll be OK. This place has never been robbed after hours. Why would it be? Even crackheads know we don't keep any money on site after we're closed. Look. Just leave the Winnie parked here and I'll drive. What do you say? It'll be fun."

"Sure," Ace said after a moment imagining what a person with a cracked head would be doing wandering around a restaurant parking lot. They'd be better off in a hospital.

"Ok. I gotta go home and wash the stank of the Colonel off me," April said with a wave. "I'll be back in about an hour to pick you guys up."

April got into a brown Buick Century with rusted out wheel wells and started it up. Immediately Ace could hear music blaring at full volume. He watched as April played air drums for a few seconds and sang along. An enthusiastic man was singing about a girl that was "built to rock." Then she pulled off into the night. Blaring guitars and shouts of "That girl is built to rock!" trailed off into the night.

Ace dropped the spent thighbone in the bucket with its eviscerated brethren. He stood, and when satisfied he was alone in the parking lot, he opened the side door on the Winnebago. The dazzler only worked on the exterior so as soon as he opened the door, he was met with the interior of *Betty*'s side airlock. He shut the door quickly behind him in case there were any people with cracked heads wandering about who might have caught a glimpse. Although, there was no way they could get in even if they wanted to. *Betty* was keyed so that only Ace and Ivan could open any doors.

Ace passed through the airlock and found Ivan walking in his direction. Ivan had dropped his human disguise and walked on tall aluminum stilts.

"Yo!" Ivan called out. "Elvis update."

"Hey. What's with the stilts?" Ace asked.

"Oh." Ivan looked down. "They're so comfy I forgot I was wearing them. I put them on in case anyone accidentally bumped into me. I thought it'd be best to be proper human height."

That made sense to Ace. The dazzler would only make it appear Ivan was normal height but he would still physically be four feet tall beneath the hologram. It would be a disaster if someone tapped his hologram on the shoulder and had their hand pass right through it.

"Good thinking," Ace said.

"Yeah! Thanks. So, Elvis update. The med computers say he's stable and his brain activity is off the charts."

"What do you mean off the charts?" Ace asked.

"Like, he's using ninety percent of his brain right now. He has active alpha, delta, theta, and gamma wave patterns. All at the same time. Which should be impossible for a guy in a deep coma."

"So," Ace said. "The guy's a heavy sleeper. Big deal. He done that spooky-ass astral projection thing lately?"

"No. Which is concerning me as well," Ivan said. "He hasn't done it since we passed Graceland. Check this out." Ivan tapped a computer screen on the wall. He issued a series of commands and the display dissolved into a rotating three-dimensional image of a mansion.

"Graceland, I presume," Ace said.

"Yeah. So, I compiled this from public records, blueprints, and the standard environmental scans *Betty* grabbed as we passed by earlier. The scans were incomplete because of this." He pointed at a section on the second floor and a glowing sphere in a room labeled "master bedroom."

"I've been researching Graceland while you've been eating your chicken," Ivan said with a sneer.

"Whatever man," Ace said. "That stuff is delicious. Why don't you try some?"

"Dude. I'm a vegetarian. You know that." Ivan always became annoyed when Ace tried to get him to eat meat.

"Yeah, I know," Ace said. "But we're on Earth. Right? Irregardless you should—"

"It's *regardless*, Ace," Ivan interrupted.

"What?" Ace asked.

"It's re-gard-less," Ivan said slowly. "Not ir-regardless. That means the opposite of what you think it means."

"What the hell are you talking about, Ivan?"

"You can say *irrespective* or *regardless* but never, ever *ir*regardless. It's not the correct word, Ace. Never has been. Never will be."

"...fuck you, Ivan."

"Fair enough," Ivan grinned, then continued, "Anyway, so, there is definitely some weird stuff on the second floor of that house. And check this out: no one's allowed up there. When people pay to tour Graceland, there is a guard at the bottom of the stairs keeping an eye on everything. People who try to go up there are told, quote, that's Elvis's floor and was his private sanctuary in life and out of respect they keep it private to this day. End quote. If you insist on going up there, you can be forcibly removed from the premises and banned for life from returning to Graceland."

Ivan continued, "Not even the people who work there are allowed up there. I read some stuff posted on message boards by former employees. One of them was a guy whose sole job was guarding that staircase. And he was never allowed up there either. Never. The only people who go up there are a few select family members and one special museum curator who brings out items to display every once in a while. And no one's been in the master bedroom or bathroom since the day Elvis supposedly died. Even when the family was still living in the house. They just sealed up the room on August 7, 1977, and left it that way. Out of respect, they say, but there's something else."

Ivan paused for dramatic effect then spoke, "That room is

sealed with some heavy duty tech. Like, non-terrestrial tech. I can't get a solid read on it so I have no idea what it is. But I'll bet credits to crabulons that whatever we're looking for is in there."

"Alright," Ace said. "So Elvis's brain activity, his lack of astral projection, and the whatever-it-is on the second floor of Graceland are all connected. How do we get in?"

"Well," Ivan said with a shrug. "I thought we'd just go break in. Like, now. Graceland is closed up for the night. Should be easy."

Ace thought about it for a minute. He wasn't one for general thievery, but the longer he sat idle, the longer it was until he got a payday. A real payday. Buckets of chicken were nice, but they didn't spend on the galactic market. Not that he knew of, anyway. Gold would be a much better commodity to exchange for goods and services.

"Alright," Ace said. "But, look. Let's do it quick. April invited us to go see some bands tonight."

"Oh yeah?" Ivan crossed his arms and narrowed his eyes. "You want to go back to her place and play some tiddlywinks, too, huh?"

"What? No!" Ace said. "I mean if you're using tiddlywinks as some kind of slang for sex. Then yes. I mean no. I dunno. I just want to get to know her. Is that so wrong? That I would want to get to know another human being for once in my life?"

"Dude," Ivan sneered. "Twelve hours ago you said you didn't care if Earth fell into a black hole. Now you're looking to play house with Mary Jane Watson!"

"I ain't looking to play house, Ivan. Just put some moves on her and see where it takes us. That's it. Plus, it's a punk show, and there's gonna be—"

"Punk show, eh?" That got Ivan's attention. "Like, a real

punk rock show? Well, say no more!" Ivan fluffed up his jacket and brushed off his sleeves, spending a little too long over the Ramones patches.

"Alright," Ace said, smiling. "Then it's settled. Let's go break into Graceland real quick and see what's on that second floor. Maybe we can get this all figured out right now. Then we'll go to the punk show."

\* \* \*

Ace put *Betty* into sentry mode and met Ivan in the parking lot of the KFC. With sentry mode activated, anyone dumb enough to attempt messing with their disguised smartship would be met with a stun blast that rendered the trespasser unconscious.

Ivan had his dazzler activated and looked like the guy April called Seth Green. He was casually watching traffic go by and humming a tune to himself. When Ace got closer, he recognized it as *I Wanna Be Sedated* by the Ramones. One of Ivan's favorites.

"You're stoked about this punk show, aren't you?" Ace asked as they turned south out of the KFC and walked down the sidewalk of Elvis Presley Boulevard.

"Yeah man!" Ivan said. "Aren't you? We can see how they do it for real. Take some notes!"

Ace and Ivan had their own punk band called The Diesel Dicks. They confused most aliens who were more accustomed to the galactic rock stylings of bands like Mustache Supernova, Dead Planet Destruction, and Zeeblezak 198. But Ace and Ivan had a good time doing it.

Ivan fabricated a recreation of a mid-1960s Mosrite Venture II guitar and Marshall Super Lead 100-watt amplifier for Ace. For the rhythm section, Ivan had a 1975 Fender Precision Bass played through an Ampeg SVT with matching 8x10 speaker cabinet and a five-piece all-white Rogers drum kit. A spot-on recreation of the instruments that the Ramones used in the 1970s.

Ivan rigged up a drum kit so he could play it with a brain controller while he also played bass. Ace played guitar and sang.

They played a few gigs at bars in the Gnarlon System. Some shady places that hosted open mic nights. They never did it seriously, though. It was more to just blow off steam and have a good time.

One night, about two years ago, they had just finished playing to a stunned and drunken crowd of miscreants spanning fourteen different genomes. A man with purple skin, two heads, and four arms approached them and introduced himself as Mustache Supernova's manager, Mr. Nick. As Ace and Ivan loaded their amplifiers into the back of *Betty*, the man began asking them about *Betty*'s hauling capacity. With the tailgate down he could see that the interior was several times larger than the exterior. Mr. Nick stared with wide open mouths on both of his heads.

"How big is it in there?" Mr. Nick gawked.

"Oh, about half a parsec," Ace said with pride. In truth, he didn't actually know the capacity of *Betty*'s trailer. Since it was extradimensional cargo space, it could, he guessed, hold just about anything of any size. He never bothered to read the manual, but then again, he never had trouble shoving anything that needed hauling into her. So, as far as he was concerned there were no limits.

After a short chat about Ace's experience as a licensed, bonded, and insured cargo hauler, Mr. Nick offered him a job to transport Mustache Supernova's bass amplifier to a concert on Flodorian Six. The amplifier was the size of a small asteroid, and they needed something with *Betty*'s cargo capacity to haul it incognito. Mr. Nick explained there were rival bands that were dying to get their eyes on the amp before its debut at the Flodorian Music Festival. The need for secrecy was a must, so they required a way to transport it hidden from prying eyes.

After coming to terms, Ace and Ivan were shocked to learn that the amp was not just the size of a small asteroid, but was, in fact, built *out* of a small asteroid. After grabbing it with *Betty*'s grappling beam, Ace proceeded to get drunk. He was convinced that they were about to be smashed to pieces from the collision. Instead, the asteroid slid into *Betty*'s cargo bay with no trouble.

Mr. Nick was so impressed with the job he hired them to haul equipment for the entire next tour.

Since the tour was nonstop, they hadn't had much time for The Diesel Dicks. They were getting rusty. It would be a real treat to see a real Earth punk band.

Ace and Ivan approached the main entrance to the Graceland Visitor Center. An old jet airplane sat parked in front with the words *Lisa Marie* written on the side. Ivan, ever the gear dork, began rattling off facts about the airplane.

They paused to admire the airplane from the road. A short beige brick wall surrounded the blacktop where the plane sat. Its blue and white painted body gleamed under the fluorescent street lights. A blue tarped gangway attached to the side of the plane, allowing visitors to ascend and enter the jet as a walking museum.

As Ivan babbled on about the interior, Ace really wasn't paying attention until Ivan said something about gold-plated sinks.

"What?" Ace asked, turning to Ivan. "He has gold-plated sinks in that thing?"

"Yeah."

*If he's got gold-plated sinks on an airplane, he must be loaded with gold!* Ace thought.

Then, as if answering Ace's thought, Ivan said, "Yeah. This guy is all about the gold."

"Come on. Let's get across the street," Ace said and started walking across four lanes of traffic. He easily dodged the oncoming cars with drivers who blew their horns and shouted insults at him. Unfazed, he made a bee-line across the street and arrived at a low fence surrounding a patch of grass next to the main Graceland property. Beyond the fence, a six foot high stone wall with iron spikes on top surrounded the perimeter.

Ace hopped the low fence and ducked under a tree with low hanging branches. Cars honked, and tires screeched behind him. Ace peeked over the fence to see what caused the commotion and watched a chimpanzee on stilts in a black leather jacket running across the street. Motorists honked and gawked and pointed. Two cars almost careened into each other as Ivan leaped over the small fence and met Ace under the tree.

Ivan leaned up against the tall wall and started frantically tapping on the controls of the dazzler strapped to his waist.

"Darn it! Darn it! Darn it!" Ivan said. "There must be some sort of interference! The dazzler can't hold the projection."

As Ivan worked at the controls, all hell broke loose. The dazzler began projecting holograms at random. For a few microseconds he appeared as an old trucker, then President Bush, then a forty foot tall fire-breathing dragon, then Seth Green. A beat later he looked like a series of rotating columns of light pulsing with every color of the rainbow. Ace had to shield his eyes for fear of being blinded. A high-pitched squeal started on the edge of audibility and grew louder with each passing moment.

"Crap! Crap! Crap!" Ivan shouted over the squeal.

The din was like a dagger piercing Ace's skull, and he dropped to his knees in agony.

"Turn that damn thing off, Ivan!" Ace shouted, but he wasn't sure if Ivan heard him. The squeal was too loud at that point.

When the columns of light resolved back into a less luminous shape, Ace could see Ivan grappling with the dazzler. The way Ivan kept jerking his hands away from the dazzler suggested that the thing was extremely hot. Eventually, Ivan grabbed ahold and let out a scream. He reared back and threw the dazzler over the stone wall. A moment later it exploded in a huge green fireball. The ground shook, and the shockwave cracked the stone wall.

When the dust settled and the heatwave dissipated, Ace said, "Holy shit! Are you alright?"

"Yeah," Ivan said, wincing. "But I burned the heck out of my hand. I don't know what just happened there. I've never seen a dazzler do that before. The thing's just a hologram projector!"

Ace grabbed the top of the stone wall and pulled himself up so he could take a look at the damage on the other side. A smoldering crater dug into the ground about ten feet across. Charred grass surrounded the crater, and it looked like the earth itself had vaporized as there was no ejection debris. The dazzler itself had been completely destroyed in the explosion. Green and purple smoke hung in the air like someone had lit a novelty smoke bomb.

Ace looked past the smoldering crater towards the mansion itself. The front was illuminated with subtle floodlights, and he could hear shouts coming from the side of the house. Flashlights blinked on and began to jiggle as four security guards ran towards the blast site. Off in the distance, Ace could hear the sounds of sirens approaching.

"We need to get out of here. Now!" Ace hopped down and motioned for Ivan to follow him. Ivan blew on his hands and shook them, trying to soothe the burns.

Traffic on Elvis Presley Boulevard was light, but it was far from deserted. After a green fireball erupted into the sky, a few cars pulled over to rubberneck. A group of about ten people gathered at the closed Graceland gates, craning their necks to get a look at what the commotion was all about. No one was paying attention to the man and the leather-clad chimpanzee on stilts running down the sidewalk in the opposite direction.

When they got back to *Betty*, Ivan rushed into the sickbay and thrust his hands under a diagnostic wand. As the med computer worked on Ivan's hands, Ace checked on Elvis's condition. Ace was no expert on the medical readouts, but as far as he could tell Elvis's condition had not changed: still catatonic and with crazy brain activity.

Ace reached over to lift Elvis's eyelid because he had seen Hawkeye Pierce do that to unconscious patients on the wartime medical TV show *M*A*S*H*. Just as his finger was about to touch the eyelid, an alarm blared causing Ace to jump back like he had just touched a hot stovetop.

"Sentry alert!" *Betty* said over the audio system. "A human female is approaching the port side airlock. Stun blast will commence in five seconds."

"Whoa, whoa, whoa, whoa!" Ace yelled, "Betty! Abort sentry mode. Damn it, Ivan I thought you turned that shit off when we came in?"

"I was a little busy with my hands being burned to a crisp!" Ivan gestured as best he could while keeping mostly still for the med computer tissue reconstruction module to work on his damaged hands.

"Yeah. Man. Sorry," Ace said, and he took a peek at Ivan's hands. Blue light was illuminating the burnt skin making them look like the surface of a frozen asteroid that'd been blasted by a fireball. Ace could see the wounds were closing and healing, but it would be at least an hour before he was back to normal.

"You doing all right?" he asked.

"Yeah. The med computer just shot me full of narcos so in a second I'll be as high as a kite. Ooo. There we go!" Ivan's voice smoothed out into a lilting sing-song.

"Lucky you," Ace said and lightly patted Ivan on the shoulder.

Ace glanced at a video display of April approaching *Betty* from the outside.

"Soooo...the punk show?" Ace asked.

"You crazy kids go have fun," Ivan slurred. "I'ma stay here and play doctor with robonurse here."

"Alright, buddy," Ace said. "You hang in there. Looks like it'll be a while before Nurse Chapel has you patched up. Try to stay still and don't go too heavy on those narcotics. I'll need you fresh and daisy when I get back."

"You got it, pal!" Ivan swayed a little and spit when he said "pal."

Ace exited *Betty* through the aft cargo bay so April wouldn't see him. He didn't want her to get a glimpse of the airlock and the uncloaked interior.

April smiled and waved when she saw him walk around the front of the Winnebago.

"Are you ready to rock?" April shouted and threw up her hands in a gesture where the index and pinky fingers were extended, and her thumb covered the middle two fingers. It reminded Ace of two antennae.

*Must be some kind of greeting gesture*, Ace thought.

Ace mimicked the gesture and replied, "Yes ma'am. I am!"

"I thought I told you to cut out that ma'am shit, dude," April said changing the gesture to be her middle finger extended upright before dropping her hands to her side. "Where's Seth-

Ivan?"

"He burned himself pretty badly, so he's, uh, seeing a doctor right now. Getting patched up."

"Damn. Is he all right?" April asked.

"Yeah. He'll be fine."

"He didn't go fucking around with the pressure fryers in the shop, did he?" April asked. "'Cause I warned you about that hot ass oil. I saw it melt the wrapper off a Snickers bar once."

"A Snickers bar?" Ace asked.

"Yeah. Some dumbass rookie wanted to make a fried Snickers bar. Like at the county fair? But the jackass didn't unwrap it or batter it first. He just tossed it in the oil. It melted that fucker, wrapper and all, into a pile of brown goo. We had to use skillets and the stovetop to make the chicken until Johnny got the pressure fryer cleaned out."

Then April spoke in an exaggerated accent making her sound vaguely like a prospector from an old Western movie, "It was like Frontier Land up in the KFC that day, I tells ya."

"Yeah. It wasn't anything like that," Ace said.

"Alrighty then. Come on then, hop in my chariot." April turned and walked toward her Buick Century. Ace followed and tried to be gentlemanly and not ogle her bottom as she walked, which was hard because the black jeans she wore looked as if they were painted on.

When they climbed into the car, April asked him, "You a Red Hot Rebellion fan?"

"Never heard of them," Ace said with a shrug.

"What!?" She looked genuinely shocked. "The hardest rockin' band in the world? Jimmy Thrillwell? Blind Tone Deaf Dougie J? Andris Rebellion? Ringing any bells?"

Ace shook his head and shrugged, "Nope. Sorry."

"Well get ready to live, Brodeo." April turned the ignition of her car and pulled out a silver disc from a square plastic case. She inserted the disc into the slot of a device in the dashboard that looked like it was installed by an inmate at an insane asylum. Multicolored tape, rubber bands, and crumpled up KFC bags were shoved in the gap beneath the component and the dashboard holding it in place.

But it functioned. As soon as April hit play audio began to pump through speakers in the doors and in the rear of the car. She increased the volume to an earsplitting level as the music kicked into a hard-driving four on the floor backbeat with a wall of sound comprised of heavily distorted electric guitars. After the initial shock of energetic power chords pounding him in the face subdued, Ace began tapping his foot and bobbing his head to the beat.

April played air drums on the steering wheel and sang along as she drove. They pulled out onto Elvis Presley Boulevard and headed north away from the KFC and Graceland. She punched down the accelerator. The Buick grumbled and shook as it propelled them down the road at forty-five miles per hour.

Once the song ended, she turned the volume down so they could talk.

"Pretty good, right?" April asked.

"Yeah. That was one dandy rock 'n' roll song!" Ace replied.

"You kinda talk weird, you know that? Where are you from?"

"Umm. You know, I'm not really sure. I was raised in an orphanage. I never knew my parents or where I was born," Ace stated it matter-of-factly.

"Shit, man. I'm sorry. Sore subject, huh?" April said with a touch of embarrassment. "New subject. What brings you to the fair and illustrious city of Memphis, Tennessee? Home of

Elvis Presley, the Blues, and the best goddamn barbeque in the universe!"

Ace contemplated the last statement about the best barbeque in the universe for a moment and was about to ask April how she could verify that claim. Did she have her own spaceship? Did she really travel outside the Milky Way Galaxy? That was a feat he'd never heard of anyone accomplishing.

"We came to, uhh, see Graceland," Ace said.

"You some sort of Elvis super fan or something?"

"No. Not at all," Ace said. "I mean, he's the King of Rock 'n' Roll, you know? So, of course, I've heard of him. But to be honest, I'm not really well-versed in all his music, and I don't know much about his life."

"Well, you came to right place. You can't so much as spit without hitting someone with expert knowledge of the King. 'Specially in these parts." April spoke with a strong twang for the last part. Then switched to her normal speaking voice, "Take that guy for instance. I think that's the fourth Elvis impersonator we've passed since we left the KFC parking lot."

Ace followed her gesture and craned his neck as they passed a man dressed in a white high-collared jumpsuit encrusted in rhinestones standing on the sidewalk. The man practiced what looked like martial arts forms and then quickly stopped and began waving his hands wildly at them as they passed.

"Elvis impersonator?" Ace asked as the man rescinded behind them. He could've sworn the man was yelling at them.

"Yeah. You know, we don't really have as many as Vegas, but there are a few. My brother's one. But don't hold that against me. He's the weirdo in the family. He and some of his friends hang out in the KFC from time to time. Kinda weird dudes. They seem to me to have a creepy fetish with Elvis. But man, are they devoted."

April continued, "One guy, who I finally got to admit that his real name was Wally, told me that, quote-unquote, *true* impersonators believe that they are chosen by The King to continue His work. And that they judge themselves on their authenticity and their ability to channel Elvis's true essence. These are the hardcore dudes who don't do it for money. Their mission is to spread the message of The King. Wally is one of those guys who doesn't just do an Elvis act. He lives Elvis, dressing as the King and spreading His word by their example. Whatever the hell that means." She took her hands off the wheel to make quick air quotes around the words "lives Elvis."

"Damn, man. There's another one." April pointed at another Elvis impersonator wearing a black leather suit. The impersonator was much younger than the other they had just passed. Yet, like the other, he waved his hands wildly and shouted.

"Looks like he's trying to talk to us. Slow down," Ace said.

April slowed down and turned the music off as they approached the Elvis impersonator on the sidewalk. Ace tried to roll down his window so they could hear what the impersonator was saying.

"Ah. Shit man. Here. I gotta do that for you. Your side is broken," April said and hit the control on the driver side door to lower Ace's window.

There was no sound, but it looked like the man was shouting at the top of his lungs.

"What the —?" April decelerated the car to a crawl. They slowly rolled past the "shouting" Elvis impersonator. Although the impersonator made no sound, Ace could tell the man repeated the same thing over and over again. Ace was pretty good at lip reading. Since there was a limited amount of movies and television shows in Ivan's media stash, he sometimes liked to watch them with the sound off. Just to see if he could still tell what was going on.

And what this young, fresh-faced Elvis impersonator mouthed, repeatedly was, "Ace. Be a ritz. Find the El Dorado."

# 6

# Strange Things Are Afoot on Elvis Presley Boulevard

Ace stood at the back of Murphy's, leaning against the bar and sipping a Pabst Blue Ribbon from an aluminum can. The beer was no Dark Star, but it wasn't half bad either. The car ride to Murphy's Pub was filled with questions from April. Questions Ace was not in any mood to answer.

Although Ace liked April, he wasn't sure he could trust her with his secret: that he was, in fact, a man from outer space looking for a supposed gold hoard and the means to save the life of the not-dead King of Rock 'n' Roll.

Ace accepted the blame for April's inquisitiveness. He told her what he had lip-read from the Elvis impersonator.

"You sure he was saying your name?" April asked repeatedly.

Ace was sure. He was an expert lip reader.

"Ok. What am I saying right now?" April asked and then began mouthing words.

Ace concentrated on her lips as they moved and spoke without thinking, "You are the weirdest cute guy I've ever met."

Ace suddenly felt a rush of heat course through his body and stammered a little.

April smiled.

Ace composed himself and tried to think of something witty to say when a voice called out from behind them.

"April Sassy Molassy!" the voice said.

April's smile dissolved into a scowl.

The voice belonged to a young man with bad skin who wore a t-shirt with the sleeves torn off. On the center of the shirt sat a skull with large spikes coming from its head in the form of a jagged mohawk and the words "The Exploited" written above it. The man had a nose ring and wore dark eyeliner. His hair was dyed blue and spiked in a tall mohawk, mimicking the skull on his t-shirt.

The man ran up and grabbed April in an awkward hug. She squirmed her way free and pushed the man back. "Yo! Hands off the merchandise, Billy!"

Billy laughed. He sounded like a weasel caught in a meat grinder. "Whatever, Sassy Molassy!" He blew a series of quick smooches at her.

April feigned disgust and said, "In your dreams, Bilbo Baggins!"

"You know you want me," Billy said, cradling his own face with his hands and batting his eyes.

"You wish," April replied and then asked. "Where's your brother?"

"You mean your lover boy?" Billy replied. "He's out back. They just pulled up and are about to load the equipment in."

"Cool it. You know me and Joey are just friends," April said. She turned to Ace and said, "Seriously, we're just friends."

Billy let out an exaggerated coo. April smacked him on the side of his head, and he stopped. The spikes of his mohawk vibrated for a few seconds.

"Shut up, Billy!" April said. Then, "So, Billy. Meet Ace Tucker. Ace, meet Billy Baker, drummer for Joey and the Lawrences and a total dweeb. You guys should talk. 'Cause even though he makes himself out to be this punk-as-fuck punk rock renegade, he's a total Elvis Presley fanboy. Anything you want to know about the King, this guy probably knows." She gestured at Billy who struck a karate pose similar to the one Ace witnessed the Elvis impersonator perform earlier on their ride to the bar.

April continued, "I'm gonna go say hi to Joey out back. Hang loose for a minute, will you? I'll be right back."

Ace agreed and watched April meander through a light crowd and exit through a door towards the back of the bar.

"So, you got questions about the Big E? I'm your guy," Billy said and proceeded to go through a whole routine of karate moves before he settled down on a bar stool. He patted the empty stool next to him and invited Ace to have a seat, then ordered two Pabst Blue Ribbons.

"Whatchu wanna know?" Billy asked and took a sip from his can.

"Well, does Elvis have anything to do with El Dorado?" Ace asked.

"El Dorado? Like Eldorado, the car? Cadillac Eldorado? Sure man. Elvis loved Cadillacs. He had tons of them including several Eldorados," Billy said and took a giant swig from his beer.

"Wait," Ace said. "Eldorado is a car, not a place?"

"Well, it's both," Billy said, "But if you're talking Elvis and Eldorado, then you're talking Caddies, man."

Billy went on to tell Ace about Elvis's fascination with Cadillacs.

"In the 1950s, few things symbolized success and the American dream more than a badass automobile," Billy said. "And Elvis's affinity for Cadillacs was legendary. He was not only the King

86

of Rock 'n' Roll, but he was also the King of Cadillac buyers, purchasing at least a hundred during his life. And he didn't just buy them for himself. He was well known for giving gifts of automobiles to friends, family, associates, and even complete strangers. Sometimes he would drive them himself for a few days before giving them away."

"He owned just about every model of Cadillac," Billy said. "Except for one of the most iconic models, the 1959 Cadillac Eldorado Biarritz. It is highly sought after by collectors today because of its giant fins and slick, streamlined design with unique sweeping chrome trim that decorated the side of the car. But I digress..."

Ace nodded and asked, "So if that was the coolest car at the time why didn't he have one? He was obviously loaded, right?"

"Ahhh. There's the real mystery, isn't it?" Billy said. "Most people say he didn't have a '59 Eldorado Biarritz because he was in the army at the time. He was stationed over in Germany during the Korean War. But some Internet rumors say he *did* own one. And not only that but it was his favorite car of all time. He would just drive it at night, and he kept it in a secret garage somewhere on Graceland. See, old tunnels are running beneath Graceland. Legend has it that they were old Underground Railroad tunnels that the original owners of the mansion used to smuggle runaway slaves to the North. And when Elvis bought Graceland and started doing some remodeling, he found them and would use them to sneak out to secret locations all around Memphis. Like some kind of Bat Cave network or something!"

Ace tried hard to follow the logic of underground train routes somehow being connected to caves where bats lived. The more Billy talked about the secret and bizarre sides of Elvis's life, the more it made some kind of weird sense.

"Ace. Be a ritz. Find the El Dorado" the Elvis impersonators said. Not "be a ritz." Biarritz. Eldorado Biarritz. Ace wasn't looking for a lost city of gold. He was looking for Elvis's prized and secret 1959 Eldorado Biarritz.

Ace still had no idea how a unique car could have something to do with saving Elvis's life. Yet, the more he learned from Billy, the more convinced Ace became that things were about to get even stranger.

Over another round of Pabst Blue Ribbon, Billy regaled more bizarre tales from Elvis's life.

"Did you know that there was a UFO sighting when Elvis was born?" Billy had a wild gleam in his eye as he spoke. "You believe that shit? A freakin' UFO was hovering right over his house when he was born. Both Elvis's father and the doctor who delivered him saw it. They said the house was bathed in this weird blue light and it stayed there up in the sky for about an hour while Elvis's momma was giving birth."

"UFO? Nah," Ace tried to feign shock and hoped he did a convincing job. "UFOs ain't real..."

"Yeah man! They are!" Billy said. "And it gets weirder. Elvis had a twin brother, but he was stillborn. They got a memorial to him in the meditation garden at Graceland, but he's supposedly actually buried in a little grave in Tupelo. But some people say the twin, Jessie, *is* buried at Graceland. They exhumed his body from the original grave to transport it, like, twenty years later. But get this. The body hadn't decomposed at all! You believe that shit?"

"Well, now that is weird," Ace admitted.

"And check this out," Billy said. "Elvis would sometimes tell stories about when he was a kid, and he was visited by extraterrestrials or angels."

"What? Seriously?" Ace asked, aghast.

"Yeah. I read about it in a book called *Alien Rock: The Rock 'n' Roll Extraterrestrial Connection.* I got it from the library. What? I got a library card." Billy misinterpreted Ace's expression as disbelief Billy could read. Instead Ace was shocked at the title of the book. It hit a little too close to home.

"No. Of course, you can read," Ace said and tried to recover. "Sounds like a cool book, is all. I'd like to read it."

"Yeah, man. It's pretty badass," Billy said. "All the greats had UFO experiences. Anyway, the first time Elvis was contacted he was in a closet, being punished for doing some stupid shit. You know how kids are. He must've been like four or five years old. And while he was there in the dark he said he felt this *presence.*" Billy accented the last word with a flamboyant magician-like gesture.

Then Billy continued, "He said there was an invisible person in the closet with him and he started seeing visions of a beloved man in a white jumpsuit singing and reaching out to throngs of ecstatic followers. It wasn't 'til much later that he realized it was himself he was seeing. He saw his own future as a great entertainer."

Ace started tapping his finger on the can of Pabst and tried to riddle through it all.

"He also had telekinetic powers," Billy said. "There have been a few stories of him moving shit with his mind."

"Like what?" Ace asked. He'd met telekinetics before loads of times. Handy folks to know.

"Clouds mostly. And ashtrays...Oh. And he could heal the sick!" Billy shouted.

"C'mon, man. Now you're just messing with me."

"No. For reals. There are reports of him praying over sick

people, and they would have dramatic recoveries. Look it up, man. Shit's out there, man, you just gotta know where to look!" Billy was taking offense to the severe bullshit face Ace was throwing him.

"Alright calm down, man," Ace said.

"I'm just saying," Billy said. "The truth is out there, and it's way stranger than fiction."

Ace would have to agree with him on that last account because at that moment a chimpanzee wearing a leather jacket covered in punk rock patches stormed into the club.

Ivan Chimpanov ran up to the bar where Ace and Billy sat.

"Whoa! Fuck yeah! A monkey! Is he your pet?" Billy said as he hopped off his barstool and squatted down to take a better look at Ivan.

Ivan punched Billy square in the nose and said, "I ain't no-body's pet, *'suka!'*"

The spikes of Billy's mohawk wiggled a few times and a gusher of blood sprouted from his nose. Billy dropped to his knees and began sobbing.

"What the hell, man? What's going on?" Ace grabbed Ivan by the collar and rushed him outside. A taxicab sat idling by the curb. The driver looked over at them and then darted his gaze straight forward. Ace could see the man was sweating profusely even though it was a chilly, breezy night and he had the windows rolled down.

"We've got some serious problems, Ace!" Ivan shook Ace's hand off with an exaggerated shrug. "Get in the cab." Ivan kept smoothing and re-smoothing the sleeves of his jacket and fidgeting with the zipper. Ace took the hint that Ivan was nervous and climbed into the backseat of the cab.

"And a good evening to you, sir!" the cab driver said with forced enthusiasm.

Ivan climbed in behind Ace and slammed the door. "Shut up, Pradeep. Just drive us back to the KFC as quickly as you can. No speeding. We don't want to draw any more attention to ourselves."

"Of course! Right away, Hanuman!" Pradeep, the cab driver said. He put the car in drive, signaled, and slowly pulled out into traffic.

"Ivan, what the shit is going on?" Ace asked.

"Let's just say there's a reason I didn't take Betty to come get you. We've got a little problem back at the KFC parking lot."

\* \* \*

Ace got a firsthand look at why Ivan had solicited the help of Pradeep, the taxi driver, when they got back to Elvis Presley Boulevard. The entire street was blocked off in both directions from the edge of Graceland to the south all the way down past the KFC a quarter mile to the north. Police turned all approaching cars away. Ivan told Pradeep to pull into the parking lot of an Advance Auto Parts store a hundred feet north of the barricade. A small crowd gathered at the roadblock and grew with each passing moment.

"I snuck out just as they were erecting the barricades," Ivan said. "And I had to disengage Betty's sentry mode because she had already knocked out *five* Elvis impersonators who shambled up to her like zombies and tried to get inside. One of those impersonators was this guy's brother."

"He is the most popular Elvis impersonator of Indian descent in all of Memphis!" Pradeep boasted. "I was driving Raj to a gig on the other side of town. Everything was normal. Just like it was every other Sunday. Raj does an Elvis show for a group of ladies at Stable Willow Retirement Community. We talked about cricket and how we were both gaining weight since we moved to Memphis. When all a sudden Raj's whole demeanor changed."

"He was mid-sentence and then all of a sudden he started doing his act," Pradeep said. "One moment he was talking about how he needed to go to the tailor and get his pants let out and the next he broke into a rendition of *Burning Love* and started doing karate moves. I almost wrecked the car."

Pradeep continued, "He was, like, *possessed*, you know? He was talking like Elvis. And he wouldn't take no for an answer. He kept shouting over and over until I agreed to take him to the KFC."

Pradeep did his best Elvis impersonation. It was horrible. "You're a beautiful audience. Now, take me to KFC! Thank you. Thank you very much! He kept shouting it over and over..."

"When we got here the police had already blocked off the area around Graceland. There was some sort of commotion on the grounds. I was trying to take a look and get a better idea of what was going on, and before I knew what was happening, Raj jumped out and ran straight for your vimana! He is a good boy, Hanuman. Please spare his life."

"I told you, Pradeep, it just knocked him out. He'll be fine," Ivan said to Pradeep. Then to Ace, he said, "The Elvis impersonators started showing up about ten minutes after you left."

As they sat in the Advance Auto Parts parking lot, Ace heard something stutter chopping the air overhead. He poked his head out of the cab and looked up. A police helicopter hovered directly over Graceland with a spotlight shining down on the area where Ivan's dazzler had exploded a few hours earlier. Too many people, cars, and trees blocked his view, but Ace could only assume it was not good.

"It's all open behind this building," Ivan said. "And some trees separate it from a neighborhood. And it's all dark back there. I'm going to sneak around back and then it's a straight shot to the KFC. I know what you're going to say, Ace. But I think you should stay here. I'll move faster without you. I got a bad feeling about this. I'm going to check on Betty." Ivan got out of the cab. "Pradeep. Listen to Ace. He's on our side."

"Yes, Hanuman!" Pradeep said.

Ace pulled Ivan close and whispered, "Why does he keep calling you that?"

Ivan whispered back, "He saw me come out of Betty. He could see clear into the ship, and he just assumed I was a Hindu monkey god, so I went with it."

"We're impersonating gods now?" Ace asked. "I'm pretty sure that's illegal."

"Desperate times, ole boy," Ivan said with a wink then took off running behind the Advance Auto Parts so fast that anyone who might've seen him would've thought it was their imagination.

Most of the cars on the boulevard turned around at the barricade, but a few pulled into parking lots and to the roadside to gawk at the commotion. A minivan pulled into the parking lot of the Advance Auto Parts, and two Elvis impersonators hopped out, leaving the engine still running. One was a thin young man in a gold lamé tuxedo who had jet black hair styled into a perfect pompadour. The other was an overweight man with a black wig falling off his head whose white jumpsuit looked as if it hadn't fit properly in years. The fat man attempted to fix his hairpiece as he waddled behind the younger man.

"Wait up! Thank you. Thank you very much!" Fat Elvis called out to the younger man sprinting down the street towards the barricades.

Fat Elvis wasn't paying attention and tripped over a concrete parking stop. He cried out as he tumbled to the ground, the black wig flew off his head. He landed on all fours with a loud thump and immediately started crying.

Ace got out of the cab and went over to the sobbing Elvis impersonator. Ace helped steady the fat man so he could sit down on the asphalt.

"Rough day?" Ace picked up the man's wig and handed it to him.

"Thanks," Fat Elvis said and fixed the wig back on his head. "I'm just trying to help the King out, you know?"

"No. Why don't you tell me about it," Ace said.

Fat Elvis lurched himself up to his feet and smoothed down the legs of his jumpsuit. His knees were caked with dirt and motor oil. He beat at the stains for a few seconds, muttering something under his breath then gave up and looked Ace in the eyes. His pupils were so dilated that the whites of his eyes were almost nonexistent.

"Ace. Find the Eldorado Biarritz." It was Elvis Presley's voice, but it sounded like it was coming from the bottom of a well. A strange reverse echo sandwiched every syllable. "The Eldorado Biarritz. Find the Eldorado Biarritz, Ace."

"Elvis?"

Fat Elvis nodded his head.

"Are you still onboard Betty? What the shit is going on?"

"It's so close. I can feel it, man," Fat Elvis said. "The Elvii are coming to help you get into Graceland."

"Elv-eye?" Ace asked.

"Yeah, man," Fat Elvis said. "That's plural for Elvis, man. Multiple Elvises are Elvii."

"OK," Ace said. "But listen. There are cops everywhere. I hope you're sending an army."

Fat Elvis turned and looked around, then up, then down. Ace followed his gaze. Fat Elvis pointed at the ground.

"Use the tunnels, man."

"Right. The tunnels," Ace said recalling what Billy said about an underground railroad running into and out of Graceland. "Where's the nearest entrance?"

Fat Elvis spun around, off balance like a marionette tugged by a drunk puppeteer. His head swiveled wildly.

"None of this stuff was here back in seventy-seven, you know?" Fat Elvis said as he stumbled out to the edge of the road to get a better look. "There. There was an entrance to a tunnel over there."

Fat Elvis struck a karate pose and pointed a hand directly at the KFC. His hand wiggled for a few moments then he said, "Over there, man. Behind that Kentucky Fried Chicken. In those woods. In the middle of the trees, there's an old stump with a TCB logo carved into the bark. That's the entrance."

"TCB?" Ace asked.

Fat Elvis broke his pose and shambled up to Ace, holding up a medallion that hung around his neck: a jagged lightning bolt flanked by the letters TCB.

"Takin' care of business in a flash, Ace. That's what you gotta do," Fat Elvis said. "Here, I'll create a diversion."

Ace was about to protest, but before he got the chance Fat Elvis turned and ran towards the barricades. Four cops stood behind them, answering questions and projecting authority. Two other cops escorted a young Elvis impersonator wearing a gold lamé tuxedo to a paddy wagon on the other side of the road. Fat Elvis pushed his way through the crowd and tried to climb under the barricades and was immediately hit with a baton, then handcuffed.

"Sweet mother of mayhem! What is going on?" Pradeep asked as the cops struggled to drag Fat Elvis's limp body over to a paddy wagon.

"I'm going to the KFC and meeting up with Ivan, uh, Hanuman," Ace said.

"Then I'm coming with you!" Pradeep said with conviction. Ace was about to protest but thought that it might be nice to have another set of eyes on the situation.

Ace nodded and led Pradeep around the back of the Advance Auto Parts.

Behind the building was all open as Ivan described. There were no lights, but the glow from the front of the building gave off enough light to see the ground reasonably well. Beyond the Advance Auto Parts sat another building. Some sort of fueling station with a giant seashell logo and the word "Shell" written under it.

The woods Fat Elvis described were about ten feet behind the buildings, with the edge of the dense foliage barely visible from the ambient light. Ace and Pradeep hugged the woods as they made their way towards the seashell station.

The air was colder at the edge of the woods. Ace smelled wild plant growth and nature. He felt drawn to forestation like it held the fulfillment of a longing deep within him. He'd been in plenty of forests on dozens of planets, but there was something different about this small clutch of woods. It was familiar to him like his own hands were. He paused for a moment to try and reason out the emotions within him.

Ace thought he heard something moving within the dense foliage. A footstep?

Pradeep must've heard it too because he said in a harsh whisper, "What was that?"

"Shh," Ace replied and held out a hand for them to stop. They were still a long way from the KFC. Beyond the seashell station, sat a restaurant called Checkers and even further down was the edge of the KFC property. He could just barely see the red fence that marked the back corner of the property.

*Snap!*

Definitely a footstep in the woods.

Ace looked around for something that he could use as a weapon. He was just about to pick up a particularly nasty looking rock when Pradeep yelped. Ace followed Pradeep's gaze as the shape of a man stepped into view from beyond the building.

"Hands up, assholes," the shape said.

A beat later the shape walked into a shaft of light. Agent Randall Calhoun of the Federal Bureau of Investigation leveled a handgun directly at Ace.

Pradeep yelped again and darted his hands straight up.

Ace casually raised his hands and thought to himself, *This guy again...*

"Well, well, well," Agent Calhoun said as he took a step closer. "Somehow I knew it would be you behind all this ruckus. You think you can come down here. To my planet and mess with the house of the King of Rock 'n' Roll? No sir."

Calhoun pulled out a pair of handcuffs as he approached Ace.

"What does he mean, 'your planet'?" Pradeep said with worry in his eyes. He tried to inch away from Ace, but Calhoun stopped him dead in his tracks.

"Hey! Whoa, whoa, whoa, whoa! Hold on there, Sanjay Gupta!" Calhoun pronounced it *Goopter*. "You stay put. I'll deal with you in a minute." Then to Ace, he said, "And you, Buck Rogers! Turn around slowly and put your hands behind your back. Any sudden movements and I'll see if you have green blood like that Doctor Spock. You got me?"

Ace opened his mouth about to correct Calhoun that it was *Mister* Spock, not *Doctor*. He was amused with himself because it was the type of thing Ivan would do.

Ivan's media stash included some sci-fi movies and shows including the entire run of the 1960s television program, *Star Trek*. It was one of their favorites. Ivan, however, took his fandom one step further and wrote *Star Trek* fan fiction in his spare time. Ace enjoyed the continued journeys of the *Enterprise* crew as told by Ivan Chimpanov but thought it got a little heady at times. And the continual romantic subplots between Kirk and Chekov tended to meander a bit.

Ace decided to hold his tongue and not correct Calhoun mostly because of the gun. Yet the butchered *Star Trek* reference convinced Ace that Calhoun knew Ace was from outer space.

Ace narrowed his eyes and began to turn around in a slow, deliberate movement as not to spook Calhoun. He slowly brought his hands down and clenched his jaw.

*How the hell does he know?* Ace thought.

Ace could feel Calhoun standing right behind him. The agent grabbed Ace by the arm and pulled it up twisting it in an unnatural position. He heard the agent holster his pistol then the clank of metal chains. Calhoun slapped a handcuff on Ace's right wrist; the cop leaned in close to Ace's ear.

"How's that feel, spaceman?" Calhoun said. Ace could smell the cop's rancid breath, which also had a hint of something sweet. Donuts?

Ace had never eaten a donut, but he recalled multiple references to police officers and their affinity for the round confections.

Ivan was particularly fond of an advertisement for donuts that appeared several times in his media stash. Commercial advertisements were prevalent throughout the galaxy, so they were easy to spot. For some reason, Ivan loved watching an ad for a restaurant called Dunkin' Donuts. It depicted a man who religiously rose before dawn to make fresh donuts for appreciative customers. Every day the pudgy man with a large mustache would waddle into the store and say, "Time to make the donuts."

"When I got the call, I didn't believe it at first," Calhoun said. "A real-life ET? In Tennessee? Well, I didn't believe it at first, but after that little stunt you pulled at the rest stop...Let's just say, I've been looking forward to our second meeting. Now hold still."

It felt like Calhoun was about to slap on the other handcuff, and Ace cursed under his breath.

Calhoun paused for a beat. "What you say, boy? Something about donuts?"

"I said, time to make the donuts!" Ace wrenched his arm free. Calhoun hadn't accounted for Ace's enhanced strength and fell backward, landing hard on the ground.

Calhoun let out a loud and comical "Oof!" when he went down. The wind had been knocked out of him. As he struggled and sucked wind, he fumbled around for his holster and his pistol. Ace was on him almost the moment he hit the ground and disarmed the man.

"Holy who!" Pradeep squealed.

"Keys!" Ace held up his one shackled hand and used the other to point the gun at Calhoun's face.

"Left—left—pock—pocket!" Calhoun stuttered between half-breaths.

"Care to help me out?" Ace asked Pradeep.

Pradeep hesitated but then knelt down and rifled through the lawman's pocket. "I just want you to know, I have the utmost respect for the law."

Calhoun gave him a look like he'd just told him his wife had a horse face.

Pradeep unlocked the handcuff and handed the keys to Ace.

"Thanks," Ace said to Pradeep, then to Calhoun. "Like the man said. I also have respect for the law, but right now I don't have time for fun and games. See that pipe over there?" Ace gestured with the gun at a large pipe running out from the back of the Advance Auto Parts into the ground. It was big and looked sturdy enough. With Calhoun's arms shackled around it, there'd be no way for the agent to follow them.

Calhoun got to his feet and did as he was told by holding his hands around the pipe so Ace could cuff him to it.

"You know this is serious business, boy? Assaulting an agent of the United States Government?" Calhoun said. "I don't care if you're from Mars and got the strength of Andre, the goddamn Giant. I *will* get out of this. And I *will* get you. And when I do, I don't care what the Shiny Man said about wanting you captured alive. You're a dead man."

"What'd you say?" Ace asked.

"I said you're a dead man, asshole."

"No. Before that. About the Shiny Man? How do you know about the Shiny Man?"

"I ain't telling you *spit*, boy." Calhoun spat on the ground for added emphasis.

Ace put the gun against Calhoun's head. "How about now, sir?"

Calhoun squinted and tried to pull away from the gun, but his head pushed up against the wall preventing his retreat.

"If I tell you anything, he'll kill me," Calhoun said. His breath haggard.

Ace cocked the hammer back on the gun. "How about now?"

"Alright! Alright! Dammit. Back off and I'll tell you," Calhoun shouted.

Ace pulled the gun away from the man's head and carefully reseated the hammer. Even though it was the first bullet-firing pistol Ace had ever handled, it had a similar size and weight to his own sidearm locked away aboard *Betty*. Except that gun fired supercharged plasma and could vaporize the side of a building if it needed to.

"Talk!" Ace said. "Is he here? What does he want?"

"All right," Calhoun took a deep breath. "I've never met him in person, OK? He's been in contact with me using some sort of telepathy or something. He told me where to find you. At first, it was just, like, an impression. Like a feeling. When we caught up with you yesterday, I just sort of *knew* you'd be at that rest stop. I didn't even know *why* we had to arrest you. I just knew I did. But when you did that magic trick—which, by the way, impersonating a president is a federal offense, son—I just thought that I was losing it. I've been under a lot of stress, so I figured I would let it drop and go see the company shrink. But since then, it's getting stronger. The messages. I can see him now. In my head. A man dressed in shiny clothes. With shiny skin. He's getting closer. And he wants you to—*ack!*"

Calhoun's eyes rolled in the back of his head, and his jaw clenched shut. He began shaking like he was being electrocuted and a frothy foam began to bubble out of his mouth.

"Holy—!" Pradeep shouted.

"Don't touch him!" Ace held Pradeep back as they watched Calhoun convulse for what seemed like forever but was just a few seconds.

ACE TUCKER SPACE TRUCKER

"Is he dead?" Pradeep asked.

"I dunno," Ace reached out and checked for a pulse. It was faint. "Yeah. He's alive. Come on. We gotta go. Ivan will know what to make of all this."

Pradeep gulped and asked, "Are you really from Mars?"

"Hell no!" Ace said as he tucked the pistol in the back of his pants' waist. "I'm from Earth. Like you. Just, I've been gone a long time, that's all."

Ace was about to leave Calhoun when he stopped. Even though Calhoun was a pain in the ass who just threatened his life, Ace felt somehow saddened by leaving an unconscious man chained to an auto parts store. Or maybe it was the fear in Pradeep's eyes when he asked if Ace was an alien. Ace had lived his whole life as an outsider, living with species who'd been crossing the stars since humankind dwelled in caves. It was all he'd ever known so in a sense he was, in fact, an alien, too.

"Alright. New plan," Ace said. "You go get help for this guy. Tell him you were going around back to take a leak and you found him. But wait for about ten minutes until I'm in the woods, OK? I gotta find this damn tree stump that marks the entrance to the tunnels."

Pradeep nodded. Ace could sense the uncertainty coming from the man.

"Listen," Ace said. "I ain't no damn monster. Just a guy looking for answers, OK? Whatever did that to him is the real enemy here. He hurt a friend of mine, too, and somehow me getting into a tunnel that leads to Graceland is part of the puzzle. I know it don't make a lot of sense, but in my experience, not much in life makes sense. So, please, just give me a few minutes and then go get him some help. Can you do that?"

Pradeep snapped out of his funk and said with conviction, "Yes.

You are a friend of Hanuman, yes? Then I will do as you ask without question. I'm sorry for my doubts."

"Alright." Ace considered telling Pradeep that Ivan was no Hindu demigod, but he figured it was best to leave it alone. "Thanks, Pradeep. You're a good guy."

Pradeep smiled and nodded then went to stand near Calhoun as if to protect him from wild dogs.

Ace walked past the back of the Checkers restaurant and entered the woods behind KFC. He reflected on how just twenty-four hours ago he attended a swanky rock 'n' roll after party. Now he swatted at small annoying insects while trying not to roll his ankle on loose branches and twigs covering the ground. Somewhere in the dense woods sat the entrance to a secret tunnel and he was determined to find it.

Ambient light from the surrounding suburban sprawl combined with a semi-full moon illuminating his path as he walked. He was startled by the sound of a giant thud coming from beyond the woods. He paused for a moment, listening. A dog barked for a moment, then receded away, lost in the wind.

*Must be the police on the boulevard*, Ace thought as he continued his trek deeper into the woods.

It only took him about five minutes to find the stump with the TCB carving on it.

Mostly because it started glowing as soon as he approached it.

The stump was about knee high and about twice as wide. The top held a carved rendition of the TCB logo like the one Fat Elvis wore around his neck. It glowed and dimmed with a gentle rhythmic pattern.

"Alright," Ace said to himself. "How the hell do you open this thing?"

Ace thought back to what Fat Elvis said the logo meant: taking care of business in a flash. Billy, the punk rock Elvis expert, had also said Elvis used the tunnels to come and go quickly without anyone knowing. Maybe the lightning bolt was significant.

Ace reached out and felt along the carved, glowing lightning bolt. Steam shot out from under the top edge then lifted up on a hinge.

When the steam dissipated a rush of cold air *whooshed* out and hit Ace in the face. It smelled musty and damp but not entirely too unpleasant. Ace looked down inside the hollow tree stump. A ladder led down illuminated by recessed lights on either side of it. About twenty feet down it terminated at a rocky floor, and a tunnel began.

Ace swung his leg over the threshold and climbed down. The rungs were cold and damp, but he made short work of the distance.

The tunnel extended before him for as far as he could see. Which was about five feet. Above him, the stump-hatch closed with a hiss.

Ace took a few steps forward towards the darkness. Recessed lights on the stone walls flicked on as he walked then flicked off when he passed creating a bubble of illumination that went about five feet ahead and behind him. After taking a few tentative steps, Ace got used to the rolling light and guessed (more like hoped) that the tunnel was a straight shot to Graceland running under and across Elvis Presley Boulevard.

Every ten feet or so a framed portrait of Elvis hung on the cold stone walls. The first one he came across was a grainy black and white photo of Elvis in a simple white karate uniform.

Elvis stood barefoot on a grass lawn with his arms akimbo. A black belt was tied around his waist. He looked young. Beneath the portrait was a little bronze-colored placard with words etched into it:

> *November 1960. First Degree Black Belt Earned*
> *As you go out into the night*
> *To defend freedom and honor*
> *Remember where it all started*

The next portrait was a color photo of Elvis receiving an award while shaking the hand of a man out of frame. Elvis was older in the picture. He had much longer hair with massive mutton chop sideburns and looked like he'd put on about twenty pounds. Elvis seemed just a tad younger and slimmer than the man currently in a coma on *Betty*. He wore a much more elaborate outfit. This time the white karate uniform had bright red satin trim around the cuffs and edges. A similar red satin belt was tied around his waist as well as another black belt. On Elvis's left chest was a circular patch with the familiar TCB logo. The logo was flanked by the words "faith, spirit, and discipline." Seven stars wound around the edge of the patch. The stars were oddly familiar to Ace, but he was more interested in the award Elvis was receiving.

Ace squinted to read the print, but then he noticed that the award itself hung just a few inches to the left of the picture.

An elaborately decorated official document from the Kang Rhee Institute of Taekwondo - Headquarters of Pasaryu Karate Association hung in a simple black frame. It was signed by Master Kang Rhee conferring the rank of Tiger, seventh-degree black belt on Elvis A. Presley on September 9, 1974.

"Whoa," Ace said to himself. "Seventh-degree black belt. Badass."

Ace continued walking and admired more photos of Elvis posing with martial artists. Then the images changed into Elvis posing with law enforcement officers. He came upon a picture of Elvis receiving what looked like a police badge from an important looking man. Next to it was a photo of Elvis seated in a chair dressed all in black with a bright white tie. He held out a police badge and was surrounded by men in suits all holding similar-looking badges.

Beneath the photo a placard read:

*Sheriff Bill Morris Confers Rank of Chief Deputy*
*We fight the good fight and take care of business*

As Ace studied the picture, the hairs on the back of his neck started to rise. He had the odd sensation that he was not alone in the tunnel.

He heard a scratching sound, like clawed feet scurrying on cold stone coming from beyond the edge of the light before him. The sound receded away into the dark. Ace approached where he thought he heard the scratching. The wall lights snapped on revealing no sign of anything out of the ordinary. Only more pictures of Elvis and law enforcement officers.

Ace walked a few more feet and stopped when he came up to a picture of Elvis shaking hands with another smiling man in a business suit. The image seemed more significant than the rest. The two men posed in front of four official looking flags. Elvis wore a black suit with long lapels and had a high-collared white shirt with the top button undone. He had a large silver belt buckle around his waist. The man whose hand Elvis shook wore an unassuming business suit. The man was smiling and looked oddly familiar to Ace.

*Maybe an actor?* Ace thought.

A new scratching sound came from behind. Like a four-legged creature approaching then stopping. Again the sound came from beyond the cone of light. When Ace spun around to face it the sound receded away from him. Ace walked back to where the sound emanated and again when the lights snapped on there was nothing out of the ordinary.

Ace shrugged, turned around, and went back to the big picture. The placard beneath it read:

*President Nixon Confers Rank of Federal Agent-at-Large*

"Agent-at-Large, huh?" Ace muttered and resumed his course.

After a few steps, the hairs on the back of his neck stood straight up.

"Hey, asshole. What the hell do you think you're doing down here?" The voice sounded like a gravel mixer filled with slobber.

Ace spun around and found the voice had come from a gruff looking snarling dog.

# 7

## You've Got Some Nerve

The mostly white dog had a few large brown and black spots spread over its torso. It stood a little over a foot tall at the shoulders, and had short stubby legs and a brown face with long brown ears that almost touched the ground. It looked well-fed, and its plump body waddled as it walked.

As Ace tried to wrap his head around what was happening, the dog took two steps forward. The familiar *clackity clack* rang out as the dog's long toenails hit the hard stone ground.

"You have a frickin' hearing problem, schmuck?" the dog said. "I asked you a goddamned question. What the fucking shit are you doing down here, asshole?"

"Ummm," Ace said. "Elvis sent me?"

"Fuck you, the King sent you," the dog said with a mocking tone. "Are you fucking kidding me?"

"It's true," Ace said. "He's up topside in my ship right now. He's the one who sent me down here. Are you a hound dog?" Ace didn't know why he asked that and immediately regretted that he did.

"I'm a fucking Basset hound, you sack of monkey shit. You ignorant dick muncher!" the dog said. "Not just any hound dog. A fucking *Basset* hound. Not a shit-eating Bloodhound. Not a

108

goddamn Greyhound, those prancing fancy fucks. They think they're so goddamn special because of their speed. Ooo! Look at me! I can run sixty miles per hour, and you can see my goddamn ribs. Who gives a shit?"

The dog continued, "No one has a better sense of smell than a Basset hound. Or better hearing. And you can take that shit straight to the mother-lovin' bank. I got a bead on your ass soon as you dropped down the ladder. You stink like fried chicken and motor oil. You hear me? I'm on to you, Fucko."

"Ace. My name's Ace."

"Good for you. My name is Hank. And I don't give a flying fuck if your name is Mary Fuck-Me-Sideways-Poppins, asswad. You still ain't told me what the fuck you're doing down here. No one but me and the King himself are allowed down here. You got it? So, take your hippie ass and your smell of despair and get the fuck outta here before I get testy and take it out on *your* testes." Hank growled and chomped his teeth.

Ace followed Hank's gaze right to his own crotch.

"Ummm," Ace said.

"That's right, dickhead. Ummm," Hank mocked him again. "Follow me, I'll show your ass to the door." Hank turned and waddled back towards the other end of the tunnel. With the dog's back to him, Ace stole a quick glance in the opposite direction to a ladder leading up and presumably into the mansion itself, maybe ten feet away.

*If I make a run for it*, Ace thought, *there'd be no way that dog can catch me with those stubby little legs.*

Hank continued down the tunnel and hurled insults at Ace. "You stupid asshole. You ignorant piece of turkey shit. You got some nerve coming down here today, *Face*. You hear me? Oh! Son of a bitch ass whore!" Hank turned to look back just as Ace was about halfway up the ladder. "Get the fuck down here, dickhead! You ain't allowed up there! Get the fuck down here!"

Ace could hear the *clackity-clack* of toenails scampering below as he pushed his way through the hatch at the top of the ladder.

"Get the fuck down here, shithead! You mother fucker! I'll bite your goddamn nuts off you sack of shit. You—"

Ace cleared the opening and slammed the hatch clamping off the incessant vulgarities flying at him. He stood in a small dark room. A closet maybe? Ace reached into his pocket and pulled out a lighter he got as a souvenir at a Mustache Supernova show on Graxon 12 last year. The lighter was adorned with the trademark image of a humanoid man whose mustache had grown to an unbelievable size, covering almost his entire face. Ace flicked the lighter and a small blue plasma flame burst forth casting the space around him in a ghostly light.

He was definitely in a closet or a small storeroom. As he moved the lighter around, he saw walls lined with metal shelves holding various weapons and tactical equipment. Handguns, shotguns, knives, a few samurai swords, night-vision goggles, rope, handcuffs...

Ahead of him was a wall with no shelves. A door. Ace reached out and pushed the door open. He emerged into a home office inside what must have been Graceland. When he stepped into the room, the door swung closed and revealed itself to actually be a bookcase. Dusty books packed the shelves that ran from floor to ceiling. There was an audible click that sounded like a locking mechanism, but Ace could see no visible way to open the door again.

A large wooden desk sat to the left with various books and papers scattered across it. A fine layer of dust covered everything. *The rumors were true*, Ace thought. *No one has touched this stuff in years.*

The air had a faint musty smell and was cool, almost frigid, like the climate control was set low to preserve the place. A piano sat along one wall and a small electric organ along another. A fish tank rested behind the desk and looked like the water had long ago consumed its once happy, swimming occupants and then evaporated. Only tiny colored pebbles, fake plastic seaweed, and larger decorative rocks remained, covered in a thin gray film.

Beside the fish tank sat a gaudy floor lamp covered in seashells with what looked like a thatched wicker lampshade.

Wood paneling surrounded the entire office broken up by artwork and two windows flanking the desk in the corner. Ace walked to the closest window. The floor-length dark blue velvet curtains were drawn shut, and he pushed one aside to look out.

He confirmed he was on the second floor of the mansion and looked out over the back of the estate. The property extended for several thousand feet. Hints of light from flashing police cars on the other side of the house danced off mature trees and a well-manicured lawn.

Ace turned to face the far end of the office. He recalled from the floorplan Ivan had shown him that Elvis's master bedroom should be to the left, around the corner of the wall where Ace came through the bookcase.

As he walked towards the corner, a buzzing sound became audible. At first, it was just on the edge of hearing, but the closer he got the louder the buzz became.

When he turned the corner, he found the source. A purple and green curtain of energy spread across the door leading into the master bedroom. A forcefield. A real nasty one that was definitely not of terrestrial origin. Ivan's scan of the mansion had been correct.

*This thing must be the source of the weird energy reading Betty picked up when they approached Graceland*, Ace thought. *But that still doesn't explain why the dazzler on Betty had failed and the second one on Ivan exploded when we got close to the property.*

As far as Ace knew that wasn't something a normal forcefield could do to a run-of-the-mill stage hologram projector.

Behind him, across a small foyer, was a set of double doors. Ace guessed those were the doors that led to the main hallway of the second floor including the other bedrooms and the main staircase to the first floor.

Ace waved his hand in front of the forcefield, careful not to touch it. A ghost image of his hand trailed across the energy curtain as he moved it. He could feel the excited air dance around his hand. It tickled a little, and he made sure not to touch the thing. Making contact would vaporize his hand in mere microseconds.

*No wonder they never let anyone up here*, Ace thought. *The first rube who came across this thing was probably burnt up the moment they touched it.*

Ace searched for a panel or terminal near the forcefield—anything that would allow someone to turn it off. It took him a few minutes, but he finally found a part of the wall that looked like it had been cut out and replaced with a new piece.

When he touched the panel, it slid up with a slight hiss and revealed a flat glass surface tilted back at a forty-five degree angle just big enough for a human-sized hand to be laid upon it. To drive that point home a small outline of a hand lazily traced its way across the glass panel. The words, "Hand of the King" scrolled across it over and over.

"Of course," Ace said out loud. "Only Elvis can open this thing."

He cursed under his breath then clamped his mouth shut. Footsteps and voices were approaching from the hallway beyond the double doors behind him.

Ace put his ear against the doors. It sounded like two men arguing with each other as they walked up a set of stairs. Heavy footfalls on the stairs got louder as they approached.

A beat later, keys fumbled on the other side of the door. As if sensing the approaching visitors the forcefield began to hum, and an electric motor kicked on. A hatch from the ceiling flopped open, and a wall made to match the wooden paneling of foyer descended hiding the forcefield from sight.

*So that's how they kept that thing hidden all this time,* Ace thought as he sprinted back for the bookcase door. *The forcefield is only visible when the hallway doors are closed.*

Ace searched around the bookcase looking for a way to open the hidden door. He'd seen enough made-for-TV movie mysteries to know that pulling on a book was most likely the way to open it.

Most of the books were on spiritual topics and martial arts. The shelves were packed with titles like *The Prophet, The Mystical Christ, The Secret Doctrine, Life and Teachings of the Masters of the Far East, Practical Karate-Do, Karate-Do for the Expert, The History of American Karate.*

Ace heard the hallway door open, and he picked a book that looked especially worn around the edges: *The Art of War* by Sun Tzu.

There was a *click*, and the bookcase swung open.

Then, Hank, the Basset hound, came barreling out hurling obscenities and barking.

"Surprise, fuck-face!" Hank said, his voice an unsettling combination of human speech and rabid dog bark.

113

Ace jumped back just as Hank lunged forward, chomping for Ace's crotch. The stubby-legged bastard was surprisingly agile. Ace dodged two more attacks and ran for the hallway door just as Agent Calhoun of the F.B.I. and an unsuspecting member of the Graceland staff entered.

Ace shouldered past the men, knocking them both to the ground, and darted out into a hallway. In front of him, a staircase spiraled down to the first floor. He cleared the stairs six at a time and landed on the first floor in a flash.

To his right was a dining room. To his left was a living room decorated with white furniture and white carpet. Beyond the living room was a small sitting room flanked by stained glass window panes depicting birds with long bright-colored feathers. Directly ahead of him was the main entrance to the mansion.

Ace flew out the door, jumping across the front steps leading into the mansion. A paved driveway ran in front of the mansion before looping back around the edge of the property and out to Elvis Presley Boulevard. Ace broke out into a full sprint. He cleared the distance across the front yard in under thirty seconds. His speed surprised him, and he silently thanked the Galactic Union bureaucracy for standardizing gravity at a higher intensity than Earth's native level.

A few cops inspecting the crater from Ivan's exploding dazzler near the main gate gawked but didn't react as Ace sped past.

In the distance, he heard Agent Calhoun shouting from the front porch, "Stop that man! And someone call animal control! There's a rabid dog running loose in here!"

Ace turned onto Elvis Presley Boulevard and ran for the KFC parking lot leaving a scene of total chaos in his wake.

The police looked like they had been doing their best to keep the growing crowd of onlookers at bay but as more Elvis impersonators and regular curious Memphians continued showing up, the crowd seethed with nervous energy. It was a riot in the making. All it needed was a little spark to set it off.

When Ace shot down the street, leaped over the police barricades, and landed in the middle of the dense crowd, it was like someone had lobbed a live hand grenade at them.

Some people screamed and scattered. Some barreled over each other and pushed their way past the police, spilling into the street. Most of the Elvis impersonators ran straight for the entrance of Graceland trampling everyone in their path.

Ace ran through the crowd and into the KFC parking lot. He glanced back as he entered *Betty*'s side airlock. An elderly Elvis impersonator was beating a police officer with a walker. As the hatch closed with a hiss, the old impersonator give Ace a little wave before continuing his walker-bludgeoning.

* * *

"A Cadillac?" Ivan asked.

"Yeah," Ace said. "That's what I think is in the bedroom. A fucking Cadillac."

The two spoke in the sickbay next to the still-comatose Elvis Presley lying on a medical table beside them.

"Huh," Ivan said. "You know. That actually makes sense. I've been hitting the mansion pretty hard with Betty's sensors for the past few hours. It's still pretty cloudy, but I did pick up a faint outline of something that could be a car. But what could he want with a car? And why is it protected by so much super advanced tech? And—"

"There's too many questions and not enough answers!" Ace said. "We gotta get back over there and figure this shit out. Something is going on here that's bigger than all of this. Has he,

115

ya know, done the astral-thing again?"

"Not since last time, when we first got into Memphis," Ivan said. "He's had a few spikes in brain activity but nothing like before."

"He's *controlling* Elvis impersonators now," Ace said and immediately felt ridiculous. But facts were facts. Fat Elvis confirmed that the comatose Elvis lying in *Betty*'s sickbay was able to possess or control them.

"That would explain why so many have been showing up," Ivan said. "And why the impersonators are so keen on protecting Graceland."

"Protecting Graceland?" Ace asked.

"Yeah," Ivan said. "They keep trying to get the cops to leave Graceland. A bunch have been doing crazy stuff and leading the cops away. Most looked like they were just looking for a reason to start rioting. When you did your Nadia Comăneci routine, they all just went nuts. I wonder what it all means."

"I don't know, Ivan! I don't know what the shit any of this means!" Ace glared at Ivan and held his elbows wide from his body with his chest thrust out. He let out a forced laugh that had a hard edge to it.

"I mean," Ace shouted. "I thought we were just bringing a zombie rock star back to his house so he could see a special doctor and then pay us off for our troubles. Remember? Gold? There was supposed to be gold, Ivan."

Ace took off his hat and ran his hand through his hair, laughing at the insanity of it all. "Also, he's got a talking dog and a security system that only Elvis can disarm guarding the place. Oh! And I ran into the cop who jumped us at the rest stop. He knows we're not from around here. As in, he knows we're from off-world. And apparently, he's in contact with the shiny asshole who shot

Elvis. And—"

"Dude. Calm down." Ivan spoke slow and gentle like he approached a pissed off tiger who just ate a circus clown. "We'll figure this out. We've been in tougher scrapes than this. Let's work out the facts we know. Ok?"

Ace let out an exasperated sigh and cracked his knuckles. "Ok...you're right. OK. What *do* we know?"

Ivan started counting on his long fingers. "One. Elvis is in a coma 'cause some shiny jerk shot him. Two. Elvis wants something that's in the mansion across the street that apparently only he can physically access. Three. There's a riot of Elvis impersonators separating us from the mansion. Four. We're in a spaceship that is currently cloaked to look like a Winnebago, but it could just as easily be invisible..."

Ivan paused for effect.

"What?" Ace said. "You're saying we can make Betty invisible and just fly across the street, land it in front of the mansion, and then just walk Elvis up to the master bedroom? What about the dazzler? It keeps fucking up every time we get close to the mansion. Last time it exploded!"

"Yeah," Ivan said. "I've had time to figure that out. All I have to do is keep modulating the neutrino dissipators, and it should hold steady. I've run a few computer simulations, and it looks like it will work. Besides, there's a full-blown riot on the street right now. Everyone's focused on that. We can set Betty down in the yard nice and easy. Then you carry Elvis up and see what the hell is in that bedroom he wants so bad."

The plan made sense.

*Why beat around the bush anymore?* Ace thought. *If anyone tries to stop me from going inside I can just say that the man is a wounded Elvis impersonator that needs medical attention. Who'd refuse that?*

"Alright," Ace said. "Let's do it."

Less than a minute later Ace and Ivan were in the cockpit readying *Betty* for atmospheric flight. This mostly consisted of Ace selecting a button on the dashboard that depicted an outline of *Betty* flying around clouds. Other nearby buttons depicted *Betty* flying around a field of stars (for outer space flight) as well as *Betty* beneath the water for deep sea trucking.

Ace turned the key in the ignition and *Betty*'s engines began to purr with a familiar, soothing sound. Ace didn't realize how much he'd missed the reassuring engine hum as he traipsed around Memphis the past several hours.

Ivan nodded and jacked into the dashboard data port in front of him. His eyelids fluttered as he went through a ship-wide diagnostic routine. Then, he broke the connection and said, "All systems are normal. I've rerouted power to give the dazzler more juice and set it to bend the light and project a mirror of the space around us. Unless someone is right on top of us, they'll never know we're there."

"Alrighty then," Ace said with a grin. "Let's get to truckin'."

Ace hit the throttle, and *Betty* slowly inched into the sky. No one seemed to notice the sudden disappearance of a Winnebago from the KFC parking lot. Or if they did notice they couldn't do much about it given the full-scale riot raging up and down Elvis Presley Boulevard.

*Betty*'s sensors detected no discernible threats in the area except the stationary helicopter hovering above the chaos. The only reason it even registered was due to its proximity to their projected flight path.

Ace was just about to cut a wide berth around the helicopter to ensure their mutual safety when the helicopter's tail began smoking. A beat later the tail exploded in an orange ball of flame.

The helicopter began spinning and plummeted down towards the crowded street below.

"Jesus tap-dancing Christ!" Ace said "What the hell was that?"

"Something exploded on that cop 'copter!" Ivan replied.

Ace would've thought the phrase "cop 'copter" was funny if it weren't for the fact he was watching a nose-diving hunk of burning death about to land on top of the riot.

Ace's fingers danced across a computer terminal in the dashboard.

"What are you doing?" Ivan asked.

"Hang on!" Ace gritted his teeth and pushed *Betty* into a power dive after the falling helicopter. He had only a few seconds before the thing crashed onto the seething horde of rioters below.

Ace fired up *Betty*'s grappling beam, the directed forcefield used for loading and unloading massive cargo in outer space. He had never used it under the force of planetary gravity. Or while flying in a 5G power dive. Or on a falling target that was on fire. But he had to try.

Ace spun *Betty* around so her aft and the grappling beam were pointed at the helicopter.

"Ace! This is nuts! The shearing force will rip Betty apart!" Ivan extended the last syllable for what seemed like an eternity. He wrapped his long chimp fingers around the armrests of his co-pilot chair and hung on for dear life.

When the grappling beam grabbed ahold of the helicopter, *Betty* shook and shuddered like she had an epileptic seizure. Ace reversed the thrust and slammed the afterburners to give them more lift.

*Betty*'s ultra-titanium hull groaned like what Ace imagined old wooden sailing ships did in a rough storm. A loud bang rang out followed by the sound of shredding metal. Then, everything settled back into a still-unnerving-but-less-frightening shuddering creak. Something had just broken inside *Betty*. Something big. They'd have to figure out what once they were safe on the ground.

*If we even make it to the ground*, Ace thought.

Ace flew the two crafts, tethered together via the glowing blue grappling beam, up over the trees that lined the entrance of Graceland. An indicator on the dashboard told Ace the grappling beam detected flames coming off the helicopter's tail. A second forcefield automatically sprang to life tight around the tail and vented the air from it. With no air, the flames suffocated and died out.

Ace tried to fly over the Graceland mansion and set down in one of the large fields behind it. The ascent was slow, and every time he inched *Betty* higher she started shaking so hard that Ace's vision got blurry.

He pulled back on the steering wheel trying to inch *Betty* higher in the sky. At their current trajectory and speed, there was no way he could make it over the mansion.

Ace backed the thrust down and held *Betty* in a tenuous hover. A flashing light on the dashboard indicated a problem with *Betty*'s anti-gravity unit. The damage made it hard for Ace to keep it steady. He had to drop the helicopter, or they were both going to crash into the mansion.

*Betty* descended, and when the helicopter was twelve feet off the ground, Ace cut the grappling beam.

The helicopter dropped and landed on the ground with a giant *thud*. It would never fly again, but the pilots were safe and no one was crushed beneath it.

Now Ace had to deal with the ricochet forces that catapulted *Betty* up and sideways when the grappling beam disengaged. The dampeners that kept the ship stable and shielded them from sudden changes in inertia had failed.

Ace felt like a fifty-ton weight sat on his chest as *Betty* flew over the mansion.

Darkness began closing in around Ace as he reached for *Betty*'s main engine kill switch. He was blacking out from the G-force.

He must have somehow hit the switch because the floor felt like it dropped out from beneath him.

A thunderous crashing sound rumbled from every direction.

Ace thought it was strange that the main view screen displayed the ground and the sky flipping over one another like a couple of drunken mud-wrestling sailors.

As a tunnel of black closed to a pinpoint in Ace's eyes he had one final thought before succumbing to the darkness, *I wonder if this is covered under Betty's warranty.*

# 8

# Schlamoozle the Carpet Tunnel

C rash gel dissolved around Ace when he woke.
*Betty's* automatic crash protocols filled the cockpit with the rubbery substance at the moment of impact, protecting Ace and Ivan from serious injury.

The gel tickled as it vaporized leaving his skin a little slimy and smelling faintly of pina colada.

"Hey, Ivan," Ace said. His voice was raspy like he'd been smoking all night long. Or screaming. Maybe he was screaming during the crash. He wasn't sure.

Ivan didn't reply. The gentle rise and fall of Ivan's chest convinced Ace his best friend wasn't dead.

"Betty," Ace said. "Status report."

No response.

"Betty?" Ace tapped on the control panels on the dash. They were all dead.

"Not good," Ace said.

Ace unbuckled the five-point harness he didn't remember buckling and got up from the pilot's chair. His head throbbed, and he had to steady himself before taking the first tenuous step out of the cockpit. The door automatically opened when he approached, which meant *Betty* still had minimal power. The doors, airlocks, and life support would function but had they been in outer space there would have been no gravity.

Emergency lights illuminated the hallway casting everything in a dim red tint. The eerie light and lack of ubiquitous engine hum reminded Ace of a sound-deadened darkroom. A place where a deranged photographer would develop his photos while wearing noise-canceling headphones. The thought made Ace question whether he hit his head harder than he thought during the crash.

Ace entered the sickbay and discovered Elvis was also saved by crash gel. The gel had already evaporated leaving the faint pineapple and coconut scent hanging in the air. The smell brought back a flood of memories of basking on red sand beaches on Zaggama 3. It was there Ace learned that every civilized planet in the galaxy had pineapples, coconuts, and booze. Therefore, everyone had invented the pina colada at some point in their history. He wondered if Earth had yet to reach that level of sophistication.

Earth was a place Ace swore he'd never go. With an entire galaxy to explore and no ties to a planet that abandoned him, he always figured it'd be best to stay away. The promise of gold was enough to make him stow those feelings. but the events of the past several hours made the possibility of a big score evaporate like the crash gel that had just saved his life.

"Humpf," Ace spat. "Elvis Presley. The King of Rock 'n' Roll. The ghostwriter for the greatest band in the galaxy. Astral projecting telepathic cyborg?"

None of it made any sense, and that was what really bothered Ace the most. An itch at the back of his brain told him that he'd find some answers in the master bedroom of Graceland. Somehow the object stashed in there would have something that could restore Elvis's health. Or maybe get Ace the answers he needed.

Ace hoisted Elvis over his shoulder in a fireman's carry, and he thanked the Galactic Union yet again for its higher gravity standard.

A fleeting thought crossed Ace's mind, *If Ivan can't get Betty back into flying shape maybe I can make a living as a circus strongman. Or a pro athlete? Nah. Ivan is the best mechanic I've ever met. There's no way Betty is grounded for good.*

\* \* \*

"Betty might be grounded for good, Ace," Ivan said. "I think the universal kooshkies are shot, and we probably threw a nitrolium rod during the crash. Without those, she won't fly. I've got to get down to the engine room and see if I can jerry-rig something together."

"Sunuvabitch!" Ace said as he shifted Elvis's bulk to make it easier to walk.

"There is some good news, though," Ivan said.

"What?" Ace asked.

"The dazzler on Betty's bumper still has power!" Ivan said. "So we're still cloaked and invisible. I was able to extend the field a little, so even the ground we just tore up in the crash looks normal. So, unless someone literally walks into us, no one will know we're here."

"Well, good," Ace said. "See what you can do about getting us back in the sky. I'm going to drag this asshole up to that bedroom and see what's behind that forcefield. With all the alien tech protecting the door, I bet there's something inside that can help us."

Ace made slow progress through the field to the back entrance of the mansion. When Ace finally did get to a door, he was met by a young cop whose voice cracked with uncertainty.

"You there!" Young Cop said and shined a flashlight directly into Ace's eyes. "What are you doing back here? You can't be here!"

Ace considered putting Elvis down and kicking the cop's ass, but there was something in the guy's voice that made Ace think better of it.

*This guy's scared out of his mind*, Ace thought. *I better try some diplomacy.*

"Sorry, officer," Ace called out. "This man is hurt, and I was told to bring him around back to wait for medical attention."

"Told? Told by who?" Young Cop said trying to cover the squeak in his voice with a little cough.

"Uh. Buford T. Justice...? The Sheriff?"

"Who?" Young Cop asked.

Ace could see the flash of recognition in the cop's eyes as he tried to recall the name, Buford T. Justice. "Did you say you talked to the sheriff? When did that happen? I just saw him out front."

"Look, officer," Ace said with a sigh. "This guy is getting really heavy. I don't know how much longer I can hold him. Can I at least set him down if we're going to be out here chewing the fat all night?"

Young Cop shined his light on Elvis's limp body draped over Ace's shoulder, then gestured to a small white metal bench with his flashlight.

"Put him down over there. And I'm going to need to see some I.D."

Ace put Elvis down on the bench and let out a cry, grabbing his knee like he hurt it. When the cop came over to check on him, Ace stood straight up and drove his elbow under the cop's chin.

Young Cop flew back a few feet and landed hard on his back.

The cop's flashlight and nightstick clanked on the concrete path as they tumbled away.

A minute later, and for the second time that night, Ace handcuffed a cop to a utility pole.

Ace decided to dress in the cop's clothes like he had seen many protagonists do in TV shows and movies. As Ace gingerly put his first leg in the police uniform, he made a shocking realization. The young cop, in his terror, had wet his pants.

"Oh! Come on!" Ace said. "Ughnn!"

Ace cursed himself for his decision and tried to remind himself that urine is mostly sterile. Also, he'd been waist deep in much more foul alien filth in his time as a roadie for Mustache Supernova. But it didn't help the gross-out factor.

Once he settled into the cold pee pants and got used to the squishy wet sensation, he finished with the rest of the uniform. He stashed his own clothes and hat behind a bush, hoping to retrieve them on the way out. He left Young Cop handcuffed and in nothing but boxer shorts. Ace felt bad for a split second then shook the feeling. Ivan was right. These were desperate times, and they called for desperate measures.

Ace threw Elvis over his shoulder and walked through the back entrance into the mansion. He came into a tiny vestibule and then turned right into a kitchen. A bank of video displays encased in clear Plexiglas sat on a white plastic laminate counter that wrapped around the length of the kitchen. Old black and white cathode ray tube displays showed video of the chaos ensuing in front of the mansion. He paused for a moment to watch police wrestle and detain Elvis impersonators running amuck on the lawn.

Ahead and to his left, a staircase led upstairs. Ace recalled from the floor plan Ivan showed him this was a second semi-private staircase that met the main stairs leading up to the second floor and the master suite.

As he ascended the stairs, Ace heard a commotion coming from ahead. It sounded like people were running back and forth, throwing themselves against a door. When he got closer, he could make out that the running wasn't on two legs but from four.

*They must've locked the dog, Hank, in there*, Ace thought.

Behind the double doors were the office and the forcefield protecting the master bedroom. Ace had to get in and get through Hank somehow.

After several minutes trying to come up with a plan, Ace noticed the frequency and intensity of blows coming from the other side were weakening.

*He's getting tired*, Ace thought.

Ace set Elvis down in a slump and waited for a lull in the banging. He could hear heavy panting and cursing in between the sloppy licking of dog chops.

Ace knocked lightly on the door. "Hank. It's me. Ace."

"Ace? You. Silly. Mother. Fuck-er!" Hank shouted in between huge gulps of air. It sounded like an asthmatic trying to speak while running on a treadmill surrounded by ragweed.

"Open. This. God. Damn. Door!" Hank gasped.

"OK. Listen, Hank," Ace said. "I'm gonna open the door. But you have to calm down. OK? I don't want any trouble. I've got Elvis with me. He's hurt, and we need to get into the bedroom."

"The—King?" Hank stopped panting for a second then resumed. "Fuck. You. The. King. Is. Off. World. Ass. Hole."

"No, he's not, Hank," Ace said, annoyed. "That's what I was trying to tell you before. He got hurt, and I'm here to help him. He told me to bring him here and help him find the Eldorado. That's what's in the bedroom, right? The Cadillac?"

There was a long pause as Hank's panting slowed.

"Open this fucking door, asshole," Hank said in a calm, collected voice. Ace took that as a sign that Hank had finally calmed down.

When Ace opened the door, he found that couldn't have been further from the truth.

The moment Ace pushed the double doors open, Hank flew through the air snapping and snarling. Hank plowed into Ace's chest but was off center, so he wound up grazing Ace and flying into a wall. A blur of fur, floppy Basset hound ears, and slobber landed on the ground with a sickening *thud*.

At first, Ace thought Hank was knocked out, but the low moaning told him otherwise. Hank shook his head, and his giant floppy ears made loud *thwack*ing sounds. Slobber flew from his lips splattering the wall and floor around him.

"Asssssshooooooole!" Hank slurred slow like a punch drunk boxer, and his head swung back and forth like a seesaw.

Hank lazily raised his head and stopped short when he saw Elvis slumped in the corner. There was a moment of human-like confusion on Hank's face then the pure joy of a dog seeing his master home after a long day at work. Hank's tail wagged furiously as he waddled over to Elvis as fast as his stubby legs could carry him. He let out excited yips as he ran and started licking Elvis's face once close enough for his giant slobbery tongue to reach.

In between licks, Hank said, "E! It's you! It's really you!"

"Yeah. That's what I was trying to tell you this whole time, man," Ace said as he fought a rising sense of nausea from the sloppy affection being doled out.

Hank stopped licking and started sniffing Elvis.

"Dude. He's hurt." Hank sniffed Elvis from top to bottom.

"That's what I've been saying," Ace said. "We need to get him in the bedroom. Before he went into his coma, he said to bring him to the Eldorado."

"We need to get him in the master bedroom," Hank said, not paying attention to anything Ace had said. "You! *Trace*! Pick the King up and help him through these doors or I'll bite your nuts off."

"Whatever you say, man," Ace said.

Ace squatted down and picked Elvis up under his arms and walked the unconscious man through the hallway door. Hank followed, and once they were all in the foyer, Hank used his body to push the hallway doors closed one at a time. A beat later the false wall that hid the forcefield began rising into the ceiling. When the wall was tucked into the ceiling, a flap closed with a *click*.

The shimmering curtain of energy danced before them in all its deadly beauty.

Ace walked Elvis over to the wall with the concealed handprint pad, careful not to get too close to the shimmering forcefield. He shifted their combined weight to one side and tapped the wall panel with his free hand. The panel rose up revealing the glass handprint pad with "Hand of the King" scrolling across it.

Ace grabbed Elvis's floppy arm at the wrist and slapped his palm against the handprint pad. The glass turned solid green, and a happy arpeggio sounded out on a tiny hidden speaker. The forcefield evaporated. A faint smell of ozone hung in the air as Ace walked Elvis past the threshold where the super-excited energy current raged moments before. Ace realized he was holding his breath and let out a long exhale.

The bedroom door began to swing open, and Hank barked, "What are you waiting for, *Mace*. Get him in there."

Ace walked through the door with Elvis.

A pristine, bright purple 1959 Cadillac Eldorado Biarritz convertible sat in the dead center of the room.

"Wow," Ace gasped. "It's real. And, and, it's...beautiful!"

"The Cadillac," Hank said like a salesman on an advertisement, "is well known throughout the world as the unmatched combination of power, presence, and luxury. Its towering tailfins make this flamboyant Caddy one of the best-known icons of the 1950s. The Eldorado model added to this sensational shape with unique sweeping chrome trim that decorates the side of the car. The Biarritz was the crown jewel of them all and the most expensive open-air car for 1959. Only one thousand three hundred and twenty of these were ever built. This, my friend, is the King's prized possession."

Ace had to admit this car had it all. Two huge sharp chrome tailfins with dual bullet taillights. A jewel-like grille pattern and matching deck lid beauty panels. A custom gold Cadillac hood emblem with diamonds set within it.

And that was just the exterior.

With the top down Ace could admire the radiant interior, which featured white leather seats with Elvis's TCB logo embroidered on the headrest. The carpet, Hank told him, was made of purple lamb's wool. Ace didn't ask if there were actually purple lambs or if the wool had been dyed to the vibrant shade. It didn't matter. It was beautiful.

A center console sat in the middle of the long front seat sporting a large ashtray made out of crystal. In the same position in the back seat, situated dead center, sat another console holding a crystal booze decanter filled with a dark brown liquid and two high ball glasses.

When Hank saw Ace staring at the booze decanter, he said,

"Those are full of Pepsi that never goes flat. The King rarely touched alcohol."

"Uh huh," Ace muttered under his breath, recalling the beer Elvis poached from him at Sleazon's party. The start of this whole mess.

"So, what are you waiting for, dickwad," Hank said. "A written invitation? Put him in the car, asshole."

Ace opened the door and did his best to sit Elvis down in the driver's seat.

Elvis's lifeless body slumped over to the passenger side.

"Now what?" Ace asked.

"Are you some kind of a halfwit or something? Put his fucking hands on the steering wheel!" Hank's face looked like a dog's version of a disgusted teenager trying to get their clueless parent to use some new cutting edge technology. Ace resented it but let it drop. He tried to reach over Elvis and sit him up, but from where Ace stood outside the driver's side door, he couldn't get the leverage right.

Ace walked around the car and climbed into the passenger side, lifting Elvis up in the process. Hank used his body to close the driver side door. It was a good move because as soon as Ace got Elvis upright, the unconscious man started listing toward the door. If it had been open, Elvis would've fallen straight out.

Ace reached over Elvis and sat him upright yet again, this time being careful to balance out Elvis's weight. As Ace worked to make sure Elvis would stay upright, Hank jumped into the back seat and poised himself on the edge so that his face was directly behind Ace's head.

"Work faster, asshole," Hank panted. "Put Elvis's goddamn hands on the steering wheel, shithead."

"Whoa!" Ace said. "Did anyone ever tell you your breath smells like hot garbage?"

"Fuck you, *Stace*," Hank said after a beat. "You gonna put his hands on the steering wheel or do I have to bite your goddamn nuts off?"

"Alright, alright," Ace said then slapped Elvis's hands onto the purple and chrome steering wheel.

The effect was instantaneous. Elvis tightened his grip in a white-knuckle clench like he was being electrocuted. His wide eyes flickered wildly, and his lips moved like he was speaking, but as of yet, there was no sound. His rigid body shook with tiny lurching movements.

After several uncomfortable seconds, Elvis moved his right hand off the steering wheel. At first, Ace thought Elvis was holding his hand out for Ace to take it. Ace started to reach for Elvis's hand, but Hank stopped him.

"Don't fucking touch him!" Hank barked.

As if on cue, Elvis's hand darted out for the keys hanging in the ignition. He turned them and jammed his right foot on the accelerator in one swift motion. The Eldorado's engine came to life in a burst of sound like a thousand wild animals roaring in unison.

The smooth purple dashboard began to glow, and a three-dimensional holographic computer control system sprang to life. The controls were similar to the displays on modern spaceships like *Betty*. Ace recognized them as Valdovian-designed heuristic computer systems, but they looked way more advanced. Some of the displays made sense to him, but others were a complete mystery, like nothing he'd ever seen.

Elvis's hand stayed on the keys in the ignition, and his foot pushed down on the accelerator in a quick staccato thrusts. With each pump, the engine got louder, and the tone sounded less like a standard internal combustion engine.

The intonation increased upward until it reached an ear-piercing high-pitched whistle. It continued further still until the sound was outside Ace's range of hearing.

Ace felt a gentle vibrational hum reminiscent to that of *Betty*'s engines.

"Does this thing have a dark matter propulsion engine?" Ace asked under his breath.

Ace was just about to ask Hank what the hell was going on when Elvis flinched and shuddered like he had just woken out of a deep sleep.

"What the holy mother of grace is hamalama ding dong?" Elvis shouted. He looked up then down and then locked eyes with Ace. "What the hell am I doing at Graceland? Who are you? Why are you here?"

Ace tried to answer but was interrupted by Elvis shouting, "We gotta get out of here! Shaboing! Schlamoozle the damn carpet tunnel, man! The carpet tunnel!"

Elvis paused as if waiting for Ace to answer. All Ace could do was shrug and look to Hank for help.

"I'm as clueless as you are, *Face*," Hank said with as much of a shrug as a dog could give.

"Ah. Snork it!" Elvis yelled.

Elvis's fingers tapped out commands on the holographic controls hovering a few centimeters above the smooth purple dashboard. His fingers moved so fast they were a blur. The top of the Eldorado started to rise up from behind the back seat and began to extend over the interior of the car. The headlights sprang to life, casting harsh light around the bedroom. Ace saw the whole room was decorated in red shag carpet. A giant oversized bed with red satin sheets was ahead of them.

The bed lifted up into the wall behind it, and the floor dropped away revealing a ramp into the darkness below. Tiny running lights blinked on illuminating the ramp as it gently sloped into a flat runway that extended out of sight.

Ace tried to work out the physics of it all. He had only been on the first floor for mere seconds as he dashed out the front door, but he was pretty sure there wasn't a structure large enough to accommodate that ramp.

*Unless the entire ceiling of the first floor just dropped into the ground,* Ace thought. *There was no way this was physically possible. Ughh. It makes my brain itch!*

"It's transdimensional lift technology, you pea brain," Hank said in apparent response to Ace's confusion.

"What?" Ace asked.

"The ramp!" Hank said. "It's a transdimensional lift! It operates outside of three-dimensional space. Are you some kind of noob or something?"

Ace thought about it for a moment, and it did make a little bit of sense. *Betty* had extradimensional space that allowed her to be much bigger on the inside than the outside.

*This could be a different application of similar tech*, Ace guessed.

Elvis finished typing out commands as the ragtop clicked into place on the windshield. All the windows rolled up, and a gentle, sweet smelling cool breeze began blowing out of the air vents in the purple dash.

The holographic controls displayed information and symbols that Ace couldn't read. He tapped the translator implant behind his ear to see if it could make sense of it. The translator simply replied with the chime saying it was functioning normally.

*Why can't the translator read this?* Ace thought.

"Buckle up, buttercup," Elvis said as the Cadillac burst forward and down the ramp at breakneck speed.

The Eldorado emerged from a tunnel in the center of Grace-land's front lawn. A hatch in the grass opened to form a ramp, and the car flew out at a tremendous speed. As soon as the car hit the lawn, Elvis hit the brakes, which put them into a power slide that chewed up grass and threw dirt everywhere.

Ace had a tight grip on the armrest with one hand and the side of the center console with his other. His feet were jammed so hard into the floor he thought they might break through.

Elvis whistled an upbeat tune.

Hank howled in the back seat at the top of his lungs.

When the car finally came to rest, Elvis turned to Ace and said, "That was pretty cool, huh, mister?"

Ace jumped out of the car and bent over, slurring, "Oh man...I think I'm gonna be..."

Ace puked for the next minute and a half straight.

# 9

## Expeditiously Expository

When his nausea subsided, Ace looked at the chaos surrounding them. A downed helicopter teemed with rescue workers. Elvis impersonators ran wild, fighting with police and each other. A crater the size of a washing machine smoldered in the corner of the property from where Ivan's dazzler exploded a few hours ago.

Near the crater, Ace recognized a familiar face wrestling with an Elvis impersonator dressed in a rhinestone encrusted jumpsuit. April Massey, the KFC cashier, dragged the impersonator by the arm towards Elvis Presley Boulevard.

"Hey, April!" Ace called out and ran across the lawn to meet her.

"Ace? Why the hell are you dressed like a stripper cop?" April said.

Ace ignored the question but felt self-conscious about the tightness of his borrowed cop pants.

"What are *you* doing here?" Ace asked.

"Oh. You know. Trying to get my dipshit brother here from going to jail, that's all." April smacked the Elvis impersonator on the back of his head.

"Ow!" the man yelped.

"Yeah, Barry, ow!" April said as she gave him another whack on the back of the head. "The show got canceled. Billy kept raising hell about a monkey hitting him in the nose. I figured you guys got into some kind of fight. He's kind of a dick so I wouldn't blame you. I figured you just split after popping him one. But Billy wouldn't shut up about the monkey. He went nuts when no one would believe him. One thing led to another, and the bartender had to call the cops. Only the cops told him they weren't coming because a bunch of Elvis impersonators were rioting in front of Graceland. And I *knew* my dipshit brother would be there. I just knew it!"

She hit Barry in the head again. "So, I came down here and sure as shit. Here's Barry!"

"You don't understand, Sis. He needs our help!" Barry said as he tried to pull away from April. She tightened her grip and pulled him back closer to her.

"No way, Jose!" April said. "How much weed did you smoke today? What the hell is wrong with you, Barry? A freaking police helicopter just crash landed at Graceland. We need to get out of here." April smacked Barry on the head again.

"I'm not sure he can help it," Ace said to April.

"What?"

"The impersonators. I don't think they can help themselves," Ace said. "Come on, let me show you something."

Ace turned to lead April back towards the Cadillac, but it was gone.

"What the—where'd it go?" Ace asked.

"Where'd what go?" April asked.

"The Cadillac! The Eldorado Biarritz. It was right over there." Ace pointed to where the car sat moments before, but in its place, three Elvis impersonators were pummeling a cop.

"Dude. Are you smoking reefer, too?" April asked. "What the hell is going on here tonight?"

An explosion erupted from the far side of the mansion. Barry grunted, wrenching himself away from April, and took off running.

"Barry!" April sprinted after Barry leaping over a pair of wrestling Elvis impersonators in the process.

Ace was about to follow when someone behind him yelled, "Eat it, pig!"

An Elvis impersonator in a skin-tight black leather suit tackled Ace, knocking him to the ground. Ace rolled onto his back and used his legs to throw the impersonator off with a sharp kick.

Black Leather Elvis squealed as he launched twenty feet into the air. His arms and legs flailed around looking for purchase, but there was nothing but empty space until he crashed into a tree with a sickening *thump*.

Black Leather Elvis collapsed to the ground in an unnatural ball of limbs and leather.

Two other Elvis impersonators were about to attack, but after seeing what Ace had done to their friend they started backing away while patting the air in the universal "calm it down" gesture.

"Barry! Stop! Wait!" April yelled as Barry disappeared behind the mansion.

April followed hurling an impressive and colorful string of obscenities as she ran.

Ace brushed himself off and ran after them rounding the corner just in time to see Barry tearing off for the field where *Betty* had crashed.

In the field, a purple Cadillac Eldorado Biarritz approached a floating rectangle of light with a ramp coming out of it.

*Betty!* Ace thought. *What the hell was Ivan doing? What the hell is the Caddy doing?*

If April saw the Cadillac disappear into *Betty*'s cargo bay, she didn't let on because she continued to run after Barry while lobbing profanity in his direction.

Barry stumbled and ran for the light. Between gulps for air, he screamed, "Wait! Take me with you! Take me with you!"

Scores of Elvis impersonators appeared from around the other side of the mansion. Every color, shape, size, and era of Elvis impersonator all running and yelling, "Take me with you!"

Ace quickened his pace, trying to outrun them and get to *Betty*.

Barry tripped and landed face first on the ground. April stopped behind him just as *Betty*'s dazzler switched off. Ace caught up to them and heard April whisper under her breath, "That's impossible."

An eighteen wheeler with cartoon rocket nacelles extending from its back trailer hovered in the sky before them all.

The hover looked stable, but showers of sparks rained down on the ground below it. *Something weird is going on with Betty's engines*, Ace thought. *Ivan must have jerry-rigged the hell out of something in the engine room.*

Over the chorus of stampeding Elvis impersonators, Ace heard a familiar voice shouting in his direction.

"Jesus Christ!" Agent Calhoun said. "What the hell is that?"

Calhoun tackled and pinned Ace to the ground with shocking efficiency, leaving Ace temporarily dazed.

"Hey, man! Get off of him!" April shouted.

Calhoun fought to stay on top as Ace tried to free his pinned arms from Calhoun's death grip.

April jumped on Calhoun's back and started shouting directly into his left ear, "Get off! Get off! Get off!"

In the chaos, Ace fought to wrench his torso up. He flailed upward trying to headbutt Calhoun but missed and wound up connecting with the agent's chest.

For a moment everyone stopped and looked at Ace like he had three heads. An embarrassing whiff but Ace didn't think it was *that* bad.

Calhoun and April's eyes widened but remained otherwise entirely still. Ace felt the hairs on his arms and back of his neck beginning to rise. His stomach knotted up as a bright blue light surrounded them.

Ivan had engaged *Betty*'s grappling beam.

It felt like a blanket of blue cotton candy and even had a faintly sweet, sugary aroma that left Ace concerned for his safety. He always heard you weren't supposed to use a grappling beam on living beings for risk of brain damage.

*That sweet phantom scent might be my brain melting,* Ace thought.

Ace tried to sit up but was utterly immobile with Calhoun sitting on him and April wrapped around Calhoun's back. There was no sensation of weight anymore, so he guessed it was the beam itself that kept the three piled together like some sort of weird sculpture.

It wouldn't have been so bad except Ace's gaze remained locked with Calhoun's. An intense fear and burning hatred seemed to resonate from the frozen agent.

Ace wanted to turn away but couldn't. He tried to close his eyes and enjoy the ride, but he couldn't do that either. He was stuck.

Fortunately, the ride ended in about ten seconds. The grappling beam disengaged, and Ace, April, and Calhoun crashed in a pile on the floor of *Betty*'s cargo bay.

When the beam released them, April and Calhoun began

screaming. Ace scurried away from them and stood up.

"April. Try to stay calm..." Ace was drowned out by the sound of the two screaming and *Betty*'s aft cargo door snapping closed.

Ace felt a sudden lightness in his tummy like riding a fast moving elevator that just shot up forty floors in under a second. An intimately familiar sensation. It meant Ivan had punched the engines and *Betty* rocketed skyward at escape velocity.

They were headed into outer space.

In the center of *Betty*'s cargo bay, Elvis's purple Cadillac rested unoccupied with the top down surrounded by stacks upon stacks of Mustache Supernova's stage gear. Amplifiers, PA speakers, lighting rigs, sound monitors, and various stage equipment had all been pushed away to form a perfect circle around the Cadillac.

The Cadillac's hood was up, and four long cables ran from the engine into the wall near a computer access panel. Ace wanted to take a closer look but needed to calm April and Agent Calhoun down first. The screaming had stopped, but they were both breathing heavily and speaking in short staccato sentences, not making any sense.

Somewhere in the back of Ace's memory, he recalled something called Acceleration Displacement Syndrome (A.D.S.), a condition that some non-spacefaring species get the first few times they accelerate past the speed of light. Something in their brains wants to make sense of the laws of physics breaking down around them but fails to cope. Since Ace had been flying faster than light his whole life he had never experienced it.

These two, however, looked like they were trying to breathe underwater and solve a jigsaw puzzle wearing oven mitts. It could be A.D.S., or maybe they were still freaking out about the grappling beam. Or the sight of *Betty*. It didn't matter. It was starting to annoy Ace.

"Guys," Ace said. "Please try to stay calm. I can explain everything."

April suddenly stopped babbling and her face melted into a calm, serene smile.

"OK. That's better," Ace said. "What the—?"

Calhoun had the same sudden placid doe-eyed expression.

The two sat down like both their bodies had suddenly become very heavy. A beat later they both slumped over unconscious with smiles plastered on their faces. Ace went over to check on April and noticed a tiny dart sticking in her neck.

Ace plucked the dart out of April's neck and recognized it as a Sleepinol X-14 Sedative Dart. A high-grade animal tranquilizer.

"Betty! Did you just tranq these people?" Ace asked.

"Yes, Ace." *Betty*'s voice sounded perfect. Like her old self again. Whatever repair measures Ivan took to get her up and running must have fixed her artificial intelligence interface as well.

"Their adrenaline, cortisol, and norepinephrine levels were extremely elevated," *Betty* said. "The male subject was about to have a stroke, and the female was on the verge of a psychotic break. I diluted the sedative, so they are sleeping comfortably now. I will monitor them and make sure they are OK."

Ace had tranquilizer guns installed in the cargo bay a few years ago when contracted to transport Beluvian gnarl boars to an eating festival in the Razlaton Sector. The festival catered to "adventurous eaters." The "adventure" being the guests eating food that also wanted to eat them. They went through half their complement of sedatives during the trip because the gnarl boars kept waking up and trying to eat each other. They lost three whole beasts to their hungry brethren.

"Well, I'm not going to just leave them in the damn cargo bay,"

Ace said. He hoisted April up and over his shoulder and brought her to the sick bay. Then did the same with Calhoun.

Satisfied the two were safe in their med cots Ace stormed out and straight for the cockpit.

Ivan sat in the pilot's seat with his long fingers draped over the steering wheel. Elvis sat in the co-pilot seat and Hank the Basset hound lay between the two on the floor. They all stared at what looked like a paused scene from *Gilligan's Island* on the heads up display. Mary Ann, the sweet Kansas farm girl, smiled with bright eyes and pigtails.

All three were talking over each other, arguing.

"I'm telling you, E. She had no right to be there," Ivan said, pointing at Mary Ann.

"What do mean, no right? She was there for the three-hour cruise!" Elvis said.

"OK. Right," Ivan said. "A three-hour cruise. With two millionaires, a movie star, and a professor! All people who obviously have money and can afford a three-hour pleasure cruise. What the hell kind of money does Mary Ann have? What was her job?"

"She was some kind of store clerk or something. Wasn't she?" Hank asked.

"She was a farm girl from Kansas," Ivan said. Each word dripped with contempt and disgust.

"Right. A farm girl!" Elvis said. There was a long pause while Ivan waited for Elvis to say something else.

Ace cleared his throat.

Everyone ignored him.

Finally, exacerbated, Ivan said, "What the heck was a farm girl from *Kansas* doing on a cruise with a millionaire and a movie star!?"

"Uhhh..."

"I'll tell you what!" Ivan said, raising his finger to make a point. "Sabotage!"

"What?" Hank and Elvis said at the same time.

"Yeah. Think about it. Everyone else had a reason to be on that boat. Gilligan and the Skipper were working. The Howells were out for a pleasure cruise. Same with the Professor. Just like Ginger, who was a frickin' movie star by the way! All people who make enough money to pay for a three-hour cruise. How the hell would a farm girl from Kansas have the kind of dough to rub elbows with those kind of people? She wouldn't! She was there for another purpose. She was there to sabotage the Minnow and make sure they got shipwrecked!"

Ace and Ivan had the same argument years ago. Ivan would never let it drop. He was always convinced that Mary Ann was some sort of saboteur working with nefarious intent.

"Wait a minute, man," Elvis said. "It was a storm that got them shipwrecked!"

"Yeah? So?" Ivan replied. "She's from Kansas. She knows how to read the meteorological signs and predict when a storm is coming. I bet she did something to make sure the tiny ship was tossed! Listen, man. The Skipper is a pro sailor. He's a salty dog who's lived his whole life on the sea. He would've been able to steer clear of that storm and return them back to port safely. Unless...sabotage!"

Elvis looked back at the still image of Mary Ann and said, "Yeah, but why? Why would she do that? Why maroon them on that island?"

"Well that's the real question, isn't it?" Ivan pointed at Mary Ann on the heads up display. "But I don't trust that cute 'suka.'"

"*Gilligan's Island* again?" Ace said with a cough.

The three turned around.

"Ace! Care to weigh in on this?" Ivan said with a jovial smile, pointing at Mary Ann.

"No, Ivan. I wouldn't. But I'll tell you what I'd like to know, goddammit—" Ace barked.

Ivan's smile dissolved.

"What the fuck is going on here?" Ace shouted louder than he'd meant to, but the stress he carried in his gut just forced its way out.

If Ivan had been standing, Ace would have grabbed him by the collar of his precious jacket and shaken the shit out of him. It probably would have caused a fist fight, and Ivan was pretty good in hand-to-hand combat. So Ace felt relieved Ivan remained out of arm's length. Ace had the habit of writing checks with his mouth that his ass couldn't cash. Ivan was usually the one to back him up. But not this time.

"What do you mean?" Ivan asked.

"What do *you* mean, what do I mean?" Ace shouted back.

Ivan looked at Elvis, then at Hank, then back to Elvis. "You didn't tell him?"

"Hey, man. He jumped out of the Caddy before I got a chance, remember?" Elvis held up his hands in defense.

"Don't look at me, Monkey Man," Hank said. "I was just worried about keeping the King safe. I didn't know yous guys weren't on the up and up."

Ivan turned to Ace and sighed. "Alright. Let's go to the kitchenette, Ace. You're gonna want to have a drink when you hear this."

* * *

Ace went to his cabin to change out of his cop disguise and into his customary jeans, t-shirt, and hat. He threw the uniform into the garbage chute but kept the gun he lifted off Calhoun and the other cop gadgets in a little pile on his bunk. He didn't know if handcuffs, a flashlight, and a nightstick would come in handy but thought they'd make excellent souvenirs once this whole ordeal was over.

Ace loaded up a small portable cooler with beer and followed Ivan, Elvis, and Hank into the cargo bay. He trailed a few steps behind sipping on his beer and feeling more like an outsider than he usually did.

The Cadillac sat powered on and idling. Ace didn't notice it last time due to the commotion of dealing with April and Calhoun's freak out.

Ivan pointed at the Cadillac and the four large cables running from its engine into the walls of the cargo bay.

"As soon as the Caddy emerged from the tunnel," Ivan said. "The two ships established some sort of ad hoc recovery network and were automatically drawn to each other. Some sort of failsafe that has to do with the Valdovian tech in both machines. Once it got into the cargo bay, Betty and the Caddy became physically connected via these hyper-conduits."

"Yeah," Elvis said. "She's got one hell of a repair system on board. It's what jump-started my nanobots, too! That shiny jerk fried 'em pretty good. But once I touched the Caddy, the 'bots got a reboot signal, and they fixed me up good as new."

Elvis patted his side. Smooth, unbroken skin peeked out from the charred hole in his shirt. The spot that looked like black melted plastic had vanished.

Ace thought about offering Elvis a fresh Mustache Supernova T-shirt but decided against it because Elvis kept running his mouth. He babbled on and on about seventh generation nano-cyber systems *this* and Higgs replicating quantum fluctuators *that*. How the nanobots were repaired by the systems on the Cadillac's particle something-or-other-resuscitator. Blah, blah, blah.

Ace kept nodding trying to at least appear interested but then glanced around the cargo bay, bored.

He took a long pull from his third Dark Star, enjoying the slight buzz he felt coming on. The flavor was light-years better than the Pabst Blue Ribbon he drank in Memphis. The cool carbonated elixir felt great as it rolled down his tongue and throat. He let his mind relax and wander until he noticed Elvis staring at him as if waiting for the answer to a question.

"Sorry. What's that?" Ace asked with a slight burp. "You're going to have to start over. What the hell did you just say is built into this car?"

"A super-secret experimental time machine from the future," Elvis stated flatly.

"Uh huh. And how'd you get it?"

"Lemme just start from the beginning, OK?" Elvis said with a sigh.

On the day of Elvis's supposed death, two extraterrestrials from the future appeared outside of Graceland.

"They were all starry-eyed and giddy at first," Elvis said. "They kept going on and on about my destiny among the stars. Uniting the cosmos. Bringing peace to the galactic systems. Weird stuff like that."

"I thought they were just coked out super fans or something. I was kinda in a cranky mood because I had to take a monster dump and was on my way to the john. I didn't have time for that stuff." Elvis's voice cracked a little.

"I told them to get the hell off my land." Elvis looked to the floor and his shoulders slouched. "One of the ETs used something he called a mindtap to show me the future."

Elvis took a deep breath then launched into his tale:

In 2384 a Valdovian working as a delivery boy for a sandwich shop called Zimmy Zon's invents a device that allows him to deliver a customer's food before they even order it. Although simple in its design, able to only travel thirty minutes into the past, the device makes Zimmy Zon's motto "Outlandishly Expeditious" more on the nose than anyone could've dreamed.

It revolutionizes food delivery and the galaxy itself. Now only having the intention to order could result in fast, delicious sandwiches showing up at your door in the hands of a smiling Zimmy Zon employee.

Zimmy Zon's becomes the biggest company in the Milky Way and begins to look for expansion opportunities. They decide to take a plunge by entering the nearby market of the Andromeda Galaxy. Up to this point, all attempts at trade and normalized relations with Andromeda had failed. Zon Zimmerson, founder and CEO of Zimmy Zon's, makes the first delivery himself.

It is a complete disaster.

The Greys, a species of sandwich-hating humanoids, take Zimmerson's sudden appearance as an act of war. They kidnap and torture him, gleaning enough information to build their own rudimentary time machine. They begin waging war across various points of time and space throughout the Milky Way.

Millions die.

Valdovian scientists eventually create an even better time machine, giving the Milky Way a significant lead in temporal warfare. Whereas the Greys' device is wildly inaccurate, sometimes transporting its passengers decades outside of their target date, the Valdovian model achieves accuracy down to the microsecond and has an unlimited range. The Milky Way rejoices after their covert missions dismantle the Greys' war effort and a tenuous peace is achieved. But espionage is rampant and time travel is exceptionally tricky and confusing.

The Greys begin work on a weapon of temporal mass destruction meant to prevent the Milky Way from ever existing, thus achieving ultimate victory.

In a last-ditch effort to avoid the Greys from getting their hands on the superior technology, the new super advanced Valdovian timedrive is hidden somewhere no one would think to look for it: twentieth century Earth.

# 10

# Long Live the King

"They told me the second floor of Graceland became
known as the most secure place in the galaxy following
my death," Elvis said. "As the mythos of my private
abode spreads over the decades it became apparent that it's a
perfect hiding spot. They installed upgraded security measures
that only I could disengage and plopped the timedrive into my
1959 Cadillac Eldorado Biarritz. How could I say no to a time-
traveling Cadillac?"

Elvis walked over to the trunk of the car. "You wanna see the
timedrive?"

"Sure," Ace said.

Elvis popped the trunk relieving a small glass cylinder about the
size of a loaf of bread with the words "Zimmy Zon's. Outlandishly
Expeditious!" printed on it. Within the glass, a substance that
defied explanation wriggled and swooshed around. At first, it
looked like some sort of suspended liquid or plasma, but after
blinking a few times, Ace thought it looked like a solid snake-
like object turning in and over itself. Then a semi-transparent
gas. Then a torrent of sand swirling in a wind tunnel. It glowed
with every color of the rainbow while simultaneously being
completely pitch black. The more he stared at it, the more his

mind screamed to look away.

"Jesus!" Ace turned his face away.

"Yeah. It's pretty freaky." Elvis closed the trunk. "So, after souping up the Caddy with some other cool space tech, they stashed it in the master bedroom at Graceland, helped me fake my death, and blasted me into outer space. They figured it would be best to keep the Caddy and me separate. You know, layers of security and stuff."

"They gave me these kickass nanobots to keep me alive. But it's been, like, forty years...I kinda forgot all about the whole thing. You know? You know what it's like with them 'Nova guys, man. It's all space booze and space pills. Things get fuzzy after a while. You know Mustache Supernova was just a crappy garage band when I started working with them? Hell, they're the biggest band in the galaxy now!"

"For fuck's sake!" Ace said. "This keeps getting crazier and crazier. I'm either getting used to it, or I'm in shock! But you know what? Screw it. Who am I to judge? I've got a Russian cyborg chimpanzee for a sidekick...But a time machine? Man!"

Ace drew in a deep breath and blew it out slowly.

"OK," Ace said with as much calmness as he could muster. "So, what's our next move?"

"Well," Elvis said. "I was told if anyone in a shiny suit ever showed up, I'm supposed to recover the Caddy and take it to the nearest Valdovian Space Car dealership to await further instructions."

"So, we're just supposed to take it to a car dealership and then, what? Wait?" Ace asked.

"Yeah. I guess," Elvis said. "They weren't real clear on that part. Just that I needed to get the hell off Earth and take the Caddy to a Valdovian Space Car dealership. Then...they'd take care of the rest."

"What the shit?" Ace spat. He paced back and forth for the next ten minutes, muttering profanity under his breath.

Deep down Ace knew this impossible quest would never pay off, but until that moment he clung to the idea that somewhere, somehow there'd be money at the end of it all. Some sort of compensation for all the trouble. Yet, *craziness* seemed to be the only real currency.

"Alright. Fine!" Ace said. "So let me ask you this: what's stopping this shiny asshole from just grabbing us now that we're in outer space? The one thing we had going for us is that Earth is protected by the Galactic Union's shield. And the Caddy used to be on Earth. Inside the shield! We're sitting ducks out here."

"Well, not necessarily," Ivan said. "Once the Caddy got hooked into Betty's hyperdrives they started behaving like one cohesive ship. The Caddy is acting like the main engine now, and because of the attached timedrive, we are temporally cloaked."

"Tempura what now?" Ace asked.

"Temporally cloaked," Ivan said. "We are out of phase with local space-time."

Ace raised his eyebrows and cocked his head.

"OK..." Ivan said, slowing his speech like he was speaking to a child. "It's like how you know when we go faster than light we drop out of normal space and fly through hyperspace?"

"Yeah?" Ace had no idea how faster than light travel actually worked but decided to play along.

"It's sort of like that, but we are in hyper*time* as well," Ivan said, making hand gestures Ace guessed were supposed to make the concept clearer (but didn't). "We are moving outside of the normal space-time continuum right now. We are enclosed in a localized bubble that is outside the regular universe. As far as that real, normal, universe is concerned, we don't exist."

"Well now that *is* handy," a voice said from behind.

At the entrance to the cargo bay, Agent Calhoun clutched April by the arm and pressed a gun against her temple.

"Nobody move and nobody gets hurt," Agent Calhoun said. His voice sounded different than the last time Ace heard it. Of course, Calhoun was shouting and running at the time, but now something else seemed amiss. The timber and cadence of Calhoun's voice had a forced, percussive, almost unnatural thrust to each syllable.

"Eat me, asshole," April said with a shrill staccato and all the bravery she could muster. Tears welled in her eyes, and her lips trembled when she spoke.

"You do have quite the mouth on you, don't you?" Calhoun said and pushed the gun a little harder into April's temple.

April let out a gentle squeal and pursed her lips tight.

Ace's body tensed up. Flush heat swept through his body. He glanced over to Ivan and Elvis. Both froze so as not to provoke the man with the gun. Even Hank stopped his incessant panting and drew long calm breaths through his nose. It sounded like a leaky air compressor blowing through a wet noodle.

"Easy, now," Ace said as he brought his hands up. "Just put the gun down, and we can talk about this in a calm, rational manner. I'm not even mad you stole that gun from my bunk or that you're threatening my friend there. It's nothing that a couple of *rodeo clowns* can't handle..."

Agent Calhoun narrowed his eyes and tilted his head.

Ace looked around and then cleared his throat. "Umm...I said it's nothing a couple of *rodeo clowns* can't handle," Ace said.

"Rodeo. Clowns," Ace said again after a beat. "Row. Dee. Oh. Cah. Luh. Ow. Nuh. Sss."

"Rodeo clowns," Ivan said after Ace glanced over at him.

Ace mouthed to Ivan, "Why isn't the passphrase activating Betty's security protocols?"

"I don't know," Ivan mouthed back. "There should be stun beams, tranq darts, and kill drones raining down on him by now."

Last year, after an incident with a stowaway, Ace programmed *Betty* to activate a security protocol based on a passphrase. But, now, there was nothing.

"Betty?" Ace whispered.

Calhoun smiled when *Betty* spoke through the ship-wide audio system, "Yes, Ace?"

"Why aren't you blasting this asshole or flinging darts at him or something?" Ace asked.

"I'm sorry, Ace. I can't do that right now," *Betty* replied.

"What?" Ace shouted.

Calhoun's smile broadened further than Ace thought a human face would allow the skin to stretch.

"Sorry, Ace," *Betty* said. "My systems have been overridden. There is a new ownership matrix in place. You no longer have authority to give commands to any of my systems."

"What the— who—?" Ace said.

"Me," Calhoun shouted, interrupting Ace.

Calhoun shoved April towards Ace.

April held her hands out to prevent her from knocking them both to the ground. Ace caught her and steadied her next to him. She smiled a thank you.

Calhoun gestured with his gun as he spoke. "I suggest you stay perfectly still. With a single word, I can kill you all. I am in complete control of this vessel and its systems."

"How is that even possible?" Ivan asked.

"Turns out your dimwitted partner was right, Mr. Chimpanov,"

Calhoun said. "Outside of Earth, you are open to *his* signal."

"Whose signal?" Elvis asked.

"The one you call the Shiny Man, of course," Calhoun said as he walked over to a computer display screen. "Betty! Show them."

The screen lit up with an image of *Betty*'s exterior. It zoomed in a few times revealing a small impossibly shiny device stuck to *Betty*'s hull like a lamprey sucking on the skin of a shark.

"This device has been on your ship ever since your last encounter," Calhoun said with pride.

"That's what the Shiny Man shot at us when he knocked us out of hyperspace after Sleazon's party!" Ivan said.

"I thought you said we were fine, Ivan!" Ace said.

"I thought we were. Ace," Ivan said stressing each syllable. "But apparently that shiny jerk is from the future, and I'm not all up on stuff that hasn't been invented yet!"

Ace and Ivan pointed fingers at each other. An avalanche of accusations poured from their mouths until April screamed at the top of her lungs, "Will someone please tell me what the fuck is going on here?"

The arguing stopped. Ace and Ivan glanced at their feet like two boys caught fighting by their mother.

"It's really quite simple, Miss Massey," Calhoun said as he holstered his gun and reached into his pocket, pulling out a small silver-colored device. "I've been waiting for years for this moment. Working, manipulating, waiting."

Calhoun pushed a button, and a cloud of silver energy erupted around him. The field brightened until it became a swirling current of pure white light. Ace had to shield his eyes from the brilliance.

When the blinding light subsided a man covered from head to toe in impossibly shiny metal stood in Calhoun's place: the Shiny

155

Man in the flesh.

Elvis said something inaudible under his breath.

Hank growled with menace.

Ivan cursed in Russian.

April cursed in English.

Ace shook his head and wished he never agreed to go to that party at Sleazon Nebula's house.

The Shiny Man smiled, again displaying an exaggerated inhuman stretch to his face. "A similar technology to, what do you call them? Dazzlers? Except my device does not simply project a hologram. It changes my appearance at a physical level."

The Shiny Man put the device into a fold in his shiny pants and continued, "I had to get to Earth before the Galactic Union erected the protection shield. And as you know, *our* technology is not as precise as the Valdovians."

"Ours?" Ivan said. "You mean the Greys of Andromeda!"

"Very good, Mr. Chimpanov," the Shiny Man said. "After traveling from the future, I crash landed in Roswell, New Mexico in 1947. A curious rancher happened upon the crash site. I killed him and assumed his physical identity then faded into obscurity."

The Shiny Man's face twisted with rage. "Years! I've waited years for you to arrive! I was careful not to alter the timeline. Do you know how hard it was to refrain from blasting this criminal when he was a child? It would've been so easy. But instead, I encouraged him. I nurtured him from near and far. My influence always on the fringe of his every success. All to get to this point in time."

"Who are you calling criminal, you shiny fuck?" Hank barked.

Elvis's head hung low, and he drew in deep breaths. "He's talking about me, Hank."

"Yeah. I know," Hank snarled. "But no one talks to you like

that! Just let me at him, boss. I bet he's got shiny nuts under that tin suit. I'll grind them into pencil shavings!"

"It's alright, Hank," Elvis said. He raised his head and tears welled up in his eyes. "I've been expecting this for a while now."

"So," Elvis said to the Shiny Man. "How's this gonna go down?"

The Shiny Man shrugged. "How would you like it to?"

"Ah, hell no! That ain't happening!" Hank barked and leaped into the air, his tiny legs propelling him like a meaty rocket towards the Shiny Man. His giant floppy ears lay pinned to the side of his head and neck as he flew. He let out a growl like a hungry bear. A trail of slobber flew from his flapping jowls like a jet contrail.

The Shiny Man swatted Hank away like a fly with casual indifference.

Hank sailed backward, crashing into Ace knocking them both to the floor with an undignified pile of fur, slobber, and swear words.

April and Ivan helped Hank off Ace's chest. Ace spent the next few seconds picking dog hair out of his mouth and wiping it off his face.

"That. Mother...fu..." Hank passed out.

Before anyone else could react the Shiny Man shouted, "Contain them all except Elvis Presley!"

A series of metal pylons sprang up from the floor like pistons. They thrust their way into the ceiling and created a cage sealing off everyone but the Shiny Man and Elvis, another security measure Ace installed after the Beluvian gnarl boar incident last year. Ace thought if transporting wild animals became a regular gig they should at least have some sort of modular pen or cage system. It cost seven hundred credits under the table, and Ace thought it was money well spent. Until now.

Ace pulled at the cage's bars with all his might, but they were solid ultra-titanium and didn't budge a nanometer.

Elvis stood still with his eyes closed in what looked like some sort of meditative state. His breath was slow and even. His fists were clenched.

In one slow, elegant movement he raised his hand up above his head then brought them down together in front of his chest. He bowed at the waist and assumed a fighting stance. His rear foot turned ninety degrees to the side with the leg bent at the knee. His front foot slid out in front of him with the leg slightly bent. He held tight fists in the center of his chest. His head locked straightforward, and his eyes were calm but focused.

"I dislike death," Elvis said. "But there are some things I dislike more than death. Thus, there are times when I will not avoid danger."

"What ridiculous philosophical drivel are you spouting?" the Shiny Man asked.

"Mencius. Also known as Master Meng. Third century BCE Chinese philosopher," Elvis replied. "Basically it means I am not afraid of you and if death is inevitable, so be it. Honor and goodness are on my side. So bring it, you shiny piece of Andromeda space trash!"

The Shiny Man darted forward so fast he was a silver blur. He rained blows down on Elvis in a torrent of violence. Elvis blocked each punch with stunning speed and accuracy. The two looked like a tornado of punches, kicks, blocks, and thrusts. It reminded Ace of watching a kung fu movie fight scene at twice the normal speed. Or a whirlwind of two fighting cartoon Tasmanian devils.

Ace couldn't see any individual strikes. Just a blur of motion accompanied by a constant chorus of grunts and skin slapping skin like meatballs raining on a cheap metal roof.

Suddenly, the Shiny Man shrieked in pain and pushed away from Elvis, opening up several feet between the two panting combatants. A silver sheen glazed the Shiny Man's cheek like he leaked tiny droplets of mercury. Ace guessed it was either sweat or blood and from the look on the Shiny Man's face, it was probably blood.

The Shiny Man touched his cheek and brought his hand down to look at the silver wetness.

"Impossible," the Shiny Man said.

"Yeah. Sorry about that," Elvis said, his breath already returning to normal. "These nanobots I have coursing through my veins travel to different parts of my body depending on what I need. They're mostly in my arm and leg muscles now. They've made me pretty fast. Oh. And I've been studying martial arts for over sixty years now, so, you know, I'm pretty good at it. And, just so you know, I got you with a *uraken strike*. A back fist. I think the kids today call that a *bitch slap*!"

The Shiny Man's face twisted with fury as he roared.

He reached deep into a pocket of his shiny suit and drew a laser revolver.

"Elvis!" Ace called, too late. "Look out!"

The Shiny Man fired so fast it looked like a continuous eruption of crackling energy.

The deluge of superheated death hit Elvis square in the chest in an incredible radiant flare.

When the onslaught ended Elvis stumbled backward. His shirt was completely vaporized from the laser fire and a black splotch spread out over his chest.

But there was no blood.

Elvis swayed like a punch drunk boxer, and his eyes lacked

focus. All the color had drained from his face, and he looked like he was about to pass out.

The Shiny Man dropped the laser revolver into his pocket and sauntered up to Elvis. He rapped his shiny knuckles upon the burnt plastic-like coating covering Elvis's chest.

"Looks like your nanobots have all swarmed here to protect you, King," the Shiny Man said. "The ones that you have left are probably trying to repair the massive internal injuries you've sustained. Don't worry. They won't have long to work."

The Shiny Man grabbed Elvis by the hair and dragged him across the cargo bay to the garbage recycler. He opened the hatch and hoisted Elvis inside.

The Shiny Man spat.

His saliva had a silver sheen to it as it flew from his mouth and landed square on Elvis's lifeless face.

Then he closed the hatch and hit the button that broke waste material down to a slurry of reusable matter for *Betty*'s fabricators.

"The King is dead," the Shiny Man said dripping with sarcasm. "Long live the King."

# 11

## Everyone, Meet Ray-Ray

The garbage recyclers broke matter down to its base components and shuttled off the compounds to holding tanks for later use. By now all that remained of Elvis Presley was nothing more than a paste to make new tools, machine parts or anything else *Betty*'s fabricators could devise.

Ace's chest ached. The world seemed to slow down as he gripped the cage bars and stared at the floor through blurred eyes. He felt cold and had a heaviness in his arms that caused him to drop his hands to his sides and slump against the cage.

*Sure, Elvis was a pain in the ass,* Ace thought. *But he was a human being. He deserved better than being melted down to fabricator goo.*

"I've been manipulating you from the start," the Shiny Man said. "Leading you to Earth. Keeping you on task with Elvis's supposed astral projections. That was me in control of your ship's holoprojectors. The Elvis impersonators? Me again. They were all too eager to help. All they needed was a little telepathic push. Feigning ignorance and playing along at our encounters at the rest stop and near the woods? All to help string you along to recover the time machine. You've played your part perfectly, Mr. Tucker."

Ace felt drained and whispered, "Fuck you, man."

If the Shiny Man heard, he didn't react. "I will have to admit. It was pretty clever on your part, Ivan Chimpanov, to disguise yourself using the dazzlers. Sorry if my aggrandizer field caused them to malfunction when you first got close to Graceland. They were in place all around the perimeter of the property to make sure the drooling idiot Elvis impersonators had a beacon to rally to. They don't play nice with third-rate holo-technology."

Ivan held up a long middle finger but said nothing.

The Shiny Man smirked. "Now, if you'll excuse me. It's time for phase two."

The Shiny Man exited the cargo bay, sealing the door behind him with a forcefield. The lights in the cargo bay dimmed to a low red glow casting everything in a gloomy hue that reminded Ace of a submarine movie he had once seen. The crew of that vessel was in a pickle as well, torpedoed and sinking to the bottom of the sea.

April stroked Hank's head as he snored. She looked up at Ace with misty, sad eyes but looked much less freaked out than Ace would have thought given the circumstances.

Ace sat down next to April and gave Hank a little scratch behind one of his giant, floppy ears. Hank blew out an extended sigh that rattled his slobbery gums. A little bit of spittle splashed out and hit the floor.

"So..." April said, not making eye contact. "You're from outer space, huh?"

"Yeah..." Ace said. "I wanted to tell you, but —"

"No. I get it," April said. "You're like some kind of secret agent from space, trying to save the world from unspeakable terrors. You gotta keep a low profile."

"What?" Ace jerked his head back. "Where the hell did you get that idea?"

"I dunno," April said. She stopped petting Hank and looked at Ace. "You live in a spaceship with a cyborg chimpanzee that sometimes looks like Seth Green. And you're mixed up with some sort of alien supervillain asshole who just killed Elvis Presley...Who also seems to have some sort of cyborg animal friend...Seems like space James Bond shit to me."

Ace thought about it for a moment. It did sound like some pretty cool secret agent stuff. But Ace was in no mood to conflate his coolness. "April. I'm a trucker. I ain't no secret agent."

"Trucker, huh?"

"Yup," Ace said with a lump in his throat. "We got roped into this mess by accident. And all I wanted was to get money out of it so I can pay off some debts."

April nodded thoughtfully.

"You seem way less freaked out than I thought you'd be learning all this," Ace said.

"Hey man," April said, "I'm from Memphis. You ever been on Beale Street past one in the morning? Now that's some freaky shit that will curl your hair!"

April continued stroking Hank for a few moments then let out a sigh. She slapped her hands on her thighs and stood up.

"So," April said. "Ace Tucker, space trucker. How are we going to get out of this mess?"

Ace looked up at her, baffled. "We — we can't. We're stuck in a cage, and that shiny asshole has control of my ship!"

"Oh, come on!" April said gesturing wide with her hands. "You gotta have some kind of something we can do here. Some kind of, forgive the pun, *ace* up your sleeve."

April's sudden burst of energy and hopefulness confused Ace. In his experience when life kicked you in the nuts you just wrapped them in ice and hobbled away. Fighting back never worked. No one likes a hero.

"I—I don't know," Ace said.

"Well, how about you, Seth-Ivan?" April asked as she walked over to Ivan in a far corner of the cage. Ivan was squatting down with his back to them. From how his shoulders moved it looked like he was working at something on the floor.

Ace followed April to the corner. Ivan had peeled up a part of the floor with the spike he used to jack into *Betty*'s computer system.

"Whoa," Ace said.

"Yeah," Ivan grunted and strained. "This ain't easy. This is reinforced poly-ceramic here. But if I can get this panel up, I might be able to jack into a data conduit and see what that shiny jerk did to our girl here."

Ivan peeled the panel back with extreme effort. His whole body shook, but the panel moved little by little. The conduits and cables making up *Betty*'s guts became visible. Ivan was about to get a free hand under the panel and hoist it up when a terrible scream erupted from outside the cargo bay.

The Shiny Man stormed in and threw something hard against the wall with enough force to make a dent.

"What did you do?" the Shiny Man yelled as he stormed over to the cage. Ivan was discrete and dropped the panel down. He kept his spike wedged underneath and sat crossed legged over top of the panel making it look like he was sitting on one of his hands. As far as Ace could tell, the Shiny Man didn't see any of it.

Ace walked up to the bars in an attempt to further hide Ivan from the Shiny Man's vision. "Come again, mister?" Ace said. "What can I do for you?"

"Don't play coy with me, human!" The Shiny Man spat. His face twisted in horrible rage. "I just checked the Chronomicon.

The future has not changed! The death of Elvis Presley has done nothing to alter the timeline! What have you done?"

"Hey man. I have no idea what the shit you are talking about," Ace said.

"What I am talking about, *Mister* Tucker is the future." The Shiny Man sneered when he said "mister" like it was some sort of an insult which, in all fairness, it was to Ace. "It appears that killing Elvis Presley in the twenty-first century does nothing to stop him from becoming as Prime Minister of Earth in the twenty-fourth century."

"Buddy," Ace said with a sigh. "You're not making any sense. How can a dead man be prime minister of a planet?"

"I don't know how but your involvement has made it possible!" the Shiny Man said. "You are now listed in the Chronomicon as a Time Abrasion. You have done something in this timeline that has already undone what I came here to do."

Ace tilted his head like a dog listening to air slowly escaping a balloon.

"You've created a temporal paradox," the Shiny said. "Your actions have reversed what I've done before I even had a chance to do it."

Ace blew out a long exaggerated breath. He hadn't seen this much crazy since he spent a night drinking Gortexian ale with Knees McGuffin, the drummer of Mustache Supernova. That particular bender resulted in two arrest warrants, a wedding, a subsequent annulment, and the adoption of a Parmeezian parrot named Tinkles. Ace had only been able to piece together the evening's events through stolen security footage from seven different space station databanks and the personal recollection of a minister/exotic pet dealer from the Null Sector.

Knees still had Tinkles the parrot and took him on tour ever since.

Ace still had a tattoo he didn't remember getting and made monthly alimony payments to the ex-Mrs. Tucker (a woman he didn't remember marrying).

Ace wasn't sure if the arrest warrants were still valid, but he vowed never to go back to the Null Sector without a team of lawyers. Just in case.

"Listen, guy," Ace said. "Last time I checked I was stuck in this cage like some kind of goddamn circus animal. How the frick could I do anything to mess with your crow-no-whatcha-ma-jigger?"

The Shiny Man screamed.

Ace clutched his ears. The roar was so loud it rattled Ace's teeth and sent shock waves through his skull.

When the outburst subsided, the Shiny Man returned to a calm demeanor. He spoke in an even, emotionless deadpan. "You are lucky the rules governing this situation are very clear. Your involvement has saved you and your band of caged freaks. At least temporarily. A Time Abrasion cannot be destroyed lest irreparable damage be done to the timeline. It seems we are all ensnared in this paradox together. But I am not defeated. It will just take extra measures to rectify it."

The Shiny Man turned and walked over to the Cadillac. He checked the cables running from the engine to a computer wall panel. Then he reached in over the driver's side door around the steering wheel and tapped a button.

The Cadillac sprang to life as the engine revved up. Light burst out of the seams of the trunk. The Shiny Man tapped another button on the dashboard then walked over to the computer panel on the wall of the cargo bay. Ace couldn't make out what was on the display, but it looked like some sort of navigation interface.

The Shiny Man's finger flew across the screen as he entered some sort of program.

*Coordinates, maybe?* Ace thought.

The Shiny Man tapped the screen one final time with an exaggerated flourish.

*Betty* began to shake like they were flying through atmospheric turbulence. The telltale hum of her engines took on some new odd overtones that raised the hair on Ace's neck.

"Next stop," the Shiny Man said. "Earth. Tupelo, Mississippi. January 7, 1935. To make sure I erase him from history, I will kill Elvis Presley before he is ever born."

Before leaving the cargo bay, the Shiny Man launched into a long, drawn out speech. He used phrases like "temporal splinter" and "quantum enigma." Something about restoring the natural order of the universe by destroying the Milky Way Galaxy. It was all mumbo jumbo, so Ace tuned it out.

One part of the mind-numbing story got Ace's attention, though. The Shiny Man said Elvis will return to Earth at the end of the twenty-fourth century and usher in a grand new era of humanity united. No more famine. No more hopelessness. Just a unified Earth with endless opportunity and the best Rock 'n' Roll scene in the galaxy.

Somehow, according to the Shiny Man, this was still destined to happen. Even though Ace just watched Elvis die moments ago. The Shiny Man had a device for reading past and future events, the Chronomicon, and it stated Elvis's new United Earth was still inevitable.

Hence, the Shiny Man transformed *Betty* into a time torpedo hurling through space-time so he could kill an unborn baby. Kill Elvis. Again. But for the first time. Ace tried hard to follow the logic of it all, but it made his head hurt.

When the Shiny Man finally finished his jibber jabber and exited the cargo bay, Ivan resumed working on the floor panel.

Ace went back to sulking.

"I'm going to try and jack into a low-level subsystem of *Betty*'s neural network," Ivan said.

"Well, I'm going to help," Hank said, still a little groggy but up and about. "I'm an expert on semantic computer networks. Besides I need something to fucking do else I'm gonna start bawling and shitting everywhere." Hank was taking Elvis's death pretty hard.

Ivan, eager to accept the help, said, "Yes! Please. Betty's network is screwed six ways to Sunday. If you could help me penetrate the first few layers of security I might be able to establish a subroutine to gain some sort of foothold."

Ace ignored them after that. It was just an incomprehensible torrent of technobabble.

April sat in the other corner, tinkering with what looked like a small computer hand terminal. Ace sat down next to her and asked, "You trying to hack into Betty, too?"

"No," April said. "Just playing some Angry Birds on my cell phone."

"Angry Birds?" Ace asked.

"Yeah, it's this dumb mobile game where you fling birds at these brick and wood houses that these stupid, fat pigs make. The object is to fuck up the houses and kill all the stupid pigs."

"Sounds pretty violent," Ace said.

"Nah, it's silly. Look." April scooted closer to Ace and tilted the device so he could see the screen. She moved her index finger across the screen, and a cartoon bird on a slingshot followed it. When she let go the bird flew across the screen. It panned as the bird crashed full speed into a shoddily constructed wooden house. The impact caused half the structure to collapse on the pigs within it. The green pigs exploded in a puff of smoke.

"Cool," Ace said.

"Yeah man. Fuck those pigs," April said with a giggle.

Ace wasn't sure who had the filthier mouth, April or Hank. Then Hank took first place as he spat out every swear word Ace had ever known while somehow creating new compound curses. Hank performed a true feat of linguistic gymnastics Ace didn't know was possible; a whole new level of profanity.

"I love that dog," April said.

"Yeah," Ace said halfhearted, trying to be nice and not think about how Hank threatened to bite his nuts off. "He's the best..."

"So, is he a cyborg like Ivan?" April asked.

"Huh," Ace said, "You know — I don't know."

"Hey, Hank!" April called out to Hank half-buried in the open floor panel. Only Hank's hindquarters were visible. "Are you some sort of cyborg or something?"

"Lady," Hank said, his voice sounding muffled. "I am a Basset hound."

"Yeah, I know," April said. "But how is it you can talk and stuff?"

"Oh, that," Hank said, still with his head buried in the floor. "So, I don't know, really. I woke up one day, and I was like this. Hey, Ivan. Hold that cable right over here."

Ivan complied and said, "Got it. Keep an eye on the transition conduit next to it."

"I see it, dipshit. I'm not fucking blind." Hank lisped like a pair of forceps held his tongue.

April whispered to Ace, "How is he moving stuff in there with no hands? Is he using his tongue or something?"

"Damned if I know," Ace said.

April got up to check out Hank and Ivan's progress. She got halfway when *Betty* jolted violently, throwing her off balance and almost to the floor. She held her hands out to balance.

Hank tipped over, falling into the open floor panel and yelled, "Fuuuuuck!"

Everything was still and silent for a moment. Then, the cage around them began to recede into the floor.

"You guys did it!" Ace jumped up.

"Yeah," Ivan said. "I was able to convince Betty that the cage was part of an invasive computer virus and the autonomic controls took over and killed it."

"We!" Hank said as he struggled to pull himself out of the open floor hatch with his stubby little legs. "We! Were able to convince the computer."

"Yeah," Ivan said with a smile. He pulled Hank out of the hatch and set him down. "It was a team effort. Thanks, Hanks."

"You got it, monkey man," Hank replied.

"But don't you think the bad guy is going to notice that you shook the whole ship to do it?" April asked.

"Oh. That wasn't us," Ivan said.

Ivan approached a computer panel on the wall. He extended his cyber implant spike and jammed it into a data port.

"I've gained the trust of some low-level systems," Ivan said. "I'm still locked out of the major stuff. It looks like he's got Betty's fabricators working overtime building something. The good news is he's routed most of the power away from Betty's security systems. Guess he thought we'd never break out of that cage."

"Dipshit!" Hank said.

"What's he making?" April asked.

"Looks like a tearing electron plasma inducer," Ivan said.

"A tearing electron what now?" Ace asked.

Ivan let out a sigh. "It's a type of gun that is capable of blasting a target on a cellular level."

Ace felt like a frog trying to figure out how to rebuild a starter motor on a hypercycle.

"He can cook a target from the inside out," Ivan explained slowly. "My guess is he could kill someone or give them cancer or a heart defect or something without anyone knowing he did it."

"Oh," Ace said. "Why not just blast the shit out of stuff with Betty's laser guns?"

"He's a murderous psychopath from the future," Ivan said. "I'm sure he's got his reasons. Probably doesn't want to call too much attention to himself. Make it look like a natural death."

"Hey, *Grace*," Hank said to Ace. "Pick me up so I can get a better look at that computer readout."

Ace hoisted Hank up. The information on the screen flew by far too fast for Ace to comprehend, so he started looking around the cargo bay, bored.

That's when he noticed a gray goo dripping out of the garbage recycler.

Small droplets accumulated in a little pool on the floor. The pool pulsated like sand on a vibrating drum and seemed to be inching itself ever so slightly towards Ace.

When the pool was about the size of Ace's palm, the droplets stopped falling, and the pool started snaking across the floor.

"Guys..." Ace said.

Everyone ignored him. Ivan and Hank were chattering about quantum *somethings* and trans-recta-who-knows-*whats*. Even April chimed in, asking for clarification on what Ivan would point out on the screen.

"Guys..." Ace repeated, shaking Hank a little to get his attention.

"What?" Hank shouted. "Fuck, man! What are you fucking trying to do? Make me puke? Stop shaking me."

"There's some weird stuff crawling across the floor over there," Ace said, turning so Hank could see.

"Shit!" Hank jolted, and Ace almost dropped him. "Where'd they come from? Holy shit! Put me down, *Lace*."

Ace ignored the new butchering of his name and put Hank down on the ground.

Hank sniffed the air in the direction of the snaking gray goo and wagged his tail furiously.

The goo slowed as it approached the group like it was cautious of them.

"Eww! What is that?" April said with disgust.

"Those are Elvis's nanobots!" Hank said with a little wiggle of his tail. "They must've escaped the recycler."

"*That* is a robot?" April asked.

"Not just one robot, sister," Hank said. "Hundreds of thousands of tiny microscopic robots. They all work together and were what *was* keeping Elvis alive all these years. They must have gotten rebooted because Betty's systems are tied into the Caddy. But since Elvis's body got broken down in that fucking garbage recycler, they don't have anything to work on anymore..." Hank's voice trailed off at the last part, saddened. Then he snapped out of it and said, "Monkey man, you have an electromagnetic telelink module we can use? We need to talk to these things and quick."

Ivan tapped a few times on the screen of the computer panel. "I'm still locked out of higher level systems like the fabricators. I would normally be able to make one, but I can't right now. I need some more time to get them online. But that's not the biggest problem here. The Shiny Man just left the ship."

"What?" Ace, Hank, and April said.

"Yeah," Ivan said. "That turbulence we felt a few minutes ago? That was us breaching the stratosphere."

Ivan paged through computer readouts. "Given the lack of industrialized sprawl and major pollution, I'd say we're definitely somewhere in early twentieth century of Earth. Yup. We're hovering about Tupelo, Mississippi. I'm guessing in the early 1930s."

"That's where Elvis was born! He's going after baby Elvis!" Hank shouted. "Ace, go put your hand on those 'bots!"

"Whoa!" Ace said. "Hank, you actually called me by name proper name! Wait. What!? I'm not going to touch some weird pile of robotic goo that just climbed out of another person's body!"

"They're made to interface with human DNA, assbag," Hanks said. "If they get in your system, you'll have a fighting chance against the Shiny Man! This might be our only chance to save Elvis!"

"Are you suggesting I inject myself with some crazy-ass swarm of robots and go fight the Shiny Man?" Ace asked, beside himself.

"That's exactly what I'm suggesting, you fruit! Now, do it!" Hank barked.

"He might be right, Ace," Ivan said. "Chimpanzee DNA is ninety-six percent the same as humans. But that other four percent is a big darn difference. If they only work with humans that leaves you and April. And if they give you some sort of fighting chance against that shiny jerk, one of you has to take it. He won't be expecting it. You can catch him off guard."

"I—I guess, I would do it," April said, unsure. "I took Taekwondo in middle school and—"

"No." Ace cut her off. "This is my ship, and this is my responsibility."

Ace cracked his knuckles and blew out a long sigh as he contemplated the facts. It crazily made some sort of sense. He saw what Elvis could do, how fast he could move with those nanobots in his system. Ace wasn't trained in martial arts like Elvis, but he'd been in his fair share of barroom brawls. If he could just get the jump on the Shiny Man, he knew, he hoped, he could take him. Not to mention he'd be saving rock 'n' roll itself and the supposed future of humanity in the process.

A torrent of conflicting thoughts and emotions flooded Ace, and a sour feeling in his gut began to creep up. He wasn't sure he could handle all the pressure. He didn't sign up to be a hero. All he wanted to do was go to a party, have a few drinks, a few laughs, and hit the road to the next Mustache Supernova gig. He never asked to get embroiled in some sort of cosmic plot to undo Earth's history, and he sure didn't ask to pick a fight with a super-powered shiny psycho from another galaxy.

He was right on the cusp of backing down, about to say the pressure was too much, that they should find another way to deal with it all.

Then a new emotion broke through the self-doubt and despair. Anger.

The Shiny Man had manipulated him, had stolen his ship, his home. *Betty!* The one girl he ever truly loved. The Shiny Man turned her against Ace and used her to hurt him and his friends. The Shiny Man was actively using her to try and kill the King of Rock 'n' Roll before Elvis was even born.

*What kind of a sadistic prick does something like that?* Ace thought.

174

Ace felt energized as adrenaline rushed through his body. A pounding began to *thump, thump, thump* in his ears like majestic battle drums. His body tensed up, and he fantasized about all the violent ways he was going to kick the Shiny Man's ass.

But he'd need more than his wits and the element of surprise to help him out. He took another long breath and blew it out slow, allowing the rage to coalesce into courage.

"Ivan," Ace said. Frigid wrath dripped from every syllable. "Do you have access to the Broom Closet?"

Ivan tapped on the screen a few times. "Yes. I believe I do."

"Broom closet?" Hank yelled. "You don't have to sweep those 'bots up. Just go touch them, dick nose!"

"I will Hank," Ace said. "But first I gotta get something that might come in handy. Call it an insurance policy. Go ahead and unlock it, Ivan."

Ace walked to the far corner of the cargo bay and a door labeled Broom Closet. He heard a soft click as the lock released. A puff of cool air gushed out from within, hitting him in the face like the welcome of the cool side of a pillow.

"See, Hank," Ace said. "The Broom Closet is what I call my gun locker. I'm not a big fan of guns, but at times like this, when impending doom is breathing down your neck, and the future of humanity is on the line, a good sidearm comes in handy."

Lucky for Ace he had just the pistol. He called it Ray-Ray. It had some fancy technical name but Ace called it like he saw it: it was a damn Star Trek-Duck Dodgers-Flash Gordon-ass ray gun! And it packed one hell of a wallop.

The cool metal pistol grip felt good as it rested in the curve of Ace's palm. It had been a few months since Ace held Ray-Ray in his hand. The last time was at an ill-fated truck stop in the Dramemine Quadrant.

Unbeknownst to Ace, a polymorphous lizard beast had laid an egg on *Betty*'s undercarriage when they set down on Brovidian IV. The jungle planet was home to all manner of dangerous critters. The lizard beast, looking for a shady place to incubate, stuck one of her young on *Betty*'s hull. They didn't discover it until after leaving Brovidian IV when they landed at Starward Ho's Space Truck Stop and ran *Betty* through the truck wash.

The suds and the friction caused the egg to hatch, and the lizard beast started wreaking havoc all over the place. Ace cornered the critter behind the Thirsty Singularity, the truck stop bar, and blasted the foul thing into oblivion. The owner of the truck stop was so happy with Ace's handy work that he bought a round of drinks and filled up *Betty*'s power cells on the house.

Ace nodded to himself while he reflected on the lizard beast incident. It was a crappy situation, but he stepped up and got done what needed doing. He didn't run. He found the right tool for the job and got it done.

Before he returned to the others, Ace flipped Ray-Ray on and dialed in a power setting of forty million megajoules.

*That should be enough to blast a hole the size of a dump truck through just about anything,* Ace thought.

Ace tucked Ray-Ray into his waist. The metal felt cold against his skin. The gun vibrated ever so slightly like the supercharged particles of violence were just itching to be unleashed.

"Alright," Ace said. "How's this work?"

Hank danced around like he had to pee, his long nails *clickity clacking* on the floor. "Go put your hand on those bots, asshole. Do it now!"

# 12

## You Really Are a Piece of Work

The puddle of gray goo made of Elvis's expelled nanobots swirled in a clockwise circle on the floor before Ace, Ivan, April, and Hank. Every few revolutions it undulated up towards Ace and then again to April. It seemed like the goo was reaching out for the two of them, the only humans in the room.

Ace knelt down next to the puddle of goo, and it stopped swirling around. He took a deep breath and held his hand out as if gingerly gauging the heat of a stove burner. The hairs on the back of his hand stood on the edge like a reaction to a strong static electrical charge.

Then the gray goo darted upward and penetrated Ace's palm.

It felt like shaking hands with a live wire. Every cell in Ace's body inflated with nervous, excited energy. He felt like he might explode with the fury of a thousand nuclear bombs at any moment.

Yet, as the jolt of adrenalized potential raged through his body, he felt serene and placid. The more neurotic and fidgety the energy felt, the calmer he got. The paradoxical nature of it was both unsettling and completely comforting at the same time.

On Tripulon, a planet Ivan affectionately referred to as "Hippie Central," Ace took a meditation class. The girl he dated at the time thought Ace was too high strung and need to "find his center." Through the four-day course, the instructor kept assuring Ace that if he just focused on his breath and let go of all thought, he would experience serenity and peace unlike any other. Ace was pretty sure he had maybe six seconds total of tranquility. He could never turn off the random thoughts racing through his head.

Now it was the exact opposite. Ace felt a calmness and peace of mind that he never knew was possible. Everything made sense to him now. Or it didn't make any sense at all. But it didn't matter that it didn't make sense.

"Umm. Ace?" Ivan asked. "You feel alright?"

"Ivan, buddy," Ace replied. "I feel great."

Ace stood and flexed the muscles in his chest and arms. He felt like he could easily rip a small tree in half. He felt invincible. Even the ever-present dull throb in his lower back that no amount of shiatsu could ever relieve was completely gone.

"Jesus, man," April said. "You look like you're ready to take on the world. I don't think I've ever seen a smile that big before."

Ace didn't realize he was smiling, but when she mentioned it, he felt the grin plastered across his face. He couldn't help it. He felt like he'd drunk a shot of pure black magic dynamite. He felt like he could do anything.

"Let me at this shiny jerkoff," Ace said.

The nanobots coursing through Ace's body did a great job repairing the years of abuse he had inflicted upon himself. The time they spent in his brain restoring burnt out neurons was incredible. He didn't realize how clouded and confused his mind was until they set up shop in his cerebral cortex and started dusting out the cobwebs. It was like the mental equivalent of hearing sound after pulling wads of cotton from his ears.

But it was short lived because the nanobots were programmed to move around a human body enhancing and repairing things on an as-needed basis.

Ivan remained locked out of a majority of *Betty*'s computer systems, and he couldn't land the ship. His only option was to gain the trust of *Betty*'s inventory system and convince it Ace was a crate of Bordarian cheese past due for delivery.

Before leaping out of *Betty*, Ace calculated the variables and concluded Ivan's supposition was sound.

Once Ace tasted open air some forty thousand feet above ground, the nanobots enhancing his intelligence flooded away from his logic centers and straight to his heart to prevent a cardiac arrest.

Ace screamed until the grappling beam grabbed him, an alarmingly long four seconds of freefall later.

When the initial danger passed, his newfound perception and reasoning abilities returned. He became acutely aware of everything around him. He knew his speed, the amount of wind resistance, and his core body temperature (which rapidly dropped due to the frigid air whooshing around him). He also had an innate knowledge that falling at thirty-two feet per second from an altitude of forty thousand feet would liquefy his body when it hit the ground. Actually, he didn't need thousands of advanced robots supercharging his brain to figure that one out. That was kind of a no-brainer.

The grappling beam bathed Ace in the familiar cotton candy scented blue energy field and immobilized him. His new nanobot-powered hyper-awareness allowed him to actually feel the beam wreaking havoc on his brain cells. It was a weird sensation. He'd killed plenty of brain cells over the years, through drink and other recreational substances. Not to mention the first ride he took on the grappling beam when *Betty* grabbed him and the others in the field behind Graceland. Yet now, he could actually feel the neurons degrade, their electrical capacity draining before shutting down for good.

Yet they didn't die. It was more like the neurons just passed out.

After mere microseconds, those same neurons sprang back into action after the nanobots repaired them and brought them back "online."

It was pretty cool but felt like an itchy nose that Ace couldn't scratch deep in the center of his skull.

Ace descended at about half the speed of freefall and had to trust the grappling beam would stay active until he was safe on the ground. It was designed to protect anything within it from shearing forces or strong impacts. Ace hoped that Ivan messing around with its controls didn't remove those life-saving features.

Then the sense of dread and fear melted away. A flood of warmth snuggled him like the softest, most comfortable blanket in the world. Or a hug from a buxom brunette while lying in a pool of delicious, delicious cold and frothy beer. The calm came from the nanobots releasing dopamine into his system, just as they had when they first interfaced with his body.

He felt calm and confident again, ready to take on the world.

It was almost night, and the last rays of daylight were still peaking up from the horizon. Ace scanned the ground as it rushed up to meet his feet. He was still a few seconds away from touching down, and with his improved eyesight, he could see the whole town. Little shotgun shacks separated by dusty fields and roads. A few churches. A small downtown area winding down for the evening. People on their way home for supper.

It was a nice moment until laser fire started erupting all around him. Lucky for him the grappling beam reflected the first burst of lasers flying at him.

Then Ace hit the ground and the grappling beam immediately dissipated, leaving him exposed and vulnerable. It was like having all his clothes stripped off, and a bucket of blood dumped on his head in a swarm of hungry sharks. Right as panic was about to strangle him a bolt of adrenaline shot through his body and time seemed to slow down.

A shower of laser fire flew at him, but instead of a series of flashes too fast for the eye to see he could pick out each individual bolt. His souped-up brain perceived them as ultra-luminescent red glowing sausages shot out of an automatic pitching machine and he could easily follow them all.

He leaped backward almost the instant his feet hit the ground, then sprinted over to a nearby tree for cover. Bark and leaves exploded in fiery bursts as the Shiny Man tracked him to his hiding spot and kept on firing.

"You should have left well enough alone, Tucker!" the Shiny Man shouted between blasts. "By coming here, you have opened yourself up to annihilation. You are no longer special, Mr. Tucker. Your status as a Time Abrasion will be moot after I erase Elvis Presley from this timeline by killing his pregnant mother!"

Something about the way the Shiny Man said "mother" got under Ace's skin.

Maybe it was the fact he never knew his own mother. Somehow the pain of that absence added to it all, like the threat against Elvis's mother was a threat against all mothers on the planet.

Ace's planet.

His sense of abandonment overshadowed everything in his life. But now with the future of humanity hanging in the balance, he felt different.

The short time he spent in Memphis had changed him. Inter-acting with other humans had enriched him in ways he couldn't explain. It was nothing like the shallow one-way relationships he formed with the humans in Ivan's media archive. Real Earth people were so much more imperfect and messy and amazing.

As Ace hunkered behind the tree while an alien maniac tried to kill him, a spiritual sensation bloomed within him. He relished the feeling of Earth's cool atmosphere filling his lungs. He delighted in the comforting stability of her native gravity anchoring him to the ground. He finally felt like he belonged somewhere. Like his life finally had purpose and meaning.

And here was this shiny dickhead threatening to fuck it all up.

"Not on my watch," Ace said.

Ace extrapolated the Shiny Man's position based on the orig-ination of the shots pelting the tree. The nanobots had set up shop in his cerebellum again and supercharged his cognition.

Ace pulled out Ray-Ray and started blasting. He popped off twenty direct hits to the Shiny Man's chest. The grouping was pretty great. Under normal circumstances, Ace was a pretty good shot. Now, with the benefits of Elvis's nanobots, his vision and aim were exceptional.

The Shiny Man yelped as the blasts smacked him dead in his center of mass.

Then the Shiny Man started laughing.

Ace looked down at Ray-Ray in his hand and started swearing.

The power dial on the side of the gun read "1." Ray-Ray's lowest power setting. He must have flicked the dial when he whipped the gun out from his waistband. At this power level, it was nothing more than a gun-shaped presentation laser pointer. Not even enough power to cook a wet noodle. He could maybe entertain some cats or make a room full of people go to sleep as he pointed at sales charts on a screen, but that was about it.

"You really are a piece of work, aren't you, Mr. Tucker?" the Shiny Man said.

A flash of supercharged light exploded in Ace's hand sending Ray-Ray and Ace's fingers flying through space. The energy around the bits of flesh continued to pulse and crackle as they vaporized into nothingness.

Ace dropped to the ground, clutching what used to be his hand. Pain like he'd never experienced shot up from the mangled stump and radiated throughout his body. His non-hand was pure fire. A series of venomous explosions tore through him like his whole arm lived in a meat grinder with a trillion tons of dynamite for teeth.

He could feel the nanobots trying to head off the pain by activating his pituitary gland and flooding his system with endorphins. It wasn't nearly enough.

The serene feeling of being able to take on the world was gone. In its place was the sheer terror of knowing he was about to die. The only good thing he barely had enough brain power to notice was the laser blast seemed to have cauterized his hand-stump. At least he wasn't going to bleed to death. Not yet, anyway.

"Now, if you'll excuse me I have a date with destiny," the Shiny Man said.

The Shiny Man put a hand into his pocket and pulled out his version of a dazzler and tapped it a few times.

A bright light erupted all around the Shiny Man, and Ace had to squint to keep from being blinded. When the light subsided, Agent Calhoun stood before Ace, smirking.

"Don't want the natives to get all in a tizzy," Calhoun said.

Calhoun walked away toward a little white house, leaving Ace writhing in agony on the ground like a wounded animal shot and left for dead by a sadistic hunter.

Ace had heard stories of wounded warriors calling for their mothers or watching their entire lives replay before their eyes. With the unbelievable pain wracking his body and clouding his mind, those seemed like suitable options.

Yet, all Ace could think about was fried chicken.

The heavenly scent wafted around Ace as he struggled to stand. The pain was agonizing but subsiding as the nanobots worked to dull the nerves in his arm. Ace tried not to think of the pain. Instead, he breathed in the fried chicken scented air and thought about the pure joy of eating delicious, delectable, crispy fried chicken.

At first, he thought he was hallucinating. He guessed the 'bots were flooding his brain and activating happy memories to take his mind off the excruciation of losing his hand.

But then he saw it. Gentle wisps of smoke rising out of the chimney on top of the little white house.

*Someone is frying chicken in there!* Ace thought. *Based on the position of the chimney, the kitchen is probably in the back. If I can just get around back, maybe there's a door. I can sneak in and —*

Ace stopped mid-thought and used all his concentration to try and force the nanobots to stop pumping him full of pain-deadening oxytocin. He needed them to beef up his legs and give him some of that super speed he saw Elvis use in the ill-fated fight with the Shiny Man.

When he sprang into action and started running, the nanobots responded, and Ace accelerated. He was already faster than the average human due to his muscles' acclimation to much higher gravity. But now, with the added boost from the nanobots, he was cheetah fast.

The trade-off was less help with the pain. He ignored the

intense throbbing in his arm and tried his best to not pass out as he made a wide arc away from the direction of the Shiny Man and towards a large brown house further up the street.

Once on the back side of the larger house, Ace made his way through the backyards of two neighboring houses. A moment later he reached the back of the little white house. Elvis's mother's house. There he found a small white picket fence and a single door.

*Bingo!* Ace thought.

The little white house was so small he could hear the Shiny Man walking up the steps in the front. Ace had to act fast. A curtain covered a tiny window on the door, and he thought he saw the silhouette of a person moving towards the front of the house. Ace hopped over the fence and put his ear up against the door. He heard the telltale footsteps receding from within and tried the handle on the door. It was unlocked.

There was a knock at the front door on the other side of the house.

A woman's voice responded, "Just a minute! I move slow in my condition!"

Ace pushed the door open and stayed low as he crept into what appeared to be a tiny kitchen. A small table covered with a green tablecloth sat in the center of the room. A small wood burning stove stood against a brick wall that separated the kitchen from the only other room in the front of the tiny house.

And there, on top of the wood-burning stove, was a large cast iron skillet filled with frying chicken bathed in rolling, crackling cooking oil.

*This must be the old fashioned method April talked about.* Ace thought. *Before they had pressure fryers.*

The scent was so powerful Ace began to salivate. He took one

3425

long breath, filling his lungs almost to bursting. Then he exhaled slowly and tried to focus on the task at hand. There'd be time for fried chicken later. He hoped.

There had to be at least a full chicken in that skillet. All trimmed and cut and caked with what looked like delectable seasoned flour. The chicken was just beginning to brown. Based on what April had taught him, the oil would be between three hundred twenty-five to three hundred seventy-five degrees Fahrenheit. Hot enough to get the job done.

More knocking at the front door. This time harder. Louder. More demanding.

"Well, land sakes! I'm coming!" the woman yelled.

From the front of the house, a light *twing* rang out like the woman had dropped something metal.

"Oh. Sugar!" the woman said followed by a groan like she was having trouble bending down to pick the item up.

Ace stayed low and peaked around the corner. The walls of the only other room in the house were covered in floral wallpaper. A small bed rested in one corner, and a small chest of drawers was up against the wall that separated the main room from the kitchen. A very pregnant woman in a flower-covered housedress strained to bend over and pick up a pair of kitchen tongs. One hand was planted on the small of her back as she did her best to balance and prevent herself from tumbling over face-first. It seemed difficult with the large baby bump.

The woman was Elvis's mother, Gladys Presley.

Ace surprised himself that he knew that bit of trivia. Elvis's mother's name. He was also surprised at the sudden innate protection instinct he had. He felt a sudden need to rush out and help her pick up the tongs. He was just about to do it when the front door swung open.

Gladys darted upright and let out a surprised cry, "Oh!"

The Shiny Man, still disguised as Agent Calhoun, stood in the open doorway with a sickening smile on his face.

"Good evening, Gladys," the Shiny Man said.

"Who? Who are you?" Gladys backed away from the door and stumbled, falling back into a sitting position on the bed. "What - what do you want?"

"Don't worry. This will be over very shortly. Try to relax."

The Shiny Man reached into his pants pocket and pulled out a small device that looked like an impossibly shiny small hand mirror. The device flashed once, and Gladys gasped then fell back onto the bed unconscious.

Ace knew he had mere nanoseconds to act. He spun around and grabbed the iron skillet off the stovetop with his one remaining hand. The handle was as hot as boiling lava, but Ace gritted his teeth and held it tight as he ran into the front room, screaming.

The Shiny Man stood slack-jawed and off guard as Ace charged into the room wielding the scolding skillet of fried chicken and oil.

Ace launched the contents of the skillet straight at the Shiny Man before he had a chance to raise his hands in defense. The pieces of frying meat pelted him with satisfying *thunks*, and the boiling oil covered his face, neck, and torso.

The Shiny Man dropped the device and erupted in screams of pain and surprise. He clawed at his face and clothes, trying to get the scalding oil off but it was no use. The scorching grease was too viscous and stuck to him with authority.

The Shiny Man wiped his face and then slapped his hands on the legs of his pants in an attempt to mitigate the damage, but he just spread it around. One slap also seemed to have hit the dazzler-like device in his pocket because the Agent Calhoun disguise flickered and disappeared.

With the disguise gone, Ace could see the real damage done by the coat of hot oil. The Shiny Man's face was a mess of metallic goo. It looked like someone had taken a blowtorch to a spool of solder. Each time he swatted at his face and neck, it only made it worse as more shiny flesh sloughed off onto his hands.

The screaming was the most horrific thing Ace had ever heard. Like an animal being slaughtered by a swarm of angry beavers with blender claws for teeth. The sound had a synthetic quality to it, like poorly rendered audio pumped through a meaty membrane for a speaker.

Ace threw the scolding hot skillet at the Shiny Man as hard as he could. The nanobots pumped up the strength in his good arm so that when Ace let go of the skillet, it was like a shotgun explosion.

The skillet screamed across the room at almost the speed of sound, catching the Shiny Man in the center of his chest and launching him back out the open front door.

Ace lost sight of the Shiny Man as he continued to sail backward from the force of the blow.

Seconds later, Ace heard a crash like a sack of meat dropped from the second story of a building across the street.

Ace looked down at his hand and saw the telltale signs of a third-degree burn. He shrugged it off as he could already feel the nanobots working to heal it. That level of injury they could deal with. Regrowing his missing hand they could not. That would have to come later when he was safe aboard *Betty* and plugged into her advanced medical system.

Ace went to check on Gladys. She appeared to be sleeping, and he checked her pulse. There was a strong heartbeat. A sense of lightness, almost giddiness, filled Ace.

Satisfied Gladys would be OK, Ace walked out the front door and across a little porch with a swing seat suspended from the ceiling. He bounded down a few stairs and straight away from the house to find where the Shiny Man had landed.

*If that shiny bastard is still drawing breath*, Ace thought. *It'll be his last.*

Ace crossed the little dirt road running in front of the house and into the field where he descended before the gunfight. A fresh rift tore up the dusty field where the Shiny Man had hit and kept going, like a man-sized plow, carving up the ground. Ace followed the gash until it ended. The Shiny Man lay on his back in a lifeless heap.

Ace stood over the Shiny Man and was just about to check for a pulse when a bright shaft of light encircled the two of them from above. An effusion of wind blasted down. Dirt and grime flew everywhere causing Ace to shield his eyes with his one good hand while doing his best to protect his stump from the flying debris.

A roar exploded from above like a thousand heavy metal drummers stomping blast beats on double bass drums. He felt the reverberation in his chest, and his eyes rattled from the percussive onslaught.

Through his squinting eyes and flying crud Ace saw *Betty* coming in for a landing. Her retrorockets were firing, and she was about to make a touchdown.

*Ivan must've gotten control of her!* Ace thought as an unexpected release of tension unraveled throughout his body. Tears began to well up in his eyes. From the flying dirt, he told himself.

*Betty* touched down with a giant release of steam, and the driver's side door swung open. Ace rubbed his eyes to get the dirt out and blinked a few times. The cockpit was empty.

*That's weird,* Ace thought.

Without warning, the Shiny Man punched Ace in the nuts so hard that it lifted him two feet off the ground.

An explosion of pain erupted through Ace's body, and a bright light flashed before his eyes. He landed on his back writhing in agony trying not to throw up, but he could tell it was coming any second. He took huge gulps of air trying to blow off the pain, but between the nutshot and crashing to the ground with a mutilated hand he was blacking out.

Ace rolled on his side fighting to stay conscious, but his vision dimmed around the edges. He tasted copper in his mouth and spat blood on the ground. He had bitten his tongue on impact, and it felt like it got sliced by a rusty hacksaw.

Ace used all his strength, lurched up, and broke into an off-balance run straight for *Betty*. He fought to keep upright, but it felt like a ton of steel ball bearings rattled in his skull. He tripped and stumbled then caught himself with his good hand. The impact sent shockwaves of pain through Ace's body. He ignored the agony, heaving himself back upright and into a flat-out sprint.

The Shiny Man was well ahead of him but wasn't moving all that fast. There was a chance Ace could catch him before the shiny bastard got in *Betty*'s cockpit.

Ace could feel the nanobots trying to increase his speed, but they seemed distracted trying to mitigate the pain and damage throughout his body. There wasn't time to try and convince them otherwise, so he just kept running.

*Betty*'s driver side door was wide open. The Shiny Man pulled himself up into the seat behind the steering wheel. He turned and looked at Ace, still dozens of feet from the ship. The Shiny Man's face was a twisted mess of melted goo, but Ace could make out the shape of the Shiny Man's eyes burning with hatred.

The Shiny Man tapped a few commands on the dashboard computer screen and then reached for the door to close it. When it swung shut, he rolled down the window to gloat.

"You lose, Mr. Tucker!" the Shiny Man boasted. "I have the time machine! I can return to this point in history time and time again. I *will* kill unborn Presley. There's no way to stop it!"

*Betty*'s main engines sprang to life as she cycled through the pre-launch systems check. Ace had mere seconds before she would blast off into the night sky. It was now or never.

Ace dug deep within himself and focused his mind on a singular task: leaping as hard as he could straight for the door.

Time slowed down for Ace as he rocketed into the air. He had no idea how fast he propelled himself but based on the shocked expression on the Shiny Man's trainwreck of a face, it was damn fast.

He hit the door with enough force to knock the Shiny Man out of the driver's seat. Ace swung his good arm up and over the open window, reaching for the handle.

A sudden burst of light erupted under *Betty,* blinding Ace as he groped. Ace scrambled to find the handle both for something to hold onto and to get the door open.

He squeezed his eyes shut and gripped the armrest on the inside of the door. He felt the weight of four Gs press down on him as the engines ignited and *Betty* rocketed skyward.

A thunderous *whoosh* of air blasted down all around him, and it took a herculean effort to breathe. Adding to the discomfort was the weight pushing down on his elbow as it sat hinged over the open door window. He could feel the ligaments in his arms stretching and his grip slipping. Blackness crept around the periphery of his vision.

The Shiny Man crawled back up into the driver's seat. One of his shiny hands rested on the steering wheel and the other tapped out commands on the dash.

Ace tried to pull himself upward, but there was no way. Even with the aid of Elvis's nanobots he couldn't get enough leverage or apply enough strength to overcome the weight of four Earths pushing down on him at close to ten miles per second.

When the Shiny Man finished typing in his commands, he hit a button to roll up the driver's side window.

Ace's cries were silent as they had already accelerated past the speed of sound. The window pane rose upward, pushing up on Ace's arm meat with authority. His hand slid off the handle, and he dropped back about a foot before slapping his hand on the inside of the rising window. Had it been a normal glass window his body weight would have broken it in half or pulled it out of its track. Lucky for him the window was a transparent version of the same ultra-titanium that made up *Betty*'s hull. One of the strongest materials in the galaxy. It also meant that it would have no trouble slicing through his wrist when it reached the top.

Ace tried to kick his legs up to land them on the running board, but the weight of acceleration was too much. He was pinned.

The Shiny Man had a grotesque smile on his nauseatingly melted face before it suddenly smashed against the window.

The impact of the Shiny Man's face against the window reverberated down Ace's slipping hand and through the rest of his body. Ace almost lost his grip but somehow held on.

The Shiny Man flew back out of Ace's view, leaving a disgusting splatter of shiny meat and blood behind.

The window began to roll back down. Ace gripped it as hard as his awkward position would allow. A new problem arose: when the window receded into the door there'd be nothing to grip, and he would fall. His fingers struggled to hold, and he scanned the door for something else to grab onto when the time came.

A moment before the window disappeared into the door a pair of hands grabbed Ace below the wrist and pulled him upward. His mind boggled on how this was even possible with the force of thrust pushing down on them. Then he realized *Betty* had stopped accelerating and rested in a gentle hover several thousand feet above the ground. Frigid air bit at him as he fought to climb up into the window.

When he finally got his feet on the running board, he realized it was April pulling him in. She wedged herself on the other side of the driver's seat and strained to get him inside.

Ace pressed up with his legs. He floundered over the window landing half on top of the driver's seat and half on top of April. It might've been a nice moment except April was caught in between the two seats with her knees up against her chest. Her knees drove hard into Ace's ribcage. She must've sensed Ace having trouble getting upright because she pushed him back onto the seat with both her hands on his shoulders.

Ace sat still for a moment and caught his breath. Everything hurt, but he was alive and breathing.

April climbed up in the co-pilot seat and said, "Jesus! Are you OK?"

Ace didn't answer the question. Instead, he panted, "Shiny Man?"

"Ivan and Hank jumped him," April said. "They're dragging him to an airlock. I think that's what Ivan said. I don't know. He just told me to haul you in. It all happened so fast. Holy shit! What happened to your hand?"

"Asshole shot it off," Ace replied in a matter-of-fact tone. "It hurts like hell, but Betty's med system will be able to grow me a new one."

"Whoa! No shit?" April said. "Cool!"

Ace looked over the control readouts on the dashboard computer screens.

"Man!" Ace said. "What the hell did he do to the control systems? There's some new software running, probably what that shiny prick uploaded when he compromised *Betty*. Ok. That looks like altitude. We're at a stable hover at thirty-two thousand feet. And it looks like I have internal communication. Yup the intercom looks good. Ok, April. Sit here and keep an eye on THIS readout. If it turns red, call me."

"Call you?" April said. "With what? My cell phone?"

Ace handed her the push-to-talk CB handset from the ceiling. "You know how to use one of these?"

"Yeah. I've seen enough trucker movies to know you push the little button on the side and talk into the microphone. I'm not an idiot," April said with a smile.

"Cool," Ace said. "Let me know if anything changes on the read out."

"Aye aye, captain!" April said and plopped down in the driver's seat.

"And," Ace said pausing at the door to exit the cockpit. "Try not to touch anything. I don't know what he did to Betty here, but we'll figure it out."

"Yeah, man. I'm not going to touch shit," April said with sincerity. "This is way more complicated than my Buick."

"OK," Ace said with a nod. "Just watch that screen and call me if it turns red."

Ace exited the cockpit and entered the hallway. A trail of shiny blood and goo led away in a pattern that looked like Ivan had dragged the struggling Shiny Man.

Ace followed the blood trail for a minute, expecting it to take a right turn at the first junction towards the airlock on the starboard side of the ship. Instead, there was a giant blotch of shiny blood intermixed with red mammal blood.

A chill ran down Ace's spine as he imagined Ivan getting pummeled by the Shiny Man. It could've been Hank's blood. That thought made Ace feel a little better. Then immediately bad for feeling better Hank had taken a beating. Either way, his friends were in trouble.

The trail of red blood led straight ahead down the corridor. A low moaning was audible over the telltale hum of *Betty's* engines.

Ace followed the moans until he found Ivan sitting with his back against the wall covered in his own blood

"Ivan!" Ace knelt in front of his friend. Ivan's face was a bloody swollen mess.

"Jeez, man! You look like I feel!" Ivan said spitting out a little blood with each word. "He...he cold-cocked me, man. He's so fast."

"Just try to stay still," Ace said.

"You—you gotta get him, Ace. He's going after the time machine...gonna...disconnect. Betty. Escape."

It made sense. The Shiny Man was trying to cut his losses and run.

"Just stay here and rest," Ace said. "I'll stop him."

"How you gonna...with only...one...hand?" Ivan labored to speak. He started to wipe the blood from his lips with the sleeve of his jacket then stopped, disgusted with himself. He dropped his long arm down on the floor with an exacerbated sigh.

"Just stay here. I'll think of something." Ace patted Ivan on the shoulder. He had no idea how, but he was going to make the Shiny Man pay for what he did to Ivan.

"Uhh. Ace?" April's voice boomed over the intercom system.

"I think we have a problem."

Ace leaned over Ivan and tapped on a computer panel on the wall. He keyed up the intercom system and replied, "April. I'm here. What's up?"

"That screen you had me watch?" April said. "Well, it changed."

"Holy shit! Did it turn red?" Ace shouted.

"Not exactly," April replied.

A wave of relief washed over Ace. "Well, if it's not red, then it can't be all that bad."

April paused then said, "Are the words *self-destruct* and a countdown clock bad?"

# 13

## The Double Dazzler Deception

"What do you mean self-destruct?" Ace yelled into the intercom panel.

April replied back with urgency, "Just what I said! The screen has big flashing letters spelling out 'self-destruct' and a clock counting down! Now four minutes, ten seconds!"

"That shiny sonuva—!" Ivan said. "Help me up, and I'll see if I can disable it."

Ace helped Ivan onto his feet, careful to not aggravate Ivan's wounds. Ivan wobbled and used the wall as support as he waddled over to the computer access panel. He grunted and extended his cyber implant spike from his wrist and jammed it in the data port.

"Whoa," Ace said. "You've got shiny blood on you!"

"Yeah," Ivan said. "I got that shiny jerk in the shoulder with my spike. Took a chunk out of him before he royally kicked my butt."

Ivan's eyes fluttered, and he grimaced. "OK. I see what he did here. Man. He really messed Betty's computers all up. This is gonna take a minute, but I think I can disable the self-destruct."

"You sure? Because we only have, like, four minutes," Ace said.

"Yeah. I got this. Go kick that guy's butt."

197

Ace didn't need any more of a shove. He took off running for the cargo bay, hoping that he got there before the Shiny Man could do *whatever* with the time machine. He had to trust that Ivan would be able to disable the self-destruct. With *Betty* compromised, there was no way he could do it alone. It would have to fall on Ivan to do the nerd stuff and Ace to do the ass-kicking. Just the way he liked it.

He realized the pain from his missing hand had dwindled. It was more of a dull ache now. He guessed the nanobots were back to mitigating the torment because they sure weren't helping him run any faster. It took what seemed like forever to reach the cargo bay.

The Shiny Man was in the process of unplugging the cables running into the Cadillac's engine. Only two cables remained, and the Shiny Man's back was to Ace.

*It's now or never*, Ace thought.

Ace let out a battle cry and tackled the Shiny Man. The two hit the floor with a giant *thud* and rolled over each other a few times. Pain exploded throughout Ace's body as he fought to get control of the Shiny Man and pin him to the ground. It proved harder than Ace wagered with only one hand.

The Shiny Man kicked Ace in the stomach. The blow launched him into the air and into a wall. Firecrackers exploded behind Ace's eyes, and everything went black for a second.

*Well, there's another concussion*, Ace thought when the cobwebs cleared.

"Fool!" The Shiny Man said. "You just can't leave well enough alone, can you?"

The Shiny Man stalked up to Ace, his mangled face twisted with rage. Or maybe it was the damage from the cooking oil that made his face look so haggard. Ace couldn't tell. It was hard to concentrate with the giant laser revolver leveled at Ace's head.

Ace knew he should be afraid but he wasn't. He'd come too far to be afraid of death. Now, looking down the barrel of an impossibly shiny gun, the only emotion Ace had was sadness. Maybe a little disappointment.

There was still so much he wanted to do with his life. So much of the galaxy he wanted to see. He desperately wanted to spend some more time on Earth, the one place he swore he would never set foot upon.

A new feeling swept over Ace. He'd never felt it before but he somehow immediately recognized it as gratitude. He was actually grateful for the crazy set of circumstances that brought him to Earth. Grateful for his time in Memphis and especially for being introduced to the delights of fried chicken. Grateful for getting to know April a little, though he wished he had more time to get to know her better. Grateful for seeing Graceland. Hell, he was even grateful for Hank. If this was it, he was at peace with it.

Ace closed his eyes and drew in a deep breath, waiting for the laser blast to reduce his head to a cloud of vaporized molecules.

It never came. Instead, a new voice snapped Ace out of his meditation on death.

"Hey! Shiny Man!" Elvis said. "Why don't you pick on someone your own size!"

Ace opened his eyes. Elvis stood at the entrance of the cargo bay wearing a white jumpsuit and cape emblazoned with what looked like every rhinestone in the universe. The jumpsuit was zipped open to Elvis's belly button revealing a matte of shiny black chest hair and a large golden medallion shaped like an angry bird. An eagle? No, a phoenix! Ace had seen a show about the mythical bird once. A bird that is reborn from the flaming ashes of its former self. A similar golden phoenix rising out of ruby flames lived on Elvis's belt buckle.

Hank stood, panting and slobbering, next to Elvis.

"Please, boss. Let me bite his shiny nuts off!" Hank said with a growl.

Elvis coughed and stammered for a second. His voice sounded like he had breathed in helium.

"How?" the Shiny Man turned to face Elvis, dropping his gun to his side in what must have been disbelief. "I killed you! Threw you in the recycler!"

Ace seized the opportunity to strike, jerking himself up and lunging for the Shiny Man's back. He slammed into the Shiny Man and wrapped his handless arm around the shiny bastard's neck. Ace used his working hand to keep the gun pinned to the Shiny Man's side.

Ace wrenched back on the Shiny Man's neck as hard as he could. He could feel the nanobots pumping up his strength to the point where he exerted enough force to crush a steel ball bearing. The Shiny Man gurgled and thrashed, clawing at Ace's arm.

The Shiny Man threw his elbow back and into Ace's gut. It hurt like hell, and Ace relaxed his grip uncontrollably. The Shiny Man took the oppurtunity to get his laser revolver up, and he started firing blindly in the direction of Elvis and Hank.

Elvis let out an undignified cry and dove for cover behind a stack of P.A. speakers. Hank followed yipping and dodging laser blasts with his tail between his legs.

Another elbow slammed into Ace's gut, catching him in the ribs this time. He heard a loud crack and tasted copper in his mouth. Even with the aid of the nanobots, he wouldn't be able to keep up the fight much longer. He had to change tactics and quick.

"Do something!" the voice came from behind the P.A. speakers.

The voice was definitely female and definitely not Elvis Presley.

"April?" Ace relaxed his grip on the Shiny Man who repaid the favor with another elbow in the gut. Ace started falling backward but was able to hold onto the Shiny Man's shoulder. The two stumbled across the cargo bay before coming to rest against the driver's side door of the Cadillac. The force of the impact caused the Shiny Man to lose grip on his laser revolver. It fell to the ground with a loud crash.

Ace couldn't see anything with the Shiny Man leaning back against him and the car. But he heard Hank barking and the *clickity clack* of his long toenails against the floor. The thrashing of the Shiny Man stopped suddenly when a heavy weight plowed into his crotch. The Shiny Man pushed back with so much force it knocked the wind out of Ace.

A loud crunching sound rang out over the Shiny Man's screams and the growling of an angry dog.

Hank was finally trying to bite the Shiny Man's nuts off.

The Shiny Man leaned back hard in an attempt to get away from the dog attached to his crotch. Ace felt his balance slipping. He had no choice but to tumble backward, over the driver's side door. All three of them landed on the car seat in a giant squirming mess.

The weight of the Shiny Man was torture on Ace's battered body. Ace reached out for something to grab onto. His hand hit the dashboard, and a loud beeping sound rang out over the growling, screaming, and nut crunching.

"Time circuits activated," a pleasant computerized voice said.

The Shiny Man cursed then wrenched Hank off his crotch. The change in body position gave Ace enough room to wiggle out from underneath the shiny bastard on top of him.

The Shiny Man threw Hank across the room.

Hank crashed into a stack of P.A. speakers sending dog slobber and stage gear everywhere.

The Shiny Man tapped on some controls, and the pleasant voice replied, "Time circuits deactivated."

Ace threw open the passenger side door and rolled out of the Cadillac landing hard on his knees. Pain erupted from the impact, and Ace doubled over to catch his breath. His head rested on the floor as he drew in deep breaths and fought off a wave of pain-induced nausea.

That's when he saw the laser revolver resting just outside of his reach underneath the Cadillac.

Ace dropped to his belly and reached out for the pistol with his good hand. The pistol grip was so big his fingers could barely wrap around it. He got a tentative hold on it and scooted it back from under the car ready to blast the Shiny Man to Kingdom Come.

Instead, he saw the Shiny Man holding April like a human shield with one of his shiny hands wrapped around her neck.

A single tear rolled down April's cheek. It dropped from her chin, rolled down the Shiny Man's arm, and splattered on a dazzler attached to April's waistband.

*She was using the dazzler to look like Elvis!* Ace thought.

Hank lay unconscious and snoring in front of a toppled stack of P.A. speakers.

"Drop the gun, Tucker," the Shiny Man said. "Or I swear I will snap this female's neck."

The way the Shiny Man stood, with April in front of him, there was no way Ace could get a shot off without hitting her as well. Ace bent over and put the laser revolver on the ground then stood up showing the palm of his good hand.

"See?" the Shiny Man said. "You're not a dumb as you look.

Now kick the gun over to me."

Ace complied, shoving the laser revolver towards the Shiny Man. It came to rest close to April's feet. The Shiny Man didn't pick it up. Instead, he walked April to the front of the Cadillac where the two remaining cables ran from under the hood into the wall of the cargo bay.

"Reach in and detach those cables. Do it now," the Shiny Man said, leaning April over the car by the back of her neck.

April's hands shook, and she grunted with effort as she worked. The cables came free, slinking back into the wall.

"Good," The Shiny Man said. "Now, we're going to be leaving. I'm taking the female with me as an insurance policy. And. I might get hungry during my trip."

The Shiny Man spun April around, so she had to face him. Then he pushed his mangled face up against April's hair and inhaled like a fat man lusting after a freshly baked pie.

April put her hands on the Shiny Man's chest to try to push him away, but he held her fast against him in a terrible embrace. She squirmed a little, turning so her back was to Ace. The Shiny Man hugged her and rested his twisted mess of a smiling face on her shoulder.

Then the Shiny Man's smile broke. His eyes and mouth went wide, and his head jerked back with a gasp.

April took a step back, dropping her right hand to her side. A long metallic spike covered in dripping shiny blood jutted out from the top of her wrist.

The Shiny Man's nostrils flared, and he let out a guttural roar. Then he backhanded April, sending her flying across the room and into a wall. She hit hard, and multicolored light burst all around her.

When the spots cleared from Ace's eyes, he saw Ivan lying

unconscious where April had been moments ago. Attached to Ivan's jacket was a broken dazzler, crackling with sparks and wisps of colored light. On Ivan's feet was a pair of stilts, now bent and broken from the impact.

*That wasn't April pretending to be Elvis,* Ace thought. *That was Ivan pretending to be April, pretending to be Elvis! The ole double dazzler deception!*

Ace didn't have time to admire Ivan's cleverness. He sprinted towards the laser revolver on the ground, getting to it as the Shiny Man bent down to pick it up.

Ace crashed into the Shiny Man, grabbing the shiny hand holding the laser revolver and pushed it away from them as they struggled.

The Shiny Man got two shots off. Both missed Ace by a wide margin. Sparks rained down from the ceiling in a spectacular shower.

Even with the burned up face and multiple stab wounds, the Shiny Man was strong as hell. Ace felt the nanobots pumping up his arm muscles, but it didn't prevent the Shiny Man from wrenching the gun down and sandwiching it between their chests.

Ace could feel the barrel pushing into his breastbone. He clawed at the Shiny Man's fingers, prying them from the trigger.

The world exploded in a crackling burst as a laser bolt erupted between them sending Ace flying backward.

Everything went black.

\* \* \*

"Ace...come on, man! We gotta go!" The voice came from far away and sounded like it was underwater.

The darkness surrounding Ace began to clear, and the image

of a chimpanzee with a bloody nose came into focus.

It was confusing at first.

*Is that chimpanzee talking to me?* Ace thought. *That's really weird.*

"Ace! Snap out of it! We gotta go!" the chimpanzee shouted again this time shaking Ace by the shoulders.

Ace sat up and felt like a dump truck full of quantum cinder blocks rattling in his head. He shook his head like a dog shaking off a bath and tried to make sense of it all.

P.A. speakers were lying everywhere. A purple Cadillac with its top down sat idling a few feet from him. A Basset hound, a girl, and a chimpanzee were all shouting at him. And on the other side of the room, an impossibly shiny man lay in a pool of impossibly shiny blood with a gaping hole in his chest.

Seeing the Shiny Man dead finally snapped Ace back to his senses. He grabbed at his own chest, checking for injury and found a scorched hole in the center of his shirt.

He dug into the hole and felt his bare skin below. Something was different. It was like a super dense plastic plate had been grafted to his chest. It was smooth, hard, and cold. He tilted his chin down to get a look at it but was only able to make out the top of the plate. It was black, and when he thumped on it with his fingers, it sounded thick.

"You'll have time to play with yourself later, *Mace*! We gotta fucking go!" Hank got up in Ace's face. Hank's breath affronted Ace's nostrils with the scent of hot garbage.

"Whoa!" Ace said backing off and pushing Hank away from him.

"Don't whoa me!" Hank snarled. "Get up and get in the fucking car, asshole. We only have seconds left."

"What are you talking about?" Ace asked as he stood and

brushed his hands against his pants.

"The self-destruct, Ace," Ivan said. "Somehow the Shiny Man turned it back on after I disabled it. And this time I'm completely locked out. We have ninety seconds left. We gotta abandon ship. Now!"

Ace's head was still filled with cobwebs, but the look on Ivan's face compelled him to follow the chimp's lead.

"What do we do?" Ace asked.

*Betty* had one escape pod at the front of the ship behind the main cockpit. There was no way they'd make it there in under ninety seconds.

Hank jumped into the driver's seat of the Cadillac barking, "There's a panic switch under the steering wheel. It's got a hard-coded preset location in space and time for emergencies. Everyone get in the Caddy!"

April leaped over the back of the car and landed hard in the back seat. Ivan followed and Ace slide into the driver's seat, feeling around for the switch and ignoring the excruciating pain that seemed to radiate from every inch of his body.

"What's this switch gonna do?" Ace asked. "Won't it just take Betty with us?"

"Don't be an idiot, *Trace*! Ivan disconnected Betty from the Caddy. You hit that switch, and we'll leave Betty behind!"

Ace's fingers brushed over a smooth button that was at least ten degrees cooler than the rest of the steering wheel column.

"Oh. Is this it?" Ace asked. "This little switch here?"

He pushed the button.

"Time circuits activated," a pleasant computerized voice said. "Hold on to your nuts."

The world around Ace erupted in a swirling mess of color and sound.

# 14

## The Galactic Galleria

Time travel in a Cadillac convertible with the top down is a dumb idea. Ivan Chimpanov confirmed this.

"We shoulda put the top up first!" Ivan gritted his teeth as he white-knuckled the edge of the backseat. His voice was barely audible over the noise.

"I know!" Ace shouted. "Jeez, look at this stuff flying around us! It's all a swirly mass of color and insane darkness. It's like the stuff contained in the timedrive we have in the trunk of the Cadillac!"

A hard wind blew at them from all directions like they were under a thousand giant hair dryers. Hank added to the din by letting out a series of long howls.

The wind's temperature oscillated between sweltering to frigid, and the scent of baking cookies permeated the air. Ace's stomach grumbled. He couldn't remember the last time he ate.

All around them swirling masses of colorful light and insanely dark anti-light exploded in a mindnumbing display of havoc.

"Yeah!" Ivan said. "I think we're seeing the fabric of space-time itself!"

Ace tried his best to keep his eyes focused on the inside of the Caddy. The readouts on the dash displays were complete gibberish, but based on the icons he saw, a little purple dot moving closer to a large green dot, Ace guessed they were making good time and would be arriving at their destination in a matter of minutes.

In the back seat, April looked around like a kid in a candy store with a huge smile plastered on her face.

"Well, I think it looks cool as shit!" April said.

"Say what you want, girlie!" Hank howled. "It's freaking me the fuck out!"

A few minutes later the Cadillac came to rest, and the real world began to materialize, like a dense fog suddenly melting away.

"You have arrived at your destination," the pleasant computerized voice said.

The Cadillac turned itself off. All the instruments and readouts on the dashboard went dark. It was eerily quiet, with only the wind and Hank's incessant panting audible.

"Looks like we're in the middle of a forest or something. Where are we?" Ace asked Hank.

"I dunno," Hank replied. "I just knew there was a panic switch under the dash. I don't know where it takes you."

A chime sounded out from the dashboard, and the computer panels sprang to life. Text and images flew by too fast for Ace to read. Every few seconds the displays would pause, and he was able to guess the computer was running through some sort of boot sequence.

A beat later the words, "Total system rebuild in progress. Please stand by..." appeared on the computer display.

"Hey," April said, standing up on the back seat to get a better look around. "I think I recognize this place."

"You do? Where are we?" Ivan asked.

"Yeah," April said. "These trees look like sugar maples. I'm

208

pretty sure we're in Tennessee."

Hank sniffed the air and said, "Yeah. It kinda does smell like Tennessee."

"You can know where you are based on smell?" Ace asked.

"Listen, dipshit. I'm a Basset hound, and Basset hounds have the best sense of smell of any hound out there."

"Yeah, yeah," Ace said. "You've mentioned that."

"Maybe we should get out and look around," Ivan said.

A tritone chime sounded, and the computer screens stopped scrolling. The complex ultra-advanced Valdovian 4-D control systems sprung back to life.

The pleasant computerized voice said, "Hands on the steering wheel, please... Hands on the steering wheel, please."

"I think it's talking to you, Ace," Ivan said. "You're in the driver's seat."

"Yeah, I know," Ace said. "I just kind of resent it saying hands. That shiny prick shot off my right hand...ugh. I guess one hand will have to do. Here goes."

Ace put his one good hand on the steering wheel.

The world exploded around him as a bolt of pure lightning raged through his body.

The nanobots inside of Ace sprang back to life.

Once online they began to flow away from the center of Ace's chest. It felt frigid and itchy like the blackened plastic area on his chest was rubbery poison ivy taffy pulled from the inside of an ice bath.

His body shuddered, and he was unable to take his hand off the steering wheel. The rebooted nanobots worked with feverish vindication repairing his bruised flesh and cracked ribs. A few hundred snaked up into his brain, and Ace felt a new level of understanding creep up. The 'bots had sacrificed themselves to protect him from the laser blast just as they had for Elvis back at Sleazon's party. Before taking the brunt of the laser blast, a few remained in the palm waiting to interface with the super advanced computers onboard the Caddy. The physical contact breathed new life into the nanobots, and they were now functioning at one hundred percent efficiency.

Yet, as more nanobots upped his cognitive abilities, a new level of awareness began to take hold.

*Yes*, Ace thought. *My cognitive abilities are increasing. Ahhh. Yes. Yes. I'm beginning to understand now. Time travel. Time itself. It is not a stream flowing in one immutable direction. It is more like a jagged amorphous mess of interlocking building blocks. Yesss. You remove one block further down the structure, and every block that follows can be affected. I see it now.*

Once the reboot sequence completed Ace let go of the steering wheel.

"Holy shit!" April said. "Ace! Are you OK? It looked like the Caddy just shocked the shit out of you!"

"Yes," Ace said. "I'm great. I see it all very clearly now. We can totally save Elvis. We just need to get a few things first!"

The nanobots upgraded Ace's translator implant, and the new software allowed him to glean enough information from the Caddy's onboard user manual to enter a specific location in time and space. This time, however, he put the top up and had everyone buckle their seat belts. The manual was very insistent on those two bits of safety information and kept droning on and on about indemnification against injury.

After entering in the coordinates and a quick trip through the fabric of space-time itself, the Cadillac materialized in a parking garage of the Galactic Galleria in the year 2018.

The Galactic Galleria had the distinction of being the largest shopping mall in the entire galaxy.

Ace's first stop was Proton's Popular Prosthetics where a jovial mutant named Zandar sold Ace a brand new top-of-the-line five-fingered humanoid hand.

"We normally don't carry hands like this," Zandar said. "But it came in with a shipment of Bordon neck wedges, and the whole thing was nonreturnable, so we kept it. You came at the right time, friend!"

Zandar gestured at Ace's missing hand and smiled. "And don't think just because you are, in need shall we say, that Zandar will charge you an arm and a leg! Get it? An arm and a leg! Ha ha ha!"

"Ha ha," Ace said, dripping with sarcasm. "May I see the hand please?"

"Sure, sure!" Zandar said as he took the hand out of a glass display case and gave it to Ace to inspect. "Here you are. Take a look. Feel free to take a close look, friend. I think you will find it to be of the finest Valdovian craftsmanship!"

"Valdovian, huh? Man, is there anything those guys don't make?"

"Well," Zandar said. "They are the galaxy's best engineers. And this is the only model we have that matches your natural hand. The next closest thing we carry is a three-fingered Raradon paw."

"Yeah," Ace said. "This looks good. You guys take Celestial Express, right?"

"Of course!" Zandar said with a wink. "Don't leave the phantom zone without it, right? Hahaha! I love those commercials. Yes, my friend. Right over here and I will ring you up. But before I do. We are running a special on laser-proofing on all new prosthetic purchases. It's only 400 extra credits. A fine value, I think."

"Sure, whatever," Ace said.

Zandar sang to himself as he applied a coat of laser-proof spray to the hand. When he was done, he said, "There! Here you are, my friend. I guess you'd like to wear it out, right? No need for a bag?"

"Yeah," Ace said through gritted teeth.

"Ok!" Zandar said giving Ace the hand. "You're all set, then! Enjoy your new appendage!"

Ace's new hand was amazing. His sense of touch and gripping ability were as sensitive and strong as his natural hand. It really was a fine piece of Valdovian craftsmanship. After running the hand through a series of tests and a short trip to the Caddy to look up some stuff on its computers, Ace met Ivan, April, and Hank in front of a Dippin' Dots stand where the three were enjoying the Ice Cream of the Future.

"I can't believe you guys have this stuff out here!" April said as she spooned little frozen ice cream balls into her mouth. "It's just like the same Dippin' Dots on Earth!"

"Yeah," Ivan said. "It was one of the things that slipped through before the blockade went up. Some carpetbagger from the Glorbon Cluster started selling the stuff on Earth. It was right after the Hasselhoff Incident, and it was the straw that broke the camel's back. The Galactic Union erected the shield to keep aliens from messing with Earth right after that."

Hank lapped up ice cream from a little cup and wagged his tail, "Well. Shit. It's good as fuck!"

"The Hasselhoff Incident? You mean David Hasselhoff?" April asked.

"Yep. The one and the same. Didn't know he was an alien, huh? He really ticked off a lot of people when he single-handedly brought down the Berlin Wall."

"Ummm," April said. "I don't think that's how it happened. I mean, I remember he did some sort of stunt where he had, like, a concert on top of the Wall in some sort of electric light jacket. And German people really love him. Which is super weird. Like, they really, really love him. Like he was some sort of god or something. I've heard he could get people to do anything he wanted. And oh my God, he *did* bring the wall down!"

"Yup," Ivan said. "Messing with an unenlightened culture's politics is a big no-no. Kind of like the Prime Directive in *Star Trek*. Between Hasselhoff and the sudden introduction of super advanced culinary tech, the big wigs at the Galactic Union had enough." Ivan tilted his treat cup back to get the last few frozen balls onto his tongue.

"Hey, *Face*! You look like a hundred bucks!" Hanks said when he saw Ace approaching.

"Yup," Ace said wiggling the fingers on his new prosthetic hand. "Good as new."

"I hope they calibrated that thing properly," Hank said. "Wouldn't want you to accidentally rip your crank off next time you take a leak!"

Ace ignored him, but Ivan and April giggled.

Ace was ready to get to work. "Ivan, who's the best mindtapper you know?"

"Huh," Ivan said. "I think Bleeborp still works for one of the big networks on Alpha Centauri Prime. Probably him?"

"Think he can cook up a quick vignette about a galactic apocalypse?"

"Yeah. I bet he could," Ivan said with a smile. "I think I know where you're going with this. I'll give him a call and get him to start working on it."

"Well," April said. "I'm lost. Can you two spacemen fill me in?

I feel like a fifth wheel over here."

"Not me, sister," Hank said. "I don't know what the fuck's going on either, but I don't care. This ice cream is just too goddamn good!"

"That's good, Hank," Ace said. "Because you're probably not going to remember any of this by the time it's over."

"What?" Hank said and started growling. "You come near me, and I'll bite your n—"

"Yeah. I know," Ace said, patting the air to try and calm Hank down. "You'll bite my nuts off. Look, I don't like it either but what I'm trying to do is make things right."

"Yeah!" Hank said. "We can make it right by not having any of this fucked up shit happen in the first place! All we gotta do is go grab the first time machine from the pencil neck who invented the shit. No Zimmy Zon's time machine, no going to Andromeda. No starting a war. No reason for the Shiny Man to kill Elvis."

"OK," Ace said. "But then how will we still be here right now? In this particular locale in space-time? Look, we're somehow instrumental in all of this. Think about it. We need to get the Caddy out of Graceland for it to be here with us now. We have to meet Elvis at Sleazon Nebula's party. The Shiny Man has to chase us to Earth. All of that."

"Well, then what's the point?" April asked. "If all this is fated. Why bother going back to change anything?"

"Because," Ace said. "Before I met you guys here, I went back to the Caddy and started poking around in the computer. I was able to get into a program called the Chronomicon."

"Yeah! The Shiny Man said he had one of those!" April said.

"Yes," Ace said. "It's a system for reading events of the past. And the future."

"Whoa," April said.

"Yeah. For instance, I found out what happened to Betty when we left her."

"Poor Betty," Ivan said. "What happened?"

"Well, the self-destruct worked," Ace said. "She exploded over Tupelo in 1936."

"1936? I thought we were in 1935?" April said.

"We were," Ace said. "But we jumped ahead a year when I accidentally hit a button in the Caddy while fighting that shiny dickhead. Anyway, Betty blew up in the sky over Tupelo and caused massive devastation. The papers reported it as a tornado strike because no one on the ground had any clue what had happened. Elvis was one year old at the time, and he survived, but it was a close call."

"Holy shit!" April gasped. "I know about that tornado strike! My brother was always spouting Elvis trivia, and one of his favorite bits of arcane knowledge is how the King was almost killed by a tornado when he was one year old. Wait a second...how can I know that if it just happened?"

Ace smiled. "See? Because it happened in the past, you know about it now. Time is pretty malleable. And our brains are different now because of the time-jumps. It's one of the artifacts of being a time traveler, I'm guessing."

"The Chronomicon keeps mentioning dates in the future where Elvis does all this crazy shit. He's totally alive. And there's something else," Ace said.

"What?" Ivan asked.

"All our names are in the footnotes," Ace said. "I don't understand it all because it's written in a language my translator can't fully decode. But the gist I'm getting is we're somehow responsible for...everything. We're responsible for getting him off world and faking his death. We're responsible for planting the Caddy in the master bedroom. All of it. And somehow we fix it all, so Elvis survives in the twenty-first century and becomes some sort of politician that brings Earth into the Galactic Union."

"Holy shit," Hank said.

"Which brings me back to Hank," Ace said. "We can't change anything up until right before the Shiny Man kills Elvis. Things need to play out just as they have before. But once we do make the change, everything after that moment will be different. We probably won't remember any of this. It'll be like it never happened."

"Well, fuck it then!" Hank said with a little hop. His long toenails scraped on the ground when he landed, and he kicked his Dippin' Dots cup away. "If we can save the King I don't give a shit if I think I'm Joan of fucking Arc afterward. Let's go save him and tear that shiny fucker a new asshole!"

"So," April said. "We go back and save Elvis from getting turned into hamburger by the Shiny Man. How?"

"I've got an idea," Ace said. "I'm not sure it will work, but we've got to give it a shot."

# 15

# Back to Memphis

Their first stop was Alpha Centauri Prime to pick up the mindtap from Ivan's friend, Bleeborp. The device was small and unassuming. April said it looked just like a View-Master, an Earth children's toy that allowed kids to flip through stereoscopic pictures on little discs when they held it up to their eyes. When Elvis looked into this gadget, though, his brain would be flooded with a perfect 3-D and quadraphonic vignette depicting the horrors of the temporal war with Andromeda. Since Ivan had an eidetic memory, he gave Bleeborp every single detail Elvis had told him.

Bleeborp was also a home security nut and gave them a Secure-o-Tron 10,000 Modular Security Kit. With it, they would be able to install all the advanced security measures at Graceland to keep the Cadillac safe until Ace's former self made his way into the bedroom with Elvis.

After saying their goodbyes to Bleeborp, everyone piled into the Cadillac. Ace sat in the driver's seat and Ivan in the passenger seat. In the back seat April and Hank were already belted in and ready to rock.

"Ok," Ace said. "Now that we have the mindtap, we need to go back in time and make sure each key point that resulted in our current timeline plays out the way it did before."

"Well," Ivan said. "I'm not sure it really matters what order we do it in. I mean we have a time machine, right? We can do it in any order."

"Look," Ace said. "How do we know if we do things outside of the order it's listed in the Chronomicon, it won't, I don't know, make a butterfly with nine heads in two million years?"

"There already *is* a butterfly with nine heads on Zaxon Six," Ivan said with an air of pretension. "I thought you were smart now because of the nanobots."

"I *am* smarter now!" Ace said. "Wait. Are you implying I was some sort of idiot before?"

"No," Ivan said with a cough. "Not at all."

"I swear to God, Ivan. I can totally kick your ass now. All I have to do is move the 'bots into my arms and I can kick your ass."

"Oh yeah?" Ivan said as he unbuckled his seatbelt. He jumped up on the seat and assumed fighting stance. "Try it!"

"Guys!" April yelled from the back seat of the Cadillac. "Please!"

Ivan slunk back in his seat and buckled his seatbelt with a pout. "Sorry. This is kind of how we make all navigation decisions. We always fight about it."

"Yeah," Ace said, embarrassed. "It's kind of our process."

"OK. Good," April said. "Because I thought I was going to have to turn a hose on you boys. So, for the record, I'm with Ace. If shit is in that thing in some sort of order, we should follow it. Who knows? Maybe someone in the future put it in there so we would follow it like breadcrumbs, you know?"

"Breadcrumbs?" Ace asked. "What do you mean?" He was still pretty hungry, even after his large cup of Doozbleberry Dippin' Dots.

"You know," April said. "Like Hansel and Gretel? A trail for us to follow?"

Ace and Ivan looked at each other and shrugged.

"Come on. Ivan, didn't you say you have a media archive from Earth?"

"Yes. My stash," Ivan said.

"There aren't any fairy tales in there?  Brothers Grimm? Ringing any bells?"

"I guess not."

"Ok. Well. When this is all over, I'm taking you boys to school," April said. "Anyway, the point is maybe that stuff is in there explicitly for us to follow. So things work out correctly. You know?"

"My point, exactly," Ace said.

"Makes sense to me, monkey man," Hank said.

"Ok," Ivan said. "I guess I'm outnumbered then. We do it in order. So, Sacagawea, where's our first stop?"

"Wait," April said. "You know Sacagawea, but you don't know Hansel and Gretel?"

"I have a few history shows in my stash. Sue me," Ivan said.

Ace tapped on the dashboard controls and brought up the Chronomicon. He was careful to page through the entries exactly as he had before so he would arrive at the screen in question. It was almost like his subconscious knew where to find the info he needed.

On the screen was a slew of gibberish and then a middle section written in plain text:

*Ace Tucker, Ivan Chimpanov, April Massey, Hank*
*2018, 2384, 2010, 1977, 1935, 1936.*

"What am I looking at?" Hank said.

"I'm pretty sure those are the key years where we have to do stuff to make this all play out properly," Ace said.

"Ok," April said. "Obviously 2018 is where we came from and didn't Elvis tell us that 2384 is the year the sandwich dude invented the time machine? So what about the rest?"

"Well, 1977 is the year of Elvis's faked death," Ivan said.

"1935 the year of his birth," Hank blurted out like a kid eager to answer a question in class.

"1936 is the year Betty blew up after Ace jumped us ahead one year," Ivan said.

Ace gave him a look. "I was fighting for my life, dick."

"I know," Ivan said. "So what about 2010?"

"Well," Ace said. "I can tell you one thing important that happened in 2010."

"What?" April asked.

"Mustachepalooza," Ace said.

"Whoa." Ivan flopped back in his seat like the wind was knocked out him. "That can't be a coincidence that it appears right after the date when time travel is invented."

"Yup," Ace said. "I hope you guys saved some room for some sandwiches because our first stop is the Zimmy Zon's in 2384."

"Why?" April asked.

"Well," Ace said. "If we're going to turn a Cadillac into a time machine and leave it in the master bedroom of Graceland for my former self to find we're going to need a timedrive."

"Are you serious?" Hank asked. "You think we can get the geek who invented the timedrive to just hand one over to us?"

"Yup," said Ace. "That's exactly what we're going to do."

"How are you going to do that?" April asked.

Ace smiled and said, "I'm going to get him laid."

\* \* \*

Mustachepalooza was the stuff of legends. Even in the twenty-fourth century. When Ace met Dino Valdeeznuts in the back of the Zimmy Zon's in the year 2384 and presented his modest proposal, it took zero amount of arm twisting to get Dino to agree.

Dino quickly built a second working version of his newly invented timedrive for Ace. Then he wrote out instructions for his boss to use the original he left behind and jumped in the Caddy with Ace.

Ace was glad he didn't have to strong arm the geeky Valdovian because he had four of them. All Ace had to do was show Dino his all-access Mustache Supernova backstage pass.

Their next stop was Mustachepalooza, one of the most infamous rock concerts in the history of the galaxy. Dino didn't even seem interested in seeing his invention in action. Or that it had been augmented to replace his original thirty-minute time jump limitation. He was more interested in getting the lore of Mustachepalooza correct.

"So, is it true that two million people attended the concert?" Dino asked.

"Yup," Ace replied.

"And after the show, everyone backstage had to be naked the whole time? The band, the crew, the, um, groupies?"

"That's right," Ace said.

"And Nova Johnson rigged the beverage system so that every drink served was spiked with Turbo Ecstasy? So it turned into a giant orgy?"

"That's what the history books say." Ace wasn't part of the

Mustache Supernova road crew at the time of Mustachepalooza. It was before he and Ivan joined, but he was familiar with all the details of the concert-turned-four-day orgy. It went down as the greatest rock 'n' roll party in history, responsible for six hundred births and more than a thousand cases of herpes googleplex fourteen.

Knees McGuffin lost an eye on day three. No one was exactly sure how it happened, but a polygendered Delladon was suspected as the two were inseparable during the fray.

Dino fidgeted with his four hands as the Cadillac materialized in the loading bay of the concert arena.

Ace handed Dino a laminated pass the read, "Mustache Supernova Crew. All Access."

"You know these things are damn near impossible to get?" Ace asked.

"Oh. Yes!" Dino said. "I know. I've read all the Mustachian Legends."

"Ok," Ace said, handing over the pass. "You go have fun now. And thanks for the timedrive. You're helping to save the galaxy, you know?"

"Uh huh!" Dino was already out of the car and running for the backstage entrance holding his pass out like it was a crucifix warding off vampires. The security guard waved him in, and Dino squealed with glee.

"So, are we going to stick around for the concert?" April asked from the backseat.

"No," Ace said. "By all accounts the show itself was terrible. The band was so loaded they could barely play. It's only the orgy that makes the history books. We'll go to a good one soon, I promise."

"OK," Hank said. "What do we do now?"

"Well," Ace said. "We've got to build a time machine into another Caddy in 1977, so it will be waiting for us in 2018. My guess is when we hook up this one it's going to get updated so it will behave just like the one we have in the trunk now. Remember, the original model only goes thirty minutes in the past."

"What makes you think that will work?" Hank asked.

"There's an extra cable in the trunk with a label on it that says 'attach to clone timedrive,'" Ace said.

"That's super weird. How do you even know that?" April asked.

"I saw it when Elvis opened the trunk while we were on Betty. Come on, I'll show you."

Everyone got out of the Cadillac and followed Ace to the trunk. He popped it and there, next to the crazy, swirly timedrive powering the Cadillac was a cable running from the sidewall with a little white plastic tag stuck to it, right behind the four prong connector that matched the shape of a port on the timedrive. It read, "attach to clone timedrive" in black magic marker.

"That can't be a coincidence," April said.

"Yeah," Ace said. "Someone left that there for us."

"And, fuck! That thing is crazy to look at!" April shouted.

Ace set down his dormant timedrive next to the insanity-inducing active one. Without power, the timedrive looked like a simple glass cylinder with a mess of lifeless metal filaments snaking inside. He grabbed the cable with his artificial hand and a jolt of electricity shot through his arm.

"Ow!" Ace said, pulling back his hand. "Dammit! The cable shocked me in my new hand! I just bought this thing. Better not have messed it up. Whoa. Did you guys see that? My hand glowed for a second."

The pain was gone in an instant but an almost imperceptible glow radiated around the artificial forefinger. Ace wiggled his fingers to make sure his new hand wasn't damaged. There was a strange tingling in the fingers but otherwise everything seemed normal.

"No. I missed it," April said. "I'm trying not to look. Everything in that trunk makes my head hurt!"

"Yeah, I didn't see it either," Ivan said.

Hank snorted and said, "I'm too short to see in the trunk. Thanks for reminding me, fucker."

"Whatever," Ace said. "Looks like no harm done. I'm gonna grab the cable a little further back where the shielding is better."

This time there was no shock.

When he plugged the cable into the connection port on the dormant timedrive, the metal filaments began to glow. It was subtle at first like an old vacuum tube coming to life. After a few seconds, the filaments started vibrating and the glowing increased. A bright flash like a tiny supernova erupted inside the cylinder, and the filaments morphed into the mind-bending swirling mess of darkness and light.

Ace tried not to look directly at the kaleidoscope of horrors threatening to drive him insane if his gaze hovered too long. When the psychotic movements within both cylinders synched up, Ace closed the trunk.

"OK. So, there's that," Ace said.

"Now what?" Hank asked.

"Well," Ace said. "According to Elvis a few aliens show up at Graceland on August 16, 1977, help him fake his death, and get him the hell off Earth. So we have to go do all that, then we'll build a time machine out of his prized Cadillac."

"How the shit are we going to do that?" Hank asked.

"We're going to follow the instruction manual. There's step-by-step instructions in there. Pictures and everything."

\* \* \*

It was a surreal experience for everyone when they arrived in Memphis in 1977. The beginning of the eventual suburban sprawl dotted Elvis Presley Boulevard, but nothing like the buildup in 2018. The KFC April would work at in the future was nothing more than a sparse clump of trees in a small field.

"Man!" April said as they drove. "This is so freaky! Everything looks so different."

"Yeah," Ace said. "I gotta admit, I'm a little sad there's no fried chicken..."

Hank sniffed the air like he was trying to get his bearings and kept muttering, "I remember this. How do I remember all this?"

Ivan wouldn't shut up about the Ramones. "You know, 1977 was the year the Ramones release Rocket To Russia? That's their best album, man. They're out there right now! Probably getting ready for a show at CBGB's or something! Man, we have to go when this is all over!"

"Alright everyone," Ace said as he powered down the Caddy in the abandoned barn he chose to be their base of operations. "Let's try to stay on task here, OK?"

"Right," Ivan said. "Sorry. I got a little excited. OK. So how are we going to do this thing with Elvis?"

"Well, for one," Ace said. "You and Hank are going to have to stay out of sight. We don't have dazzlers to disguise you. Hank can get by if he stays quiet but a chimpanzee walking around might turn a few heads."

"I saw a thrift store up the road a piece," April said. "Maybe Hank can sneak in there and steal you a disguise, Ivan."

"Yeah. Good one," Ace said with a smile. "Then you guys are going to have to go steal the Cadillac and bring it back here so we can soup it up."

225

"Sounds good, *Lace*," Hank said. "Will do. Where are yous guys going?"

"Me and April have to go pretend to be agents from the future."

"Well, in all fairness," April said. "We kind of are. You know? But didn't Elvis say something about the people looking like feds or undercover cops or something?"

"Good point," Ace said. "But we better look the part. Maybe the three of us go to the store then. Me and you get suits and distract the staff while Hank sneaks out with something Ivan can wear so he won't attract too much attention."

"OK," Ivan said. "In the meantime, I'll start reading through the manual on how to build the time machine into the other Cadillac."

"You can read the manual?" Ace asked.

"Yeah," Ivan said. "It's just a variation of a standard High Valdovian mixed with a little Hyberian. Like a pidgin dialect. It started making sense last time you showed us the dates. Remember? I'm good with languages."

"I'll say!" Ace said. "Even with my translator implant and the 'bots pumping up my cerebellum, I'm still a little fuzzy on a lot of things. I was going to follow the pictures."

"Well, that's why you have me, my friend," Ivan said. He plopped down in the driver's seat of the Cadillac and started paging through the computer screens. Every few seconds he mumbled a coo of surprise or understanding.

The gang set up shop in the abandoned barn, and while Ivan pored over the instruction manuals Ace, April, and Hank walked to Mildred's Second Hand Clothes.

A fat woman in a sundress stood behind a glass and metal counter. She was smoking a cigarette, and from the looks of the ashtray loaded with dozens of crushed butts, it was her main job. A small cathode ray tube television sat in the corner. The TV had two long metal antennae sticking out of the top, and the woman fidgeted with them every few seconds.

"Come on, goddammit. Lemme see my stories in peace," the woman said. The cigarette bounced in her mouth and ashes fell to the floor as she spoke. Both of her hands manipulated the antennae until she was satisfied. "There we go. I can see you now, Andy Griffith. You fine hunk of sheriff you. Hey! You can't bring that dog in here."

The woman pointed at Hank like he was the foulest thing in the world.

Ace could tell Hank was offended and shooed him outside before Hank could mouth off to the woman. "Sorry! My mistake! Go on, boy, wait out here."

Once outside Hank said, "You better cut that *boy* shit out, fucker."

Ace coughed loudly to cover up Hank. "That's good, uh, friend. Wait here, and we'll be out in a minute, OK?" Ace gave Hank a look that meant business.

Hank rolled his eyes and then let out a chipper bark.

"Thanks, pal," Ace said. He reentered the store and found April in the back browsing through a rack of suits. A lot of the styles reminded Ace of the clothes he saw on TV shows from Ivan's stash.

"God! These are so awful," April said as she slid jackets around the rack.

"I dunno," Ace said. "They look kinda cool to me."

"This?" April yanked out a tweed sport coat with elbow patches. "You think this is kinda cool?"

"Well, no," Ace admitted. "That looks like something a funeral director would wear. I'm going to defer to your judgment here.

You're the one more familiar with the styles of the time."

"Shit," April said. "How old do you think I am, dude?"

"I don't know." Ace really had no idea. Until recently the only human women he'd ever seen were actors in TV shows and movies. He realized he had no actual context for how to gauge a woman's age. Yet, something in the back of his mind told him it was dangerous to even try. Like he was about to step into a trap.

"I'm twenty-four," April said. Her voice had a hard edge to it.

"That's what I was going to say!" Ace forced a laugh and started browsing through suit jackets again.

"Uh huh. How about you?" April said.

"I'm not really sure. I was raised in an orphanage, and they'd never seen a human baby before, so they based my age off the closest analog species."

"OK," April said. "So how old?"

"Sixty-seven."

April erupted in laughter. Even though Ace knew it was at his expense, the sound was like being wrapped in a warm blanket. He couldn't help but smile himself.

April wiped a few tears from her eyes and said, "No. No way, dude. Not unless you're some kind of Benjamin Button. I'd peg you for maybe twenty-eight. Thirty at the most."

"Oh," Ace said. "OK."

A loud crash erupted from the front of the store. Racks of clothes tumbled to the ground, and the fat woman behind the counter screamed.

Hank burst into the store, chasing a cat and cursing freely, "Come back here, you son of a bitch cat! You can't talk to me that way, you box-shitting fuckwad!"

At first, Hank and the cat were moving so fast, they were a blur. Ace concentrated, and the nanobots enhanced his perception so he could track them as they wreaked havoc throughout the store. When Hank came close enough, Ace jumped down and covered him in the black sports coat he had been admiring before the chaos.

Hank squirmed, trying to get free but Ace held him fast. "Let's go!"

April yelled, "Ok. Shit, shit, shit, shit!" She grabbed an armload of clothes from the rack and followed Ace out the front door, running as fast as she could to keep up.

The fat woman behind the counter continued her screaming fit and threw her ashtray at them as they exited. It crashed into the glass door and shattered it.

"I'm calling the cops!" the fat woman yelled.

# 16

# CTRL ALT REPEAT

Ten minutes later Ace plopped Hank on the ground of their abandoned barn hideout. Hank hit the ground hard and shook off the sports coat as best he could. Between the drop and Ace squeezing the shit out of him while they ran, Hank was a little out of it.

April dropped her armload of clothes on the dusty ground, bent over, and gulped for breath. "Holy shit! I haven't run that much since high school! I fucking hate running!"

"So," Ivan said still in the driver's seat of the Cadillac. "Things went well, I trust?"

"Yeah. We had a little bit of trouble," Ace said pointing at Hank.

"That. Fucking. Cat. Had. It. Coming," Hank said between big sloppy gasps.

"Whatever, man," Ace said. "We got some clothes, but I'm pretty sure we're wanted by the police now. So, we gotta do this fast."

"Well, take a look in the glovebox," Ivan said. "There's something in there that might help."

Inside the glovebox was a pair of official-looking badges in leather wallets. Three letters were laid out over a jagged lightning bolt running through a spiral galaxy.

"That can't be a coincidence," Ace said after reading the letters.

"I'm starting to think that none of this is," Ivan said.

"What's it say?" April asked.

"TCB," Ace said.

"Whoa," April said coming in for a look. "That's kinda like Elvis's classic TCB logo, but, upgraded. Wow. Look how it sparkles! It's kind of like the galaxy is moving on the badge. Like a super badass hologram on a credit card. Cool!"

"Well. These look pretty official," Ace said. "So let's change into these suits, go to Graceland, and flash these badges. We have to convince Elvis to fake his death. And from the story he told us, two official-looking agents are the ones to do it by showing him a vision of the future war with Andromeda. Now we can use the mindtap we got from Ivan's pal to do just that."

"Is it weird that what you just said is far from the most batshit crazy thing any of us has said in the past 24 hours?" April said.

"Yeah," Ace said. "I know. Come on. Let's go."

Ace and April walked a few miles from the barn hideout then snuck around back of the Graceland mansion. Elvis was exiting the building April identified as the racquetball court. He wore a white t-shirt and athletic shorts. In his hand was a small racket.

In the far distance, they heard sirens ring out then stop.

*Most likely the police arriving at the thrift store*, Ace thought.

"Hey!" Elvis said, waving his small racket with menace. "Y'all can't be here! Get lost before I call the cops!"

"Follow my lead," April whispered to Ace.

"OK," Ace whispered back.

April flashed one of the badges Ace found in the glove box of the Cadillac. Ace mimicked her before dropping his own badge in the side pocket of his stolen black sports coat.

"Sorry to bother you, sir," April said with an authoritative tone. "I'm Agent Scully. This is Agent Mulder. We're from the government and need you to come with us please, sir."

The plan was to get Elvis to watch the vignette on the mindtap and get him to reveal the location of the original Cadillac Eldorado Biarritz. But Elvis had other plans.

Elvis dropped his racket. He reached behind his back and pulled a handgun from his waistband.

"I ain't going nowhere with you!" Elvis said. His voice quivered, and his hands shook. "I've already talked to the FBI! They told me some impostors would be coming by and try to tell me all kinds of crazy stuff about space aliens and the future and such. I ain't gonna have any of it.

Ace held his hands up in front of him. "Whoa, there! We're here to help. I don't know who you talked to before, but we're friends. We just need to show you something."

Ace reached for his pocket to pull out the mindtap, careful to move in a slow, deliberate fashion.

Elvis shot the ground in front of Ace's feet. Dirt kicked up, and April jumped behind Ace with a squeal.

"Hands where I can see them!" Elvis said. "Or I swear to God, I'll plug you good."

Ace weighed his options. The nanobots were working to enhance his perception and reflexes. He was almost certain he could get to the gun and disarm Elvis before he got another shot off. But he wasn't one hundred percent. Once he leaped forward, he would leave April exposed, and that was too great a risk. He needed to talk his way out of this somehow.

"Look," Ace said. "I know this sounds crazy, but we've met before. And we're friends."

"You shut your mouth, mister!" Elvis said. "I ain't never seen you before in my life."

"I know about the tunnels," Ace said. "I know you have secret tunnels leading into Graceland. We just need to show you something and then see your secret Cadillac."

"Secret Cadillac?" Elvis said. "I don't have a secret Cadillac, you lunatic. And I have no idea what you're talking about. Tunnels? What tunnels? You ain't making no sense! Now you stay right there."

"Elvis, please listen," Ace said.

"What'd you just say?" Elvis's face twisted with rage. Tears welled up in his eyes, and he jabbed the gun in the air with each syllable. "Why'd you call me Elvis? Why? What kind of a sick bastard are you? Why?"

"Whoa!" Ace said. "Easy now."

"What kind of sick bastard calls a man by his dead twin brother's name? Randy! Randy! Get out here!"

Before Ace had a chance to process what he just heard, Agent Randall Calhoun of the F.B.I. emerged from the racquetball court. He wore a white t-shirt and white shorts cut way too high for Ace's taste. Instead of a racket in his hand, Randall Calhoun was holding an impossibly shiny laser revolver.

"It's all right, Jessie," Calhoun said. "I'm here."

"Are these the crazies you've been warning me about all this time, Randy?"

"Yes, Jessie. That's them," Calhoun said.

"This son of a bitch just called me Elvis!"

"I know, Jessie. I heard," Calhoun said. His tone was like a parent trying to calm down a tantrum. "Why don't you just go on inside and get a beer out of the fridge? I'll handle them. They're just crazy mixed up fans. That's all."

Jessie lowered the gun and slouched like a moping child. He shuffled his feet as he walked into the mansion, closing the door behind him.

"What the fuck?" April said, still hiding behind Ace.

"Ms. Massey, I presume?" Calhoun said. "The vulgarity and dimwitted looks give you away, my dear."

"Yeah. That's me, asshole. How the fuck are you here and what'd you do to Elvis?"

"Elvis?" Calhoun said with a casual wave of his laser revolver. "He's been dead since 1935. Poor little tike. Died in the womb. When my timeship crashed in Roswell, New Mexico in 1947, I met a dying man. Myself from a future timeline. He told me everything before I put him out of his misery. Told me how you left him to die on an exploding ship in 1936. Well, he survived. It took him *years* to crawl to New Mexico. As he lay there in a pool of his own filth, he told me how he used a tearing electron plasma inducer on Gladys Presley. It succeeded in killing Elvis. But spared his twin, Jessie Presley."

"He said you had escaped with the Valdovian time machine," Calhoun continued. "That I would have to nurture Jessie Presley in Elvis's place. So that everything would appear to you as it does now in 1977. I've been waiting for this moment for thirty years. Now. Where is the time machine?"

A sound like a thousand screaming animals came from behind them. Ace turned just in time to see the Caddy materialize out of thin air. It was like he had turned on a TV show just as a car rocketed off a ramp. An explosion of light erupted all around the Caddy as it flew over Ace and April's head crashing into Calhoun at full speed.

Ivan was in the driver's seat. He hit a button, and the top retracted. Hank was in the passenger seat howling.

"Get in!" Ivan said.

Ace and April leaped into the Cadillac, landing in the back seat.

Hank barked, "Put the fucking top up!"

Ivan hit a button on the dash, and the top zipped overheard, sealing them in. Then he tapped another button and the world around them dissolved.

\* \* \*

No one said a word for long moments. There was just panting and heavy breathing as Ace and April caught their breaths. Outside the world was the now familiar craziness of hypertime.

"How'd you know?" Ace asked.

"At first I thought it was me just getting used to the language in the manual," Ivan said. "Words and phrases seemed to change on me. Like, I'd read something then go back and reread it, and it'd be slightly different. So I checked the Chronomicon. And I literally watched entire sections on Elvis Presley vanish as I read them. Eventually, everything about him in the future was gone. I searched in the past, and I found no mention of Elvis at all except in a footnote that he was the stillborn twin of *Jessie* Presley. That's when I realized we were in some *alternate* reality where Elvis was dead."

"Yeah," Ace said. "But how'd you know where we'd be standing?"

"I didn't. I just sort of guessed from memory," Ivan said. "Landing on top of the bad guy was a happy accident."

"Yeah! Monkey man here has a photogenic memory!" Hank said.

"The term is phot*ographic*," Ivan said. "And eidetic is the more appropriate term, Hank."

"Call it eye-fucking tic-tac-toe for all I care. That was awesome!"

"Agreed!" April said. "Thanks, Ivan. Now, what the hell do we do?"

Ace looked out the window at the swirling mess of color and shapes winking and exploding in and out of existence. He couldn't help but feel responsible for Elvis's death. He was there. If he had just been a little faster, he could've stopped the Shiny Man from zapping Gladys with that thing. Even with these new cognitive abilities, the oddities of time travel were confusing.

There was a tickle in the back of his brain that started to coalesce into a concrete thought. A terrible truth crept into his consciousness. He chewed on the thought for a moment before Ivan broke him out of his trance.

"We have to do something," Ivan said. "Because everything in the Chronomicon is vanishing. It's like there's some kind of temporal chain reaction in the works. And check this out."

Ivan called up the page with their names and the key dates on the screen. "This is the only remaining page. Everything else is a garbled mess or completely gone."

"They did it then," Ace said.

"What?" April asked.

"The Andromedans," Ace said. "Remember what Elvis said about the war? The Andromedans wanted the Valdovian timedrive so they could use it to prevent the Milky Way from ever forming. They must've have won and set off that crazy timebomb that blows up the galaxy. That's why things are unraveling."

"Well, then how the hell are we still here?" Hank asked. "If they nuked the galaxy a few billion years ago, how the shit are we still here now?"

"I've been thinking about that," Ace said. "I'm starting to understand how this all works. Ivan, you said it before. When we're in hypertime, we are outside of normal space and time. In here we're safe."

"Great," April said. "So we're stuck in the goddamn Twilight Zone forever?"

"No," Ace said. "Take a look at the dates. They're still there. Ivan, page through a list of possible destinations we can jump to."

Ivan tapped on the screen and nothing happened.

"Are you doing it right?" Hank asked Ivan.

"Yeah. I went into browse mode. It's supposed to show you everything. There should be roughly eighteen billion years listed here. The entire lifespan of the universe. But there are only six dates. 2018, 2384, 2010, 1935, and 1936. It's like they're locked into the Caddy."

"They are," Ace said. "We have two timedrives in the back of this Caddy, remember? They're talking to each other and keeping those dates locked in."

Ivan whispered in awe, "It's like we're in a *multiverse* machine now."

"Right. Us being here proves it. With the two timedrives working in tandem, we're immune to the effects of the Andromedan timebomb. And we have access to the original universe we came from. We just need to go back to 2018 and stop the Shiny Man before he ever gets onboard Betty."

"But, look!" April gasped. "1977 is gone. Why is 1977 gone?"

"Shit!" Hank said. "She's right. 1977 is gone now!"

"I think it's because we only get one shot at this," Ace said.

"Like volatile memory," Ivan said.

"Sure. Once we use it, we lose it," Ace said.

They all sat in silence for a moment then Hank startled growling.

"Right!" Hank said. "Well, what are you waiting for, *Brace*? Let's go fuck that shiny fucker up!"

\* \* \*

Ivan dialed in 2018, and the Caddy materialized in a familiar clearing in the woods. It was night and when Ace put the top down the sounds of police sirens wafted through the sugar maple trees surrounding them.

"Whoa. This is the same location we went when you hit the Caddy's panic button," April said.

Hank sniffed the air. "Yep. This is definitely Memphis."

In the distance, tires screeched, and people shouted. A helicopter circled above then stopped in a hover.

Everyone got out of the Cadillac and walked towards the commotion. The glow from the helicopter's spotlight cast long, distorted shadows through the woods.

"Think the Caddy will be OK by itself?" Hank asked.

"It's going to have to be," Ace said. "We're going to need to work together to get this done."

"OK," Ivan said. "What's the plan?"

"Well. I'm pretty sure we're in the woods behind the KFC. Hank, can you tell where we are?"

Hank sniffed the air and gestured with his head. "Yeah. The KFC is up over there."

Ace sniffed the air. At first, all he could smell were trees and damp vegetation. Then it hit him like a ton of bricks. The delicious smell of fried chicken. It was so strong he was amazed he didn't notice it before.

"Yup," Ace said. His mouth watered. "KFC is up that way."

"You can smell it, too?" April asked, sniffing deeply. "All I smell is woods and maybe some dog shit."

"Don't look at me!" Hank said. "I went back in 1977."

"Ew!" April said. "T-M-I!"

"Quiet guys." Ace pointed. "Right over there is the Advance

238

Auto Parts store where the Shiny Man disguised as Calhoun jumped me. If I'm right, my former self should be heading that way now to try and find the entrance to the tunnel. I say we wait until I...I mean, *he* handcuffs Calhoun to the pipe, and then we get that shiny bastard. If he never makes it onto Betty with the Caddy, then he'll never kill Elvis there *or* in 1935."

"Sounds good to me," Ivan said. "But, Ace. You have to be careful. We have no way of knowing what might happen if you run into your former self. We'll have to wait until he's gone."

"Yeah. Good point," Ace said. "OK. Let's go."

After a few minutes of walking a subtle glow from the street-lights began to bleed into the edge of the woods. They were getting close. Ace led the group and put his hand out to stop them when they were a few yards away.

A loud snap rang out into the night.

Ace turned and saw April standing on one foot. Her other foot hovered over a branch she had just broken.

He put his finger to his lips.

April mouthed, "Sorry. My bad," and gently put her foot down without a sound. Even Hank closed his ever open, panting mouth and slowed his breath so it would be quiet.

There were voices ahead. At first, it was hard to make out, but then Ace clearly heard his own voice shout, "Time to make the donuts!"

The sound of a struggle was clear as a bell. After the fight subsided, he heard his other self give Pradeep instructions on how to handcuff Calhoun to the pipe on the building.

Calhoun gave his little speech about being a victim of the Shiny Man and then cried out like he was being rendered unconscious by a mysterious force. Ace shook his head, ashamed of his former self for believing the deception.

Ace heard his former self tell Pradeep, "Alright. New plan. You go get help for this guy. Tell him you were going round back to take a leak and you found him. But wait for about ten minutes until I'm in the woods, OK?"

Ace focused his ears and heard the sound of footsteps walking away. His former self was behind the KFC now, entering the woods. There was so much dense foliage between them, there'd be no way he could see them, but Ace didn't want to wait any longer.

Ace waved for everyone to follow him, and they walked out of the woods just as Agent Calhoun was slinking an impossibly shiny hand out of a handcuff. A shimmer of light fluctuated over the hand as it came free then returned to a normal looking human hand.

Calhoun's other hand was around Pradeep's neck. A sickening crunching sound filled the air as Pradeep struggled to free himself.

Ace sprang into action. He charged forward as fast as he could, throwing a shoulder into Calhoun's midsection. It was so fast Calhoun didn't have a chance to react. He let go of Pradeep and flew backward, hitting the Advance Auto Parts wall with enough force to crack bricks. Calhoun's head hit the wall, leaving a spatter of shiny blood as he slunk to the ground, gurgling.

Calhoun wavered on his knees for a moment then collapsed face first. A matte of shiny blood was plastered on the back of his head.

The dazzler-like device that kept him disguised as a human fizzled when he hit the ground. A burst of light crackled around his body and then dissipated, revealing the Shiny Man in all his impossibly shiny glory.

Pradeep was on fours, gasping for breath. Ivan and April rushed over to check on him. Hank barked as he ran up to the Shiny Man and was about to pounce, but Ace waved him off. To Ace's astonishment, Hank actually listened to him and stopped short.

The Shiny Man was out cold.

April held Pradeep up in a sitting position as Ivan checked him over.

"He needs a doctor, Ace," Ivan said.

"OK. You two go get him some medical attention. I've got this guy." Ace tapped the Shiny Man with his foot, checking to see if he was still unconscious. The Shiny Man never reacted.

April helped Pradeep up and said, "Ivan can't go out there. They'll freak out about him."

"Shit," Ace said lamenting the loss of their dazzlers and the intolerance of Earth in 2018. He hoped in the future there'd be more room for cyborg chimps to roam free unaccosted.

Ivan didn't seem fazed by any of it. He looked back over his shoulder and said, "We can sneak him onto Betty and get him patched up in the med bay."

"How the hell are you going to do that?" Ace asked. "Your former self is on board right now with Elvis."

"E?" Hank said with a whimper in his voice. "He's over there? Now?"

"Yeah," Ace said. "He's in a coma in our sick bay and—"

Hank took off running in the direction of *Betty.* Ivan followed yelling, "Wait! Don't just run up there. The sentry mode is still active! Hank! Wait!"

Ace watched them go but didn't pursue. It was kind of a blessing in disguise. Ivan was smart enough to handle the situation. With Hank out of the way and not trying to bite the Shiny Man's nuts off, things were sure to go a little smoother.

"Think you can get Pradeep some help out there?" Ace pointed towards the direction of Elvis Presley Boulevard.

"Yeah," April said, helping Pradeep stand. "I can talk to a cop or something. They're liable to have an ambulance on the way. If there's not already one out there. I think I remember seeing a few when I came down here to find my dipshit brother."

"OK. Go get Pradeep some help, but if you see your former self, hide."

"I came from the other side of Graceland," April said. "It's barricaded. There's no way I'll run into me. Man, that's really weird to say."

"I get it," Ace said. "Be careful."

Before leaving April flashed a sad smile. "You, too."

An uncomfortable silence hung in the air like Ace was supposed to say something else, something more. He couldn't think of anything and was embarrassed for both not being able to think of anything and for the way he felt.

April nodded and turned with Pradeep. They disappeared around the corner of the building as fast as Pradeep could manage. The poor guy was coughing the whole time, and April kept telling him things were going to be OK.

Ace hoped she was right. They were in uncharted territory here. He had no idea how these changes would affect the future. Even with his increased intellectual abilities he still had no real understanding of how it was going to work. But it didn't matter. The Shiny Man had to be stopped.

Ace knelt down next to the Shiny Man. The blood on the Shiny Man's head looked like it had stopped flowing. Ace reached over the Shiny Man's limp body and rolled him over, jumping back a little in case the whole thing was an act.

Ace watched the Shiny Man's chest rise and fall in a slow even pattern. He appeared out for the count. Ace was careful as he knelt back down and was reminded of the old Glornok saying "never poke a sleeping garzlebear." Sound advice, but he knew that he had to poke this particular garzlebear. He had to search him.

Ace carefully reached into the Shiny Man's pocket and fished around. The pocket was deeper than it looked. When Ace was up to his elbow, his fingers brushed across something cold and metallic. He ran his finger along the object until he was sure it was the butt of the shiny laser revolver. The same revolver that shot off Ace's hand in 1935. It was his artificial hand that fished the laser revolver out from the crazy deep pocket. Ace had a lightness in his chest as a sense of vindication swept over him.

Ace stood and checked the laser revolver. The safety was on, and the gun seemed to have a full charge. He flicked the safety off and held the pistol over the Shiny Man.

His finger rested on the trigger, ready to shoot, but he hesitated.

The thought of shooting an unconscious defenseless man, even one responsible for so much destruction and heartache, left a sour taste in Ace's mouth. He knew intellectually it was the right thing to do. This shiny jerk was (or would be) responsible for the death of Elvis Presley. Twice! And then somehow he would be instrumental in the death of the entire Milky Way Galaxy! Trillions and trillions of lives were at stake. All he had to do was pull the trigger.

But he couldn't. It didn't seem right.

*I ain't no executioner*, Ace thought. He gave the Shiny Man a little kick, hoping it would wake him up. Maybe get the Shiny Man to mouth off to him or something. Anything. To make it more of a fair fight.

The kick did nothing. So Ace gave the Shiny Man a slightly

harder kick. "Come on! Get up!"

Nothing.

"I said, get up!" Ace said with another kick. Then, another.

"My. Aren't we testy!" a voice said from behind.

Ace spun around and saw a second Shiny Man at the edge of the woods. Instead of his usual impossibly shiny suit, this new Shiny Man wore a mangled stained white t-shirt and high-cut athletic shorts. He was covered in shiny blood, and his posture was off kilter like his spine had been twisted. He held his own laser revolver in one hand and a timedrive cylinder under his other arm.

"Aren't you going to finish the job, human?" the Shiny Man by the woods said.

"What?" Ace said. "How?"

"You hit me with your car but failed to check on the aftermath. All I had to do was hold on." The Shiny Man coughed and spit up some shiny blood. "Travelling through time fully exposed is not something I suggest. It took me this long to pry myself from the bottom of your ridiculous vehicle. But nonetheless. Here I am."

"Now," the Shiny Man by the woods said as he cocked the hammer on his laser revolver. "I asked you. Aren't you going to finish the job?"

The Shiny Man fired.

Time seemed to slow for Ace as the nanobots kicked all his physical and perceptive abilities into overdrive. From this short distance, there'd be no time to get out of the way. Ace watched with horror as the crackling bolt of superheated energy whizzed towards him.

Then the laser bolt sailed past Ace. He followed it with his eyes as it struck the unconscious Shiny Man lying next to his feet.

The bolt landed square in the midsection. A brilliant flash

erupted, and the unconscious Shiny Man disintegrated. Only a small pool of shiny blood remained on the grass as tiny wisps of energy winked out into the night sky.

"Are you insane?" Ace shouted and turned back raising his own laser revolver up to meet the Shiny Man by the woods. "You just killed your former self, jackass!"

"Oh. Don't worry. I'll be fine. Thank you for your concern, though. I'm afraid your quaint view of the timeline doesn't quite work like you think it does. He is of no consequence. See?" The Shiny Man patted his chest with the laser revolver. "I'm fine. And now that I have this cloned timedrive I don't have to worry about hacking the system on the Cadillac. All I need is a Valdovian spacecraft, and I'll be on my way."

"Betty..." Ace said.

"Ha! You are much smarter than I was led to believe, human. Did you take night classes since we met last?"

Ace straightened his arm out, trying to intimidate the Shiny Man with his own laser revolver.

"Oh come now," the Shiny Man said. "At this distance, we'll only kill each other. Is that what you want? To die here?"

"If that's what it takes," Ace said. "There's no goddamn way I am taking you to Betty."

"Oh, please," the Shiny Man said with a sarcastic bite. "You are not a hero, Mr. Tucker. You are a simple trucker. A rube. A pawn in an elaborate game that has been hundreds of years in the making. Your entire existence is for this one simple purpose. You are the lynchpin. The key. To the destruction of this wretched galaxy!"

Ace kept his laser revolver aimed at the Shiny Man and said with as much gusto as he could muster, "I ain't taking you nowhere. And you try to get into Betty unauthorized, and she'll shock the ever-loving shit out of you. "

"Oh please," The Shiny Man said. "I don't *need* you to access the ship. It will just be faster with your help. Believe it or not, *time* is of the essence here. Now that the two timedrives have been separated this timeline is coalescing. And although I am not happy about having to live the rest of my life in this alternate universe, I will take it if it means achieving my goal."

Ace heard something rustling in the woods behind the Shiny Man. A low whisper. At first, he thought it was his imagination, but then he heard it again. He focused and allowed the nanobots to augment his hearing. He blocked out the sounds of the hovering helicopter and the crowd. And there it was. Panting. Dog panting. And whispering...

# 17

# Finger-Licking Good

Ace heard Hank's sloppy jowls smacking as he whispered, "Get ready, Ace. Get ready, Ace. Get ready, Ace. 3...2..."

"Time's up, human. What's it going to —" the Shiny Man was cut off mid-sentence as Hank plowed into his back. He lurched forward and squeezed the trigger on his laser revolver.

A laser bolt hit Ace square in his artificial hand.

Ace dropped his own laser revolver and watched it vaporize in wisps of crackling energy. A shuddering vibration ran up his arm, and his artificial hand glowed red like molten steel fresh from blast furnace.

Ace cried out more from shock than actual pain. Rational thought kicked in, and he remembered he splurged for the laser proof coating at Proton's Popular Prosthetics. Under normal circumstances, Ace would've thought it was an unnecessary add-on. Just another upcharge by a salesman looking to increase his commission. But having his hand shot off by laser fire once was more than enough. Now, the extra four hundred credits was money well spent.

He felt a surge of nanobots in his arm above the artificial hand. They worked to mitigate the pain and keep the arm comfortable. There was a constant tingle behind his wrist where the artificial hand met his flesh and a large concentration of nanobots worked to keep everything together.

Hank had jumped onto the Shiny Man's back with all his weight. The force of Hank's attack caused the timedrive to slip out from under the Shiny Man's arm. Ace watched it tumble through the air in slow motion. He dove forward, snatching the timedrive with his flesh and blood hand just before it hit the ground. His artificial hand was screaming hot and charred the grass when he used it to steady himself.

Ace tucked and rolled with the timedrive close to his body. He made a full revolution and came up with his feet under him. He cradled the timedrive like a baby then tucked it under his left arm. His stance was awkward as he had to keep his artificial hand away from his body. It was way too hot to touch any other part of himself. The actual hand felt fine, and he wiggled his fingers to make sure it was still functional. Even the rest of the arm was OK, but when he brought the hand close to his side in a natural standing position, it felt like he was holding a live wire next to his leg.

Hank was on the Shiny Man's back, biting and clawing at the shiny head. Ace was just about to tell Hank to jump off when the Shiny Man wrenched his arm backward in a supernatural thrust. The Shiny Man's elbow slammed into Hank's body sending the dog sailing into the woods out of sight.

Ace heard Hank howl in pain and scurry away deeper into the woods.

The Shiny Man leaped over Ace's head, hitting the side of the Advance Auto Parts where a utility ladder ran up to the roof. Ace spun around as the shiny bastard scurried up and out of sight to the rooftop.

Ace cursed then ran and leaped onto the utility ladder himself.

He climbed as fast as he could with the timedrive tucked under his arm and his artificial hand still being loaded with crazy laser energy. The hand was hot enough to melt metal. Each time it hit the utility ladder rung it sizzled and sparked in brilliant discharges.

When Ace got to the roof, the Shiny Man was out of sight. He scanned the rooftop for movement, but there were massive mechanical structures scattered across it blocking his view.

The helicopter hovering above Elvis Presley Boulevard was a few hundred feet in the sky and much louder from on top of the roof. He could feel the wind from the rotor blades pushing down.

The noise of the crowd below was also much louder from up there. Ace thought he heard a woman cry out and a chill ran down his spine.

*April!* he thought.

Ace rushed to the edge of the roof and glanced down at the crowd of people and police below. There were hundreds of Elvis impersonators shouting and pushing against police barricades. Ace split his time sweeping the chaos below while glancing around the roof for any sign of the Shiny Man.

Ace was desperate to see if April was OK, but he couldn't have his attention distracted for too long. The Shiny Man had already proven himself to be tricky and resourceful.

He was just about to give up and leave the edge of the roof. Then he caught a glimpse of a woman standing next to a man lying on a stretcher. The ill man was about to be loaded into a red and white truck with flashing lights on top. It was April. She had succeeded in getting Pradeep some medical help, and she seemed a reasonably safe distance from the impending riot.

A slow smile spread across Ace's face, and the tightness in his gut loosened.

Ace turned from the roof line to resume his search for the Shiny Man. He heard a slight scratching coming from the other side of the closest boxy mechanical structure. Ace kept his footsteps even and soft as he snuck up to the structure.

Ace put his back against the structure and stole a quick glance around the corner. He tried to will his eyes to see through the solid siding of the boxy thing. He knew it was a long shot, but it would have been cool if that was something the nanobots could do. Who knows, maybe they could, but they were too busy keeping his right arm from falling off. The hand was still glowing hot. Sparks shot off it when it got too close to metal like the electrical charge was trying to find a place to flow.

After a beat, the scratching sound resumed. Ace slunk around the corner, keeping his back flat against the metal wall as he tiptoed forward. The noise got louder.

*He's right around the next corner*, Ace thought.

Ace took a deep breath and darted around the corner ready to fight.

A small frightened mammal with a long tail let out a squeak and ran away, dropping the tidbit it was eating.

Ace blew out a breath and was about to search the next hiding place when a loud booming *thud* rang out. It sounded like it came from the building next door.

Ace ran towards the sound but knew what it was even before he even saw it. The Shiny Man had leaped from one roof to the other and was running across the top of the building towards the KFC.

The police in the parking lot below didn't seem to notice. Further up the street someone (his former self) had just leaped over their barricades from inside the perimeter and set off a full-blown riot. The cops ran from the parking lot chasing streams of

Elvis impersonators that flooded the street towards Graceland.

The Shiny Man cleared the distance and leaped for the next roof. He was one roof away from the KFC and *Betty*.

The last time *Betty* fired up close to the Cadillac the Valdovian computer systems on both vehicles created a network that drew them together.

*That's the Shiny Man's contingency plan,* Ace thought. *Since he lost the cloned timedrive, he can just draw the Caddy into Betty like before. Then he'd have a functional time machine.*

"Having two of everything is really starting to piss me off," Ace said out loud.

Ace backed up, summoning all the strength he could in his legs. The nanobots were busy with his right arm and the artificial hand, so he had to rely on good old-fashioned muscle power. Even without the aid of the nanobots the lighter gravity on Earth allowed him to quickly clear the distance. Ace hit the adjacent roof as the Shiny Man ran across the roof next door.

Ace followed landing hard on the roof just past the edge. He had to tuck and roll to prevent himself from sliding across the rooftop. His charged artificial hand left a trail of sparking molten metal as Ace dragged it across the cut-rate roof.

The Shiny Man turned and watched with horror in his eyes.

*Is he really concerned about the hand?* Ace thought. *I bet that fucker is. With it all juiced up, I bet I could melt his head right off his neck.*

Ace followed the Shiny Man's gaze. He wasn't looking at the artificial hand. The Shiny Man's gaze was fixed on the cylinder under Ace's left arm.

*No, he's watching the timedrive. Like he's afraid I might drop it. He's leading me to Betty, but he's worried I might break the damn thing. This whole damn chase is just another trick.*

Ace could see *Betty* in the parking lot of the KFC next door. She was still disguised as a Winnebago. About ten unconscious Elvis impersonators lay around her. Her sentry mode obviously knocked them out when they tried to get inside.

*What was it that the other Shiny Man had said? That he was somehow influencing the impersonators to help him get to the real Elvis onboard Betty.*

But this Shiny Man was a different version. Straight from alternate universe 1977. He may have some but not all the knowledge about the current situation. Ace might be able to use something to his advantage.

As if on cue, Ace saw his former self run into the KFC parking lot and straight for the airlock disguised as the Winnebago's side door. If he got the door open, the Shiny Man would have a window of opportunity to gain entry.

But Ace would also have an opportunity for a distraction.

When his doppelganger was almost to the door, Ace called out, "Hey Ace! Up here! Ace!"

Doppelganger Ace stopped dead in his tracks and looked up to the roof. The look of shock and confusion plastered on his face said it all.

"What the shit?" Doppelganger Ace said.

"Hey man!" Ace said from the roof. "I know this looks weird. But don't open that door. This shiny fucker is trying to get in there!"

Doppelganger Ace looked over to the Shiny Man and then back at Ace on the roof. "What the shit?"

Ace made a mental note to stop using that phrase. "Yeah. It's a little hard to explain. But look. You gotta believe me. You can't go in Betty right now."

Doppelganger Ace looked stunned like he didn't know what to

do.

The Shiny Man said, "We don't have time for this!" He pulled out the laser revolver and pointed it at Doppelganger Ace. "Give me the timedrive, or I will kill him."

Ace wasn't sure of the right move. The Shiny Man had the higher ground, and there was no way his other self would be able to find cover. The Shiny Man had Doppelganger Ace dead to rights, and proper Ace was too far away. What would happen if his former self was killed? Would it mean his own death? So much was different now. So much had already been changed. Was that guy standing in the parking lot even the same version of himself? The Shiny Man said *this* was an alternate universe. But was it an alternate universe for him? For Ace? For all of them? If the doppelganger were actually Ace, then Ace would have memories of this moment, and he certainly did not. This was uncharted territory.

"You want this thing so bad?" Ace let his left arm relax and let the timedrive roll down the side of his body. He palmed it with his real hand, then held it out towards the Shiny Man. "Come and get it. But leave him alone."

"Shut up!" The Shiny Man said, turning to point the laser revolver back at Ace on the roof. "Give me the timedrive!"

With the Shiny Man's back to him, Doppelganger Ace took off running for *Betty.*

The Shiny Man heard the footfalls and turned to fire. He got off two shots that barely missed Doppelganger Ace, leaving smoldering craters in the asphalt.

At the same time, Ace on the roof shouted, "Catch!"

Ace threw the timedrive into the sky between him and the Shiny Man as hard as he could. It went straight up into the air at least four hundred feet.

The Shiny Man fired another series of blasts. Doppelganger Ace jumped to his side and avoided the first laser bolt, but the next five hit him directly in his chest. Proper Ace watched in horror as the blasts obliterated his doppelganger's body. A twisted mess of sizzling flesh scattered across the parking lot.

Ivan came running out from *Betty*'s side airlock, shouting, "Ace!"

Ivan ran for what used to be Doppelganger Ace.

"No!" Ace screamed at the same time from the roof. It was happening too fast. He jumped for the Shiny Man as a barrage of laser fire rained down on Ivan.

Ivan didn't even have a chance. Ace sailed through the air towards the Shiny Man while bolts of terrible energy ripped through Ivan's body.

Ivan disintegrated before Ace was three-quarters of the way to tackling the Shiny Man.

The Shiny Man spun back around and leaped into the sky. He rocketed upwards and caught the timedrive at its zenith.

Ace jumped after the Shiny Man with all his strength. He caught the Shiny Man around the waist in a half bear hug. The impact threw their combined descent into a ballistic spin.

As they flew sideways and towards the ground at a tremendous speed, the Shiny Man pistol-whipped Ace.

Ace instinctively swatted at the incoming fist and laser revolver with his superheated artificial hand. When he made contact with the Shiny Man's fist, it burst into flames and liquefied. The laser revolver tumbled away, melting as it fell.

The Shiny Man dropped the timedrive and clutched his severed melted limb, screaming that horrible scream of his.

The timedrive fell straight into Ace's charged artificial hand. He instinctively squeezed the cylinder as he caught it.

Then...everything...began...to...
Slow...

\* \* \*

At first, Ace thought it was the same effect as before when the nanobots amped up his vision to see fast-moving objects more easily. But this was different.

His perception wasn't merely better. The space around him took on a depth he didn't know existed. If he concentrated, he could see the molecules of oxygen, nitrogen, and argon wiggle and flow in the air around him. If he relaxed his mind he could see, no, it was more than that, he could *feel* the currents of energy that held the tiny molecules bonded together. It was like he had an innate familiarity to the force of nature itself. Just as known and natural to him as the skin covering his body.

A brilliant flash of light burst inside the timedrive as the inert wires sprang to life. The world dissolved around him as he slipped into the now familiar chaos of hypertime. But instead of fast moving shapes of color and dark whizzing by, exploding in and out of existence, he was suspended in a pool of the stuff. It was everywhere around him in all directions. Color and darkness. Shape and formlessness. Time and anti-time. All spread out before him in every direction. Not just in three dimensions...but all of them. Ivan had always said there were fourteen dimensions to the universe. But now Ace knew that wasn't true. There were infinite.

Ace could see, no, he *felt* every dimension of the universe itself. It was like looking at himself in the mirror. That same innate sense of recognition reflected all around. Ace perceived...every-thing. All possibilities. All actions. All potentiality.

And it was all so simple to him.

He saw all the moments that had led up to that instant as one single bubble in an eternal ocean of other bubbles. The bubbles bumped and bounced off of one another. They burst and created even more bubbles in their destruction. As each bubble-moment dissolved another endless multitude sprang into existence to take its place.

He let his focus contract and pulled his mind back into the exact moment he touched the timedrive. The energy stored in his artificial hand provided the spark that set it into motion. The nanobots flowed through the hand and created a circuit to link his mind to the timedrive.

He had become a time machine himself.

There was no fear. There was no joy. It was like experiencing a mindful breath. It merely was as it was, without judgment. His mind was a passionless force of nature. Eternal and indifferent.

But it was also hilarious.

His entire being gyrated with laughter. The whole thing was just so...silly. It made absolutely no sense. Instead of being upsetting or tragic it was utterly side-splittingly ridiculous. Rolling on the floor, crying, coughing, laughing so hard your stomach feels like it will burst *hysterical*.

Choice. Fate. Life. Death. All of it. Whimsical. Ludicrous. Insanely absurd.

And the biggest laugh was on ole Ace Tucker himself. Because the vast infinite possibilities of the multiverse were a private joke. He'd been given a glimpse but knew he wasn't welcome to stay. Ace wasn't a god. He was only a man. A man with a choice to make.

He saw his original timeline and how each jump through time and space had spun off entirely new universes. Each one distinct and separate. He saw an endless number of universes where he'd never existed and ones where he lived at every possible moment in time. Every possibility for his life was a possibility in a separate unique reality. All he needed to do was choose one.

Ace squeezed his hand as hard as he could and crushed the timedrive. A bright flash of color and sound erupted around him. Every cell in his body reverberated like he was standing in front of the mightiest guitar amplifier ever made. Wave after wave of resonating thunder passed through him.

His eyes became overwhelmed, and he could see nothing but pure white in every direction.

Then silence and darkness.

Ace felt nothing but a cramp in his stomach like he had just spent a lifetime laughing hysterically.

* * *

The world materialized around Ace. He held the crushed timedrive in his artificial hand. Wisps of purple smoke snaked up into the evening sky and dissipated. The hand felt cold. He had to concentrate to get it to move. He wiggled his fingers and let the pieces of the crushed timedrive fall. As the bits fell they decomposed into fine sand and disappeared in the grass and wind.

For a moment Ace didn't know where or *when* he was. He stood next to a red fence. In the distance, he heard shouting, fighting, sirens, the staccato chop of a hovering helicopter.

Recognition came to him in a flash—literally. An explosion in the sky above snapped Ace out of his haze. He was behind the KFC near the woods, there was a riot happening on the street beyond, and a police helicopter was crashing.

Last time Ace saved the helicopter by using *Betty*'s grappling beam. But that was then. *Betty* was powered down on the other side of a fence now. And Ace had another problem on his hands. The Shiny Man was gone.

Ace followed a trail of shiny blood to the fence on the edge of the KFC property. Shiny blood spatters went up and over the fence. Ace made it over the fence just as the helicopter crashed into the mansion at Graceland. The explosion was so intense Ace could feel the heat from the KFC parking lot a quarter mile away. The ground shook, and a thunderous fireball shot into the sky. The intensity was staggering. Like a detonation from a small thermonuclear device.

*The Cadillac in the bedroom!* Ace thought. *It must have exploded.*

Ace's doppelganger hadn't been able to bring Elvis to the Caddy yet. It was in the mansion when the helicopter hit.

The inferno raged into the night sky, and even though the KFC obscured his vision, Ace knew the devastation had to be severe. He didn't have time to grieve for the helicopter pilots or the unsuspecting police and Elvis impersonators.

The trail of shiny blood led across the KFC parking lot through the smashed entrance of the restaurant. Ace tread carefully to avoid unconscious Elvis impersonators and doppelganger guts scattered across the parking lot.

The KFC's windows facing south towards the raging inferno that used to be Graceland were shattered. Glass, tables, and chairs were scattered around the dining room from the explosion's shockwave.

Ace scanned the area for the Shiny Man. He concentrated and tried to will the nanobots to enhance his vision. But they were gone. Used up when he crushed the timedrive.

*Are they used up or are they gone?* Ace tried to remember what happened when he held the timedrive but the memory faded. Like trying to recall a vivid dream after being startled awake. Only an impression remained.

He made a choice to return to the same timeline from which he came. He remembered that much. Even with all the possibilities available to him, this one felt the most like home. Ivan was here. April was here. *Betty* was here. The Shiny Man was here and needed to answer for all the pain he'd caused. Ace was convinced he could make things right, but a debt had to be paid first.

There was a paradox at the core of it all, and Ace had to give up something of himself to achieve balance across the timelines. The nanobots were that needed sacrifice.

*But where did they go?* Ace thought. *I remember them leaving. Flowing into the timestream. But where—?*

The din of crashing metal snapped Ace out of his head. The door to the KFC kitchen was open, and a fresh trail of shiny blood led to the back.

Ace stalked into the kitchen ready to fight and was met by a flying hunk of metal to the face. Stars exploded in Ace's eyes, and pain bloomed across his forehead. A metal cooking pot fell to the ground with a clatter.

The Shiny Man stood several feet away next to the KFC pressure fryer. He cradled his shiny dismembered arm close to his body. His one functional hand clutched a second pot, ready to throw it at Ace.

Ace ducked as the second pot flew past his head striking the door frame behind him. His vision was blurred with tears and blood.

Ace's hand brushed a metal pot handle as he hit the deck. He grabbed the pot and threw it blind in the direction of the Shiny Man.

The pot clanged off the side of the pressure fryer, missing the Shiny Man who had already jumped back and away. A series of beeps rang out from the pressure fryer as the collapsible lid and rack system rose from the apparatus. Ace heard what sounded like a flame igniting and the sound of gently boiling liquid.

"You just don't know when to quit, do you human?" the Shiny Man said.

Ace stayed low and scurried behind a counter out of sight from the Shiny Man. His head throbbed like crazy, but he pushed the pain out of his mind and tried to come up with a plan. He leaned against the door of a cabinet. He opened the door, looking for a weapon. All he found were large plastic bags filled with powder labeled "Seasoned Flour."

"Just come out and let's end this!" the Shiny Man said. Ace heard haggard footsteps shuffling around the corner. From the off-time cadence of the steps, the Shiny Man was having trouble walking, like he was dragging a leg behind him. Ace knew the Shiny Man had lost a good amount of blood, but he wasn't sure how tough the son of a bitch actually was.

Ace dug his fingers into the side of a plastic bag. The plastic was sturdy, but he got his hand through and grabbed a handful of flour just as the Shiny Man rounded the corner.

Ace threw the flour in the Shiny Man's face. A cloud of fine white dust exploded everywhere, with the majority of the powder hitting directly in the Shiny Man's eyes.

The Shiny Man cried out with surprise and staggered backward. Ace leaped up and drove his shoulder into the Shiny Man's gut with all his strength. The two fell back, reeling for several feet.

One of the Shiny Man's feet landed on top of a cooking pot causing him to slip out of Ace's grip.

The Shiny Man careened backward, launching himself up. He sailed a few feet into the air and crashed down hard on the open pressure fryer. The force of the crash sent the racks flying and snapped the mechanism holding the collapsible lid up.

The Shiny Man was sandwiched butt first in the pressure fryer as the lid squeezed down on him. A loud *pop* rang out as the Shiny Man was folded in half. He thrashed his arms around looking for something to help pull him out but with only one hand and a snapped back he was unable. His feet kicked in the air, and he began to slide backward as his body was pulled into the fryer.

The Shiny Man was melting.

Ace watched with sick fascination as the Shiny Man slid into the pressure fryer.

A shrill robotic gurgling was audible over the sound of boiling oil. It turned Ace's stomach, but he couldn't stop watching until the last bit of the Shiny Man disappeared beneath the pressure fryer's heavy lid.

A thick ooze of shiny metallic goo dripped from the edge of the lid and ran down the length of the pressure fryer to the floor.

Ace brushed his hands on his pant legs. The seasoned flour came off after a few swipes. Ace tasted a bit still left on his fingers.

"Hmm," Ace said. "Finger-licking good."

\* \* \*

Ace exited the KFC and met April as she helped an Elvis impersonator to his feet.

"Go over past the auto parts store, sir," April said. "There are ambulances over there."

"Thank you," the Elvis impersonator said. "Thank you very much."

April turned to Ace and said, "That's the last of the impersonators. I came down here right after the helicopter crashed. I saw you chase the Shiny Man. Did you get him?"

"Yeah," Ace said with a grin. "I got that shiny bastard."

"Good." April nodded and looked towards the direction of the inferno at Graceland. "I heard they're calling firefighters from all over Shelby County to help with the fire. Did you do that?"

"No. I think that one was just bad timing," Ace said.

A combustion engine approached, roaring over police sirens in the distance. It grew louder until a purple Cadillac Eldorado Biarritz pulled into the KFC parking lot. Ivan was in the driver's seat. Hank sat shotgun with a swollen eye making his droopy Basset hound face look more comical than usual.

When the Caddy came to rest, a beep sounded from *Betty*. The hologram shimmered as the back of the Winnebago opened up forming a loading ramp.

Ivan rolled down the driver's side window and said, "I don't think anyone minds a chimp driving a car with all this stuff going on."

"You're probably right, pal," Ace said.

"So," April said. "Now what?"

"Ivan," Ace said. "Didn't the Shiny Man say there was some device he attached to Betty when we first met him?"

"Yeah. It's what gave him access to her computers once he was onboard in the other timeline."

"Well, that sucker is dead," Ace said. "And I'd feel better if you find that thing and destroy it."

"Way ahead of you, Ace," Ivan said with a smile.

After Ivan found and destroyed the device, he drove the Caddy up the ramp into *Betty*. He told Ace and April about how he chased Hank through the woods, but Hank gave him the slip. Hank circled back around, saw the Shiny Man about to shoot Ace, so he attacked and received a sharp swat of Shiny Man retaliation. By the time Ivan found Hank unconscious in the woods, the helicopter had crashed. Ivan decided to pull the Caddy around to the KFC in case they needed a getaway vehicle.

Onboard *Betty*, Ace retrieved Elvis from the sick bay and met everyone in the cargo bay. The Caddy idled with its top down in the center surrounded by sound equipment and stage gear.

Ace plopped Elvis in the driver's seat and slapped the King's hands on the steering wheel. Like before Elvis appeared to be electrocuted and his lips moved in a silent speech. His body shook with tiny lurching movements for several seconds.

Elvis sat there vibrating for a few moments then blinked twice and said, "Whoa!"

"Elvis!" Hank barked and jumped onto the man's lap. A flurry of tongue and floppy ears flew wildly around Elvis's face.

"Easy now, Hank!" Elvis said as he playfully pushed Hank off his laps. "I just woke up."

Elvis checked his side where the nanobots had congregated and hardened to save his life.

"Huh," Elvis said rubbing his repaired flesh. "Good as new."

Elvis hopped out of the Caddy and extended a hand out to Ace. "Do I have you to thank for saving me?"

"Well," Ace said. "You can thank all of us. We all helped."

"Thanks, everyone," Elvis said. "Thank you very much."

"Listen, Elvis," Ace said. "We need to talk."

\* \* \*

In the kitchenette, Ace plied Elvis with beer and a sandwich. As Elvis ate with ravenous intent Ace filled him in on all the craziness that led up to that moment.

Elvis seemed to take the insanity of multiple timelines, alternate universes, and doppelgangers in stride. He was most animated when he learned of the Shiny Man's grisly fate.

"You cooked him?" Elvis let out a whoop. "Damn, son! Nice

263

work!"

"Yeah," Ace said. "Thanks."

"So," April said. "Now that the Shiny Man is dead what do we do?"

"Well," Elvis said in between bites of peanut butter and banana sandwich. "The aliens who sent me off-world in 1977 said I'm supposed to take it to a Valdovian space car dealership and wait for further instructions. So I guess that's what I need to do."

"The closest one I know of is in the Boltar System," Ace said. "About eight hours from Earth via hyperspace."

"Can't we just use the Caddy and boop us over there?" April asked.

"I guess we could," Ace said. "But, honestly, I've had enough of that thing to last a lifetime. How about we do it the old fashioned way? I could use a nap."

Elvis put the last bit of sandwich in his mouth and drained his beer.

"She's right. I gotta take the Caddy there. Now," Elvis said. "I really appreciate all you guys' help. But now that I'm awake and near the Caddy, I can feel her calling to me. I gotta go. I gotta get her to that space car dealership. Alone."

Everyone was silent, except for Hank's incessant panting, as they walked back to the cargo bay.

When Elvis climbed into the Caddy and closed the door Hank whimpered, "I just don't see why I can't come with you, boss."

"Aw, Hank," Elvis said. "You're a good man. But this is something I gotta do on my own. Don't ask me how I know. I just do. Ever since I woke up, I've been having all these strange thoughts. They don't make much sense yet, but I just know I have to leave you guys. Now. I gotta get the Caddy to that dealership."

Hank hung his head and nodded solemnly. His long ears

dragged across the floor.

"Thanks again for everything. Thank you very much," Elvis said with a little wave. He turned the ignition and revved the engine. When light became visible through the seams of the trunk, Elvis tapped on the dashboard controls.

A heartbeat later, the Caddy disappeared in a flash of color and sound.

Ace let out a heavy sigh and shook his head.

"Ladies and gentleman," Hank said. "Elvis has left the build-ing."

The four stood in the cargo bay silent for a long time. Even-tually, Ivan walked over to a stack of P.A. speakers and patted one.

"Well. I guess we have to get the gear to the next show," Ivan said.

"You're right," Ace said halfheartedly. "They're probably pissed we're late. Probably will dock our pay for the delay, too."

"Who? Mustache Supernova?" April asked.

"Yeah," Ace said. "Their road manager is kind of a dick."

"Well," April said. "I wouldn't mind seeing that rock show you promised."

"April," Ivan said. "Are you coming with us?"

"I don't have any reason to stay on Earth," April said. "I mean there's another one of me out there now. I actually saw her kicking the shit out of my brother before the helicopter crash. They got out just before Graceland went up."

"I would agree," Ivan said. "Having two of you in one place would be catastrophic. The chance of coming into contact with one another is too high."

"Well, I'm coming, too," Hank said. "This world can't handle two Hanks!"

"Actually, Hank," Ace said. "I think the other you was in Graceland when it exploded."

"Oh." Hank looked down and then shook his head. His floppy ears *thwack*ed against his head loudly. "Well, fuck it. I'm still coming with you."

Ace tried to change the subject. He smiled at April and said, "It would be cool to keep the team together."

"Aww," April said with a singsong. "We're a team now?"

Ace blushed.

"I'm just fucking with you, man," April said. "There's no way I can go back to working some shitty fast food job after all this. I wanna see what the rest of the galaxy has to offer!"

A loud chime rang out, and *Betty* spoke over the intercom. "Ace. A priority one message is incoming."

"Priority one?" Ace asked. "What does that even mean?"

"It is a coded transmission from a representative of the Galactic Union, Ace," *Betty* replied.

"What?" Ace was shocked. "Who?"

"The Chancellor himself," *Betty* said.

"Chancellor Hollendas? Really?"

"No, Ace. Not the Chancellor of 2018. The message is from the year 2406."

Ace felt a tightening in his stomach. He cleared his throat and mumbled, "Can you patch it into the cargo bay, please?"

"Acknowledged," *Betty* replied.

Ace, Ivan, April, and Hank stood before a computer screen on the wall. The display flickered and stuttered before resolving into a video image of a green alien wearing an elaborate purple uniform.

"I have a stable vid-link to 2018, your majesty," the alien said.

A voice from off camera replied, "Thank you. Thank you very

266

much."

The video winked out and then back on revealing a smiling Elvis Presley. He had aged only slightly but now had a shock of white hair in his immaculately styled black pompadour. He was wearing a purple jumpsuit with a high collar. On his lapel was a design of a lightning bolt running through a spiral galaxy. The letters TCB flanked the design. It was the same design found on the wallets in the Cadillac.

"Cool. Yeah. I see 'em! Thanks, Gorblezon," Elvis said to someone off camera. Then he turned to the camera and said, "Hey everyone! It's great to see you."

"Elvis! What the sh—What's going on? You just left." Ace tried to stay calm but he was pummeled, tired, hungry, and more confused than he thought was even possible.

"Yeah, man," Elvis said. "Time travel is tricky, you know? You kinda have to stop thinking in linear terms. There are no straight lines. No cause and effect. Time is more like a field of possibilities rather than a flowing river."

"Okaaaay?" Ace said drawing out the word to three syllables.

"For instance, *right now* agents from the TCB are talking with my former self at Graceland in 1977." Elvis made air quotes when he said "right now."

The display switched to an overhead view of two men in black suits, hats, and sunglasses talking with Elvis Presley in the garden outside of the Graceland mansion.

"They're convincing me to fake my death and get the hell off world. This is step one of what's known as The Protocol. A kind of reset switch that makes sure I can become the leader of the Earth in a hundred years. You guys were on the right track in the alternate timeline, but we've already got it all covered. By *tonight* —" more air quotes, "The Caddy will be stashed on the second

267

floor of Graceland. I'll catch a lift on a space cruiser bound of Nezoolar 14 and get outfitted with my nanobots. By *next week* I'll be working as a ghostwriter for the newly formed Mustache Supernova."

The camera changed showing new scenes that matched what Elvis described. Then it showed a stately looking man in a suit sitting at a desk signing a piece of paper. He was flanked by two Valdovians.

"*Right now*, in 1987, President George H. W. Bush is signing the Protection of Earth Act. As the leader of Illuminati, and secretly all of Earth, he signs a cooperative agreement with the Galactic Union to keep out alien life and erects the blockade around Earth. Bush also pardons David Hasselhoff for interfering with Earth politics, but as a refugee from the Galactic Union, the Hoff must remain on Earth indefinitely. We're actually still trying to work that one out. He's starting to cause problems again."

"So, all of this is some kind of preordained fate thing?" April asked.

"No, not at all." Elvis's smile faded. "Everything was very much up in the air until recently. If you hadn't come along the future of Earth and the galaxy would be very different. Some of the changes you made are rippling across time and space as we speak. But like a said, time is pretty flexible. You're going to have to get used to it if you're going to work for us at the TCB"

"The TCB?" Ivan asked.

Before Elvis could answer Ace said, "Work for you? Man. I don't know if you've noticed, but we're all pretty banged up from this little adventure. What makes you think I'm going to work for you?"

"Because you already do." The voice came from off camera and sent shivers down Ace's spine. It was his own voice.

An older Ace Tucker came on the screen. He had long hair, a few wrinkles, and a cool eye patch. Ace was impressed with how badass and tough his supposed older self looked.

"What the —"

"Hey, Ace. Yeah. I know this pretty weird and I would've liked to do this in person, but there's this funny little thing about meeting your former self. The Universe abhors a paradox, and the results are pretty terrifying."

Ace was impressed that his older self used a word like "abhor." Ace must read more in the future.

"Oh...Hi, April," Older Ace said.

April paused and looked at the Ace standing next to her, then to the older version on the screen. "Uh... Hi?"

"It's good to see you," Older Ace said. An uncomfortable silence spread as Older Ace just stared with his one good eye.

From off camera, Elvis said, "Um. Ace. I think maybe I outta handle it from here."

Older Ace nodded and blinked a few times before stepping off camera. Elvis's sizeable smiling face took his place.

"So, April," Elvis said. "How'd you like to join your friends and work for the TCB?"

"What *is* the TCB?" April asked.

"The Temporal Continuity Bureau. As the only one of the group who has lived a full life on Earth, you're a fundamental part of the squad. Your knowledge of Earth culture and history is very much needed. If you agree, if all of you agree, we can start your training here in the year 2406. We may have won this battle, but I fear the war still rages on. It will only be a matter of time before the bad guys try to undo parts of galactic history so they can get an advantage. Ha! I just made a funny. A matter of *time*! Get it?"

"So, what then, we're supposed to be some sort of time police or something?" April said with reverence.

"You got it, Agent Massey!" Elvis said. "Look. You guys have the tools. You have the talent. All you need is a little training, and you can keep on truckin' through time and space making sure everything stays cool."

"What tools?" Ace asked. "You left with the Caddy. Betty isn't a time machine."

"She is now," Elvis said.

The entire ship shook as a burst of sound and light exploded behind them.

A small glass cylinder filled with a swirling mass of insanity sat on the floor. A timedrive.

A metal cable sprang from the wall and attached itself to the timedrive. All the lights winked out and then back on. *Betty*'s telltale engine hum modulated and took on a new overtone, a fifth harmonizing with the root note. It reminded Ace of a guitar power chord.

The cable receded back into the wall, pulling the timedrive with it.

"See?" Elvis said. "Betty's got her own timedrive now. Easy peasy."

"What do you think, Ivan?" Ace asked.

"Elvis," Ivan said. "When do we have to report for training?"

Elvis laughed. "Man. You're in a time machine! You can go anywhere in time and space that you want. I've uploaded the coordinates to TCB headquarters into Betty's nav systems. Just fire them up, and she'll bring you here."

"So, can we hit 1974 first?" Ivan asked.

"Sure!" Elvis said.

"What's so special about 1974?" April asked.

Ivan turned to her and grinned. "The Ramones played their

first show at CBGB in New York City on August 16, 1974. We have to go!"

"Oh! Shit yeah. I'm down!" April said, slapping her leg with enthusiasm.

"You kids go have fun," Hank said. "I'm going to take a nap."

"What do you say, Ace?" Ivan asked.

Ace thought about it. He never did get to see the punk show back in Memphis, the night all hell broke loose and this crazy adventure took a turn. He really did still want to see some authentic Earth rock 'n' roll. And the chance to see the actual Ramones in their heyday at CBGB was too good to pass up.

Ivan ducked around a pile of stage gear and came back holding a new dazzler. He clipped it to his jacket then began fiddling with the controls.

A moment later a young human man with long, bowl-cut, straight black hair stood in Ivan's place. He wore a leather jacket covered in punk rock band patches. Ivan looked just like a punk rocker out of the 1970s, the heyday of punk rock.

"So, Ace," Punk Rocker Ivan said. "What do you say?"

"All right," Ace said with a grin. "Let's rock!"

# Author Notes

Please take a moment to rate and review this book on Amazon. Believe it or not reviews go a long way to help establish and propel authors' careers.

https://www.amazon.com/James-R.-Tramontana/e/B077J3MF17

If you follow me on Amazon and rate this book, I'd be eternally grateful.

\* \* \*

Ace Tucker Space Trucker began as a novel then was turned into a serialized audio fiction podcast that I make entirely myself. I do all the voices, sound design, music, etc. It's a totally immersive audio experience. Check it out at www.acetuckerspacetrucker.com

\* \* \*

Special thanks to Benjamin Lande for the amazing Ace Tucker Space Trucker cover art. Extra special thanks to Bill "*Batman Bigelow*" Svitavsky and Deanna "*Best Editor to Ever Walk the Earth*" Destito for proofreading and editing this monstrosity.

# About the Author

James R. Tramontana is a writer, a rocker, a nerd and a nice guy. His notable victories include winning a ghost chili eating contest, a fight with an entire toga party and a mime competition. Learn more at www.jamesrtramontana.com